NECESSARY EVIL

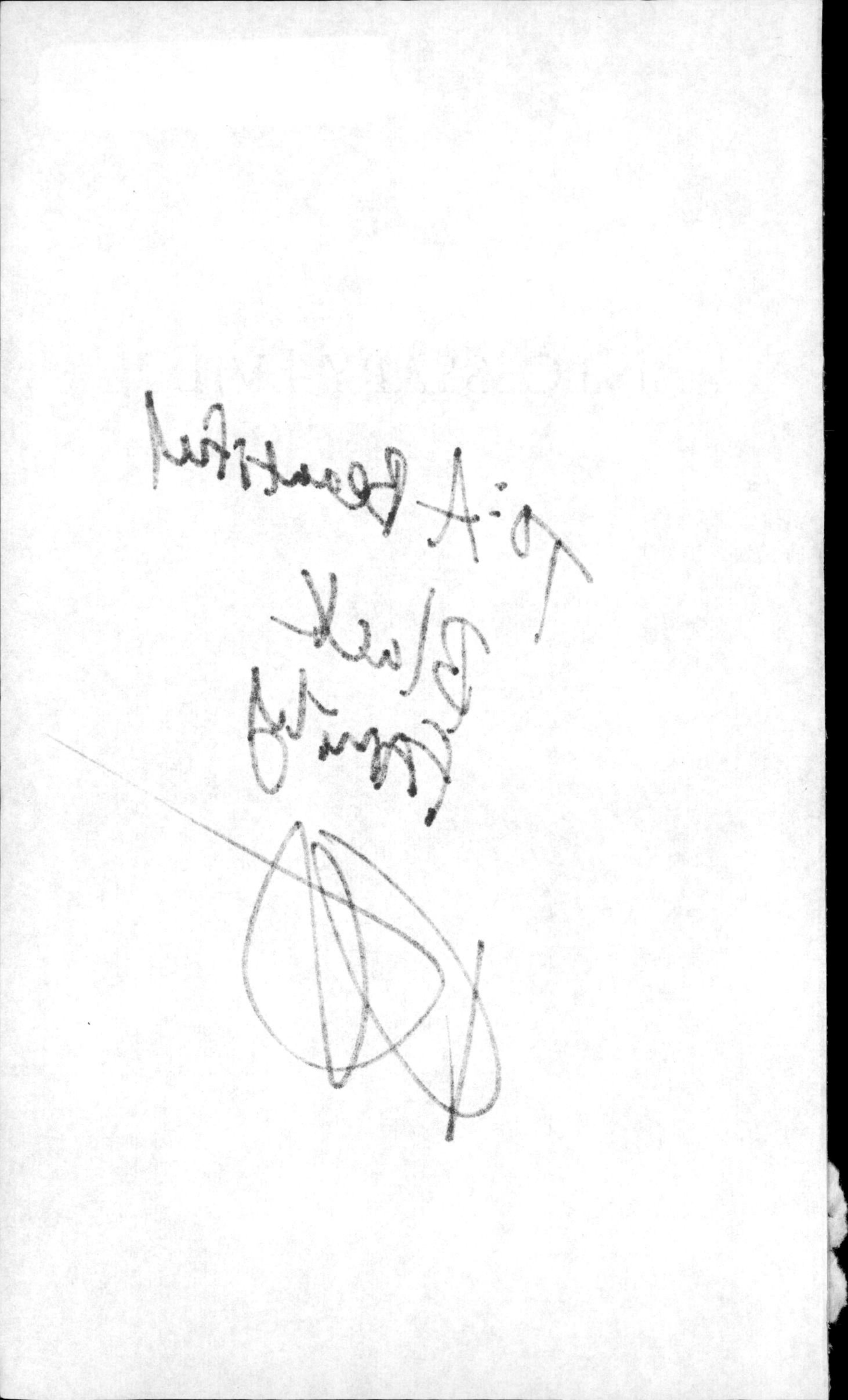

NECESSARY EVIL

KAREEM (INFNITY) HAYES

Published by: I.N.F.360Inc.

Print by: RJ Communication.
Printed in the United States of America
ISBN:978-0-578-08125-0

CONTENTS

DEDICATION

IN loving memory of Sumayyah, my eldest daughter's mother. My dear friend Jason Morales who was unjustly murdered. Jamaica, Queens, the community that supports me, and Harlem, New York, the community that raised me. This for my aunt Michelle Hayes up in heaven, who told me I had finally become a man and changed my life. For every fallen warrior for every brother behind the wall and for every black entrepreneur.

PROLOGUE

ALTHOUGH this book is fiction, it is based on knowledge of legendary accounts and events. Names, locations, and actual events have been altered. The story revolves around the perils of growing up in the inner city's "melting pot" and the racial ecology of the New York's drug trade. What's even more important is that this is a story of the ghetto. In any ghetto from Harlem to Liberia, from Queens to Afghanistan, pain is the same. Hustling is not the choice career for most young black men. It is the inherited life style associated with poverty and desperation. It is a cycle of genocide that is destroying the moral fiber of families all over the world and the worst thing about it is that those people who profit the most suffer the least and never have to set foot in the trenches. This story uses fiction as a mirror to our cold hidden truths.

In the mid 80's to early 90's three young black boys of kindred spirit's bonded at an early age in the bowels of Brooklyn and learned the streets together. They fought, bled, hustled, and ate together until their bond was severed by fate. Individually, they each went through the drug game's male "Rights of Passage" and earned their keep as men. After years away from each other Jamaal (Freedom), Basil (Supreme), and Darren (Fire) are thrust into a deadly twist of circumstances that pits brother against brother and ultimately tests their discipline, their loyalty and will to kill. Should a man be judged and persecuted for being successful at adapting to his environment? In a predatory environment would you rather be the predator or the prey? Immersed in a cold blooded business like the drug game you must have the ability to make sharp precise decisions without any emotion. You must be prepared to do whatever is necessary.

Thus the story "Necessary evil"

JAMAAL

SEPTEMBER 1982-----"You thought I'd crumble you thought I'd lie down and die! Oh no not I! Walk out the door, etc." by the late Gloria Gaynor blared out the speakers.

That's how you knew Jamaal's mom Margie had been fighting with his pops last night, not to mention her swollen eye looked like she went 12 rounds with Larry Holmes and lost. Despite that, she was still at peace as this was her little baby Jamaal's first day of school. She just finished warming the Farina. You could smell leche con sada and cinnamon in the air. The sweet aroma stirred Jamaal in his sleep but failed to awaken him.

To see Jamaal so tranquil like a sleeping angel pleased Margie. She knew he was the only thing that was still pure in her life. Margie was a fine Dominican "redbone" girl, her lips were pink and soft, her hair hung shoulder length and resembled jet black silk. She was a rare black beauty on Bedford Avenue and Clarendon. When all them West Indians came over there to Brooklyn, nothing like Margie came with them, she was one of a kind. She was rare, at least that's what Musa (Jamaal's father) thought when he met her. She still could remember how handsome he was in 1976; 5 foot 10 inches, all muscle. Musa was a high school track star and everybody in the neighborhood thought he was going to the Olympics. He was tough and confident, with good reason. He basically supported his mother and seven siblings. They moved to New York from Peach County Georgia back in the late 60s. Soon as Musa got up here all he knew was work, school and more work. He never so much as picked up a joint or a beer, that's what made him stand out. At the age of 18 he was a full grown responsible young man and Margie knew it. She would walk to school and he'd harass her, but she kind of liked it.

"Come on Margie, why you got to ignore a brother. You know you my wife! What a brother got to look like, Julio Iglesias for you to speak to him?"

"Gu'ate! cono estupido! (Shut UP! Stupid!)" Margie replied giggling.

"Okay well have a nice day Pocahontas!" Musa said while fixing his tan polyester shirt with the butterfly collar and dark brown trim.

She loved when he called her "Pocahontas" but she always kept walking silently appreciating the complements. See, men in Santo Domingo were not like Musa. Back home she was considered a nigga, a "perrito," a "negrito" -you know, lower class. But in the ghetto of old Flatbush, Brooklyn, New York, she was, "Pocahontas," a fair skin pigtailed goddess with good hair that didn't need a perm or a straightening comb. (*A lot of folks have been indoctrinated to believe that the lighter a person is the prettier they are. This horrible stereo type is not exclusive to the black community; it is present in every aspect of society.*) That's what Musa liked about her most, she was naturally beautiful.

Coming out of her day dreaming Margie's eyes became watery wondering where they went wrong and how they fell from innocence. That's when Jamaal jumped up off the couch bed military style, the way his dad taught him. Jamaal said, "Good morning Mommy!"

She jumped, still a little groggy from her flash back. "Don't cry mommy," Jamaal said while hugging his mother. He was always receptive to her feelings, being five years old with a 19 year old mother, they shared a brother and sister/son and mother relationship. Jamaal was accustomed to hiding his mother's money from her when she went on a weekend run just to stop her from spending all the food money. He was too young to understand the situation but he hated being home alone which was the case most of the time. The only thing he hated more, was watching his father beat his mother's ass or worse, his ass. Jamaal loved his father but shared an equivalent hatred for him. His mother's dark swollen eye infuriated and confused him. "Why would daddy want mommy to be hurt and look ugly?" He asked himself with angry tears. He firmly pressed his face against her C-section scarred abdomen wrapping his wiry little arms around her hips. He felt her pain and hugged her tighter with all his strength as if to say, "I wish I could protect you."

She looked down at his curly black wool and rubbed her fingers through it and gently raised Jamaal's head. His eyes were flooded with the tears of a traumatizing child hood. His soul screamed out to her trapped behind the spectrum of tears and blurred vision. He felt this insatiable fire in his gut, like fireflies were bouncing off the walls of his abdomen, a sharp pulse was shooting right down the middle of his eyes. To see the sorrow well up in his charcoal eyes only added to Margie's guilt. She shook it off and said, "I love you Papi. Aye calendo (oh cutie) don't cry its okay. Now get ready to take a bath and get dressed. You are going to take your ass to school. Whew! Finally."

Jamaal said, "Okay mommy, I love you" while running to the bathroom in his Superman underwear. That's how fast he snapped out of the grief. After all this was a normal morning for Jamaal. His mother's eye swollen, her breath reeking of liquor, a million cigarette butts in the ashtray and the internal feeling of unfocused anger. His parents' relationship was abusive and violent. Jamaal was a first hand witness seeing his mother choked and strangled to the point where she fainted. It hurt him inside because he couldn't protect her from his father who would hit on her like she was a man. Jamaal adjusted to violence at an early age, it became routine. His pity for his mother and his primordial need to protect her festered along with his bubbling hatred for his father. He wasn't worried about his first day of school, he thought it'd be fun. He was more concerned with his mother's safety while he was away.

Margie scooped Jamaal from the tub reminiscent of the Virgin Mary holding baby Jesus, cradling his thin frame as she dried him off. This was a special moment for Jamaal and he could tell by the way his mother was acting, she rubbed him with Keri lotion from head to toe, put baby powder on his "wiggy" a little on his neck. She dressed him in his new Bugle Boy jeans and shirt to match his fresh new pair of black Avia sneakers. To top it off, she put a little baby oil in his mini afro to bring out the curl. Yeah, Jamaal felt new and whatever this school thing was, it seemed exciting already. Oh, and no black child is complete without having the crust dug out his eye with a licked thumb.

Margie coos "Aye Papa, mi macho. You're so handsome. Dama un beso" while she puckers her lips and gives Jamaal a big kiss "My baby looks like Michael Jackson boy!!!" Jamaal blushed "No I don't!" "Papa I hope you ready to go to school and make me proud. Now run to the third floor and tell Rita to hurry up!!" Margie commanded.

FIRE

RITA was Darin's mother, Jamaal's best and only friend. The Desmond's-Rita, (Darrin's Mom) Bulla, (Darrin's father) and Magnum (Darrin's uncle) lived in apartment 3B, right above Margie and Jamaal. They moved to Brooklyn New York in 1979 from Trench town Kingston, Jamaica for one reason, Bulla and Magnum had to flee the country. They were at war with the local police force and Darrin was always sick from chronic sickle cell anemia. See, even though Bulla and Magnum was financially stable and powerful enough to get a private physician, they knew Fire would get better medical treatment in America. Bulla was a very serious stone faced dread. His eyes were beady and always red. His hair was knotty brown and hung to his waist. Despite Bulla's short slim frame there was something frightening about his eyes, you could see death in them.

Magnum, on the other hand, was clean-cut, at least his face. His hair always had crazy parts and designs. Straight rude boy Brown suede Wallaby shoes, brown slacks, brown nylon T-shirt and a furry brown Kangol worn loosely off the head. Rita was beautiful, not a regular beauty, more like an angelic beauty. Some say that a person's locks can reflect their persona, like a mystical crown of some sort. That must be true to an extent, because Rita's locks were the exact opposite of Bulla's. While his were clumpy, disheveled and abrasive, hers were neat, curly and elegant. She had a clear smooth complexion with big eerily dark brown eyes. Her voice sounded like Dionne Warwick with a Jamaican accent. She was a little older than Margie but much more mature and wiser. I guess that's why she was Margie's surrogate mother, since Margie's mother died from a diabetic seizure some years earlier. Rita always had something to say to make her feel better. Darren, or Fire, as everybody called him, had Rita's face and Bulla's attitude. I mean, he was a little bad ass but frail as a feather, his mother called him Lil Fire because he was born premature weighing 4 1/2 pounds; clinically he was dead for 10 seconds with no heartbeat or sign of life. Rita cried mourning what appeared to be a stillbirth but this delicate newborn responded bellowing cries of life to defiantly announce his entry as though he fought his way back from the dead. Yeah he was a Lil Fire all right, with a soul made of lofty flame. How and why Jah gave Lil Fire the spark of life?

Rita knew that sooner or later her husband's life would affect them, but felt her husband was a good man. The Jamaican authorities and Trench town's local police labeled him and Magnum menaces to be killed on site. There were numerous articles in the local Jamaican newspaper "The Daily Gleaner," accusing them of being weed dealers, drug smugglers and freelance hit men for the infamous "Shower Posse." For the children of Trench town who lived in little tin sheds with wooden beds he was a hero. Bulla was named after a cake he always wanted as a child but was so poor he could not afford it. So he always shared his wealth with the unfortunates from his hometown.

Anything from fish, meat and clothing would be dropped to the ghetto once a week. Bulla hated Babylon (Government, police etc.) and never wanted to leave, but he listened to

Magnum and Rita. Magnum had ulterior motives to spread their operation to America. Rita knew that if they stayed in Jamaica her family would end up dead. Bulla was a devoted Rasta and never wanted to leave his homeland but he was pleased to have his family safe.

"Emancipate yourself from mental slavery none but ourselves can free our minds have no fear for atomic energy cause etc.........) Bob Marley's "Redemption Song" rattled the speakers in apartment 3B.

Jamaal could hear the music as he ran up the steps. Jamaal loved going to Fire's apartment cause it was always fun up there. Jamaal thought all that "bummba clod" talk was funny. Knock! Knock! Jamaal hit the door. "A who dat"! Magnum's voice was deep and harsh but Jamaal was used to it. Jamaal tried shouting over the music

"It's Jamaal!"

Magnum sang out "Rita! Fire! De lickle Cooley bwoy from downstairs at de door!" Fire ran to the door wearing a fly little royal blue valor Pierre Cardin suit, bumping Magnum's leg in passing before flinging the door wide open. Jamaal stood there with the gap tooth Kool-Aid smile. Jamaal was slapped in the face with the thick aroma of sword fish and ackee, and he spoke fast. "My mom wants to know is y'all walking to the bus stop with us"?

"Mummy Margie wan know if we go wak wit dem to de bus stop" Fire said hollering above the music. Rita stood in the hall leading to the doorway with her hands on her hips and answered "Yes bwoy, invite ya fren inside! Ya have no manners like ya fader. Bulla turn down de musik and Magnum fix Fire an Jamaal a plate ah foo! Jamaal, Fire sit down and eat while mi wrap mi locks!" No matter how tough you were when Rita made a demand you met it and that's just how it was. The music was turned off and 2 steaming hot plates were made and the boys sat down as they were told.

Jamaal and Fire were like two peas in a pod. They couldn't wait to start school together, they already were local block terrorists and it was time to expand. Throwing bottles off the roof, dirt fights with other kids on the block but Fire and Jamaal preferred to use rocks rather than dirt. They really didn't care about a butt whooping. For one, tiny Fire was so frail and sickly with puppy eyes that Rita never let Bulla give him the good old ass whipping that his father felt he deserved. As for Jamaal's mother she either was not home or to high with a hangover to scold him.

Now his father was a different case. Musa came around a couple of times a year whenever he had time off from school and found reasons to thump on Jamaal and his mother. These ass "whoopings" did not count as discipline. They were more like torture and just made Jamaal loathe him. Internally longing for the day he could repay him.

Yup they were terrorists even though they were five years old each; they usually hung out with kids twice there age. It wasn't on purpose, they just moved like older kids.

They moved to 2491 Bedford Ave. around the same time and started out as rivals. Jamaal never really had many toys simply because his mother felt sniffing coke was more important. So when Jamaal went into the hallway and saw this "coconut boy" (*that was his insult for Fire*) with all types of toys he was just jealous. He walked over to him and patted him on the head asking.

"What's your name?"

"Fire" "That's a stupid name!" Jamaal says snatching Fire's

Superman doll. In that instant Fire jumped up and yelled. "Give me mi toy now!" Jamaal answered with a punch to the gut that would have made Mike Tyson proud.

Jamaal's father had given him three rules to win a fight. One-always swing first. Two-one punch to the gut and one punch to the head if they are your size. Three-one kick to the nuts and one punch to the gut and one punch to the head, or pick up a stick or something if they are bigger than you. These rules help Jamaal, but he really didn't need it to beat Fire. After that gut punch Fire buckled over like a woman going through labor pains. Fire ran upstairs huddled over in pain. Jamaal, impressed with his new Superman toy, continued to play in the first-floor lobby. You would never think he just beat up some little kid.

"AHHH!" Fire screamed and Jamaal's eyes switched from his new toy to this scrawny little kid screaming at the top of his lungs with fountains of tears flowing. "Give me mi toy!" It was a rage that Jamaal had never seen in another child. The little wiffle ball bat in Fire's hand didn't scare Jamaal either. Jamaal yelled "Shut up! Coconut!" Fire took off running down the flight of steps at Jamaal and knocked him upside his head, putting a speed knot in the middle of Jamaal's fore head. Jamaal was shocked and retreated into his apartment Superman doll in hand. Fire forgot about his toy, and made his way back up stairs satisfied that he avenged himself.

Margie barked at Jamaal, "What's wrong with you, why you holding your head, and where you get that toy?!" Jamaal responded with his whiny voice crying while he spoke. "Da coconut boy from upstairs hit me with a bat!" Margie responded instantly talking to herself and putting her clothes on. "Fucking banana boat mother fuckers I can take all the banging them monkeys be doing but hit my baby with a bat, ugh, ugh, Aye, no!" Margie was dramatic; whenever she was going to fight she would start crying and talking to herself. "Jamaal! Stay yo ass inside. I'll be right back!" Margie stomped out the apartment, scarf on her head and face all greasy. Jamaal followed her to the doorway where he stood hoping to hear whatever ruckus his mother caused. To his surprise there was no yelling, hair pulling or punching. Instead, the two young women seemed to be conversing in a civilized fashion. This only meant trouble for Jamaal because he was wrong in the first place.

Now Jamaal crept from the doorway down the hall into living room, to await the verdict. This would be his first time seeing Rita. She wore a long, red, black and green dress with her locks wrapped neatly into a bun covered by a silk red scarf. Her dress had lion patches on the shoulders and she seemed to glide like a feline when she walked. When the two women entered the apartment, they were talking and giggling like two old high school buddies. Fire had the same angry look from their conflict earlier. Margie kneeled over and looked Jamaal dead in his eyes and said with her (*I'll beat your ass voice*) "Why did you take this little boy's toy?"

Jamaal replied staring at Fire, "Cause he hit me!" Fire screamed "No! You a liar!" That's when Rita intervened holding the two boys apart.

Rita laid it out simple "Listen, this is how I see it. You all are both lickle black bwoys and should not be fighting over nonsense. Now since Jamaal have a lump pon him head he gwon keep de toy." Fire interrupted, "But mummy he…"! Rita snapped at him before he could finish his rebuttal, "Shut up nah! And don't interrupt me again."

Jamaal stuck his tongue out to tease Fire. "Right now we

live in a de same place so we must get along. So set aside ya differences an shake hands like men." The two boys reluctantly shook hands. Margie threw in her piece "Jamaal you too damn big to be picking on this little boy. Don't you see how small he is? From now on he's your little brother and you better watch out for him or I'll a beat your ass." Margie never hit Jamaal she just talked shit in front of people to make herself look like a real parent. "Now you all got two choices either you go play in the hallway or y'all can go in my room. Me and Rita going to talk grown-up stuff. Ya go in the room and play nice."

Fire and Jamaal ran into Margie's room and in a matter of moments, they went from arguing about who had Sheila E. as their wife, to doing front flips off the dresser and landing on Margie's bed. Rita and Margie rolled bamboo joints of yard weed.

Somehow Rita and Margie hit it off, guess the connection was being in a foreign place with few friends. Plus the fact that Musa and Bulla were similar creatures, Bulla was no woman beater but just like Musa he was never there. Musa was away at college staying with some other woman. Bulla might be home physically but mentally he was all to distant. He was a killer with a killer's thoughts. It was hard for him to love her like he used to five years ago. Back then he wasn't as cold as he is now. That's what hurt Rita. She was always there for him even though it could have cost her life. Then they had a chance to put the past behind them but he still acted like a shell shocked Vietnam vet stuck in his war days. Rita finally had someone to talk to. As for Margie she met a mother figure and she told Rita everything. The streets turned Margie inside out. She was innocent at first, but once she started riding the white pony with some local girls, it was over. Rita soon found out that Musa resented Margie, yet still loved her. He went to college on a track scholarship at 19 in a time when it was really hard for most brothers to get into college. He made a choice for the future of his family, either stay in Brooklyn and be a manager at McDonald's or go to Delaware State College for four years, obtain a degree and get some real money. Musa could not control Margie while away at college. So whenever he would visit all hell would break loose. He was a bomb set to explode; coming home for Christmas, catching Margie doing her usual, having a card game with a bunch of chicks and homeboys, Rick James's song -- Super Freak, bumping in the background, doing a couple ounces of cocaine divided into sniffing lines all over the living room table that he bought. There were marijuana joints, cigarettes lit everywhere with his son Jamaal playing on the floor. Musa was athletic and he was no street thug but he was militant. Musa "What the fuck is this!" Flipping the living room table over, punching the guy closest to Margie and bitch slapping Margie. If this situation didn't end with police coming because Musa beat the shit out of whoever Margie's boyfriend was at the time then it would end up in him kicking Margie's ass. This was the early 80s, before O.J. when things were different.

They would make up but Margie loved to party and use drugs. Musa couldn't stop her so he beat her. That hurt her and it made her party and use drugs more. In turn he beat her more etc... Margie told Rita everything, in turn Rita told Margie everything and a big sister little sister friendship was born while Jamaal and Fire formed their own sinister union.

BASIL

LET'S fast forward to 1988 when crack was one of the US economy's strongest allies, and the ghetto's arch nemesis. Michael Jackson was still human and Michael Jordan was on his way to become one of sports greatest living legends. Children like Fire and Jamaal who were born out of the late 70's baby boom, abandoned kiddy television shows like The Smurfs and Sesame Street for shows with more mature themes like He-Man, and Voltron. WWF wrestling and Kung fu flicks on channel 5 at 3:00 pm, were all visual stimulus of choreographed violence. That merely served as a back drop to Fire and Jamaal's reality of violence.

P.S 197/Huddy Annex over on Kings Highway was a huge predominantly European/American Jewish school, with 20% being Black/10% Hispanic. Five days a week before, during, and after school Jamaal and Fire got to satisfy their thirst for mischief. They would walk to the bus stop together and that's where it all began. Knowing that money was a necessity at an early age Jamaal developed the perfect setup, getting Fire to talk first. Fire looked so little and harmless that any naive school kid would trust him revealing their toys, goodies, and cash. Just when the innocent kid thought he found a new buddy Fire would turn on him, take his stuff and if he tried to fight back Jamaal would jump in. Jamaal knew this strategy would always work as he was tall, intimidating and could always seal the deal.

Together they would share the spoils. They managed to get all the Voltron Lions, all types of GI Joe action figures, Snake Eyes, Duke etc. They always had pretzels, chocolate milk and sodas during lunch time as a result of extorting their classmates.

They also shared the penalties, well kind of. Most of the time Jamaal would be the one to get suspended because Fire was being hospitalized at least several times out of a year and couldn't afford to be absent. The school administration showed Fire leniency due to his medical condition. Overall, between school and their neighborhood they were considered problematic.

It was a good day at PS 197/Huddy Annex it was only 30 days into a fresh school year Halloween was just around the corner and by that time Jamaal had the whole school on lock. There were little sets of bullies all over the school but even older students respected those two little guys, because they even robbed the sixth graders. Jamaal and Fire had two desks in the back of the fifth grade Class room 503. They were doing their usual hijinx drawing silly pictures, catching people with an occasional spitball and writing "I like you" letters to girls. Their teacher, Miss Hessman (*who Jamaal called Miss Hissman, the Snake Lady*) was a narrow faced, long nosed Italian woman who was tall and thin with a very nasal speech. She used to sit behind her desk squinting, behind wire framed glasses. That morning, she stood up in front of the classroom and right after they pledged allegiance to the flag, she made an announcement "Now settle down class we have a new student entering the school today so I want everyone to make him feel welcome." Jamaal and Fire loved when new kids came in because they were considered fresh meat. Basil was led into the classroom holding the Teacher's Aid's hand.

The Teacher's Aid was an 18 year old Puerto Rican girl named Jasmine and no one could tell Jamaal that she wasn't his girlfriend. Whenever she went to Class 503 she always gave Jamaal a wink of the eye to let him know he was special. She also called Jamaal's mother and smoothed things over whenever he got into mischief.

Jamaal hated Basil instantly. For one, this kid was the only fifth grader taller than Jamaal. Plus he just walked in with Jamaal's wife holding her hand!

These three facts made Jamaal loathe him and if Jamaal dislikes someone so does Fire and vice versa. Right away Jamaal and Fire began to plot at their desks inevitably deciding to stick to their template. Fire would befriend Basil during free time and they would jump him for his stuff around lunchtime. Basil was big for his age with a long face and short nappy hair. He could pass for a young Michael Jordan but he walked funny because he wore leg braces as a baby to help his extreme bowleggedness. Yet he figured out a way to make his limp look cool, and possessed a proud presence.

Standing in front of the class Basil was asked to introduce him self "Hello my name is Basil Vaughn Payne I am 10 years old and I'm from Barbados and I want to be a lawyer when I grow up". Jamaal knew this my might be more of a challenge than usual. Uncannily articulate for his age; Basil spoke with a confident air that let you know he was not timid at all. So the rest of the school day went on the same way. The self-assured, out spoken young Basil would raise his hand for every other question. He answered all the questions and this was his first day. How did he enter school in the middle of the year and know so much? Fire was furious because answering the questions and being the teacher's pet was his job! Oh lunchtime couldn't come soon enough.

Miss Hessman said, "Okay class now it's time for lunchtime I'll go and get your lunches, those of you who have lunch from home can get your lunch boxes". Jasmine gave a nod to reassure Miss Hessman that things would be under control. They would usually eat in the cafeteria but it was under construction, lunch time meant chill out time, for the students. Jamaal and Fire get up from their seats simultaneously Jamaal walked towards Jasmine to distract her while Fire stomps straight up to Basil whose desk seemed to be surrounded by the whole class. "Every body's joking and laughing with Basil, like he had been in this school since kindergarten!" Fire thought, infuriated he bumped his way through the crowd

"Hey Bwoy! You African booty scratcher!" Fire couldn't help it he had to call Basil out. Basil looked confused but replied on reflex, "Your mother is a African booty scratcher"! Nobody in the school and nobody on his block spoke to Fire like that. Fires eyes squinted with rage as he leapt across the desk, and wrapped his hands around Basil's throat. The new kid quickly realized that he underestimated little Fire and there was not much he could do sitting down. Jasmine finally noticed the commotion and snatched Jamaal by his collar at the same time. She knew if Fire was fighting then Jamaal was involved. Jasmine was thick and strong so though Jamaal struggled he couldn't get loose. Jasmine dragged Jamaal over to the fight ordering him to grab Fire. Basil got up from his seat and was ready for more but Jasmin held him back, rubbing his chest to calm him down. Jasmine ordered the class to calm down or she'd tell Miss Hessman they were misbehaving. Every one knew that Miss Hessman went to go get lunch but she also took her cigarette & coffee break. Jasmine considered it a blessing because Fire and Basil would have surely been suspended.

Jasmin felt the school was racist, it seemed like the Black and Latino Children were always getting into the most problems. Further more the school liked to label them "Hyper", "Problematic" or "Manic Depressant" She knew she couldn't do much to change it but she just tried to do her little part by keeping the boys out of anymore trouble. Jasmine sat Fire and B asil at the desk in the back.

Jasmine spoke in a stern whisper "Now listen you three, I don't care why the hell you were fighting, but you better make friends quick. If Miss Hessman was here you'd all be suspended. You hear me? Only a month into the fifth grade school year and Fire gets suspended. I bet your mother would like that!" Fire nodded his head because he definitely didn't want his mother to hear about him fighting. Besides he felt like he won this round' anyway. Jasmine was on a role "Basil would your parents like it if you got suspended on your first day?" Basil surely didn't want that to happen. His parents were very strict. So he nodded, "no", but in the back of his mind he knew he had to get Fire back and it didn't take much for him to know that he would have to fight Jamaal to.

Satisfied for now Jasmine turned to the class. "Now sit and wait for your lunch!" Jasmine went back to her usual crossword puzzle activities but kept a close eye on Jamaal, Fire and Basil.

Basil took a long cold hard look into Fire's eyes. Fire stared straight into his eyes. That solidified it, they had beef. They turned away from each other like two boxers going to their corners after the bell. Basil sat down at a desk alone; the rest of the class looked at him with pity, knowing he was in for another fight. Miss Hessman walked in reeking of cigarettes and coffee.

The class picked up their lunch trays and as usual Jamaal and Fire claimed the extra trays. Jamaal and Fire sat in the back of the class scheming at their desks.

Jamaal spoke low between bites of "mystery meat". "Why you didn't fuck him up man"? Fire whispered back, "Cause he' a little tough." Jamaal said, "I'm a beat his ass, watch. But we gonna wait til we on the school bus. Fire you a little punk. I can't believe you can't beat him." Fire sucked his teeth, "Just a little more time and I would have killed him. I'm still going to beat his ass later."

Basil was definitely going to have problems on the school bus but there was a lot they didn't know about Basil. He was born in Barbados and his father, Basil Payne, Sr. was an architect and his mother was a nurse. Basil was no poor kid. He lived in East Flatbush on 32nd St between Avenue J and K., to be exact. It was a mostly Jewish neighborhood. He had everything a kid could desire, except freedom. His parents were strict disciplinarians. So every time he had a chance, he would disobey them, out of spite more than anything. Due to the area he lived in he always played alone. But don't think that Basil is not a fighter because of his privileged yet isolated upbringing. Basil knew how to handle bullies. That's how he ended up in PS 197. He bashed a classmate over the head with a metal ruler in self-defense. The other student receives 150 stitches across his forehead. So Basil was officially banned from the private schools in the Brooklyn district. His father's only choice was to send him to public school. Basil loved it. He didn't have to wear that stupid uniform anymore and didn't have to be the only black kid in the class.

SHOW DOWN AT 3 O'CLOCK

IT was pouring cats and dogs that day and all the teachers' aides and bus monitors ushered the children on to the school buses. Jasmine gave a heads-up to the bus monitor for bus number 503. She told her to keep a close eye on Fire, Basil, and Jamaal. All of the children of class 503 were seated in size order. Fire was always the smallest in his class, so he was supposed to sit in the front and he did for about two stops. Then he'd make his way to the back where Jamaal always held him a seat. But this day had a awkward turn of events and Basil, being the new tallest kid in fifth grade, sat right next to Jamaal. He clearly wanted Jamaal to know he had no fear but the bus monitor remembered what Jasmine told her and separated the boys. By moving Basil over one seat as though it would deter them from conflict.

When all the kids were seated the bus monitor made her way back towards the front to begin her futile attempt at keeping the students in order. She couldn't control the chaotic behavior plus she could not see the back clearly. After the bus passed a couple of streets, Fire snuck to the back of the bus where he joined Jamaal to start their daily routine. The two little bastards opened the windows and spit at pedestrians while screaming obscenities. They also indulged in some extra curricular activities, taking turns calling Basil an "African Booty Scratcher."

Basil was at the end of his wits filled with frustration and insult. His opposition was overly obnoxious and bold. Basil was bubbling over with rage and tried to ignore them by staring forward rocking back and forth in his seat. Basil wasn't scared; he was just getting in his zone. Fire forever the irate instigator gathered up a "lungy" in his mouth (*a lungy is a large glob of saliva mixed with the mucous snot you've sucked back from your nose*) and spat directly in Basil's face. It splattered across the side of his face resembling thick Chinese egg drop soup. Fire taunted "Aah hah look at the….." Before he could finish his sentence Basil kicked him dead in his face with his muddy sneakers leaving a wet dirt print on Fire's cheek. The impact knocked Fire into Jamaal who was still looking out the window. Jamaal turned around and was surprised Fire started the fight so soon. Jamaal stepped forward to defend his friend and wrestled Basil to the ground. The two boys tussled on the bus floor Fire seized the chance to pounce on Basil's back and bite him because his blows didn't faze Basil. Every student on the bus was pushing and shoving to get a better view of the two on one death match.

The bus monitor was a sweet young lady and she didn't like to yell but things were getting a little to out of hand. She told the children to, "Sit the fuck down!," at the top of her lungs. It's a shame that she had to go to that extent but it got results. Everyone calmed down and jetted to their seats with the exception of the death match participants. She tried to pull Fire off of Basil's back Fire held on to Basil like Sgt. Slaughter the WWF wrestler, in a "cobra clutch" like fashion giving Jamaal enough time to land a right hook on Basil's jaw that dazed him. The punch didn't bewilder Basil enough to stop him. Basil kicked wildly as the monitor grabbed him and landed one to Jamaal's chest. Leaving a Lotto sneaker print on Jamaal's Cotler shirt, as he fell back into his seat. Before he knew it the bus came to a sudden stop. Basil was slightly subdued with his left ear in the bus monitor's firm grip. He still managed to wiggle away from her and point at his Father waiting at the bus top. "That's my Dad," he shouted as he rushed to the open door way, I guess wanting to explain the situation to his father before the bus monitor, because he sped off the bus. This didn't bother her in the least bit. Once she made a report to the school of course her report would lead to the suspension of all three boys.

Disheveled with his He-Man book bag draping down to his forearms, Basil was huffing and puffing, not out of exhaustion but more so out of angry adrenaline. Jamaal and Fire watched Basil closely through the window and when he gestured towards their seats they ducked down in there big green seats. If you ever road "The Cheese Bus" then you know it takes a little while at each stop. The two cowered low in their seats trying to hide. Basil Vaughn Payne Sr. pushed through moving parents and students alike getting on the bus while dragging Basil by his shoulder. The bus driver and monitor tried their best to uphold the Board of Education Policy, where you shouldn't allow an angry parent the opportunity to confront a child or children who have been in a conflict with their own child without the proper mediators present. Their words fell on deaf ears as he ignored them and continued on his path. Basil Sr. was slightly insulted by the implication that he would harm someone else's child or speak inappropriately. By now, Fire and Jamaal could see him coming.

Jamaal spoke in a loud whisper. "What are we gonna do!" Fire replied "We fight dem!" Jamaal scheming, "This is what we're going to do. I'll fight his pops! And you fight Basil. But check this out, if Basil's pops don't want no static, then we going to chill."

Their eyes widened as they stepped from behind their seats. Basil Sr. was a very tall man and every step he took seemed to make him look bigger. The boys stared up at him in awe. He stood a good slender 6ft 6 inches wearing an all black pin striped Brooks Brother's suit and custom made black leather shoes. His eyes were narrow and stern and his nose was long and slender, his head was completely shaved. A light goatee decorated his pointy chin. He walked strait at them like a drill sergeant dragging his captive. At that moment Jamaal almost admired Mr. Payne. He was different; Jamaal had never seen a real black man in a suit that didn't look like a punk. Jamaal liked his style, when Jamaal likes your style he'd listen to you, when Jamaal listens so does Fire. Basil Sr. stood towering like a giant of some sort, he spoke with a deep serious tone. "First and foremost, you boys look like two chickens, stand up at attention and stick your chests out!" They stood up like they were in the marines. Basil Sr. continued while releasing his son's shoulder, Basil Jr. stood still out of respect for his father suppressing any desire he could possibly have had for revenge.

Basil Sr. barked, "Look me in the eyes when I tell you that Basil was not raised to fight over foolishness." Fire started to giggle but was quickly nudged by Jamaal who continued to stand at attention

Payne Sr. continued, "I'm not playing with you young man! My son was sent to this school for to get a education. I should hope that your parents want the same for you." Kneeling down, he lifted his slacks, checking his 14kt Cartier tank watch simultaneously. Then he pulled all three boys into a huddle saying, "You are three little black kings in a system that is set out to destroy you. Hold out your hands, now look at them, see, they are all brown. Why fight with each other? Get your education and share with your brother, help your brother." Fire glanced over at his partner and to his surprise Jamaal's eyes were tearing. Jamaal had an old spirit that was touched with a chill overwhelming him to cry, especially when powerful words came from an adult who he respected.

Mr. Payne kept his eyes locked on Jamal's when he said "You know what I'm talking about, don't you son?" Mr. Payne gave him a nod of reassurance, stood up and turned around with the finesse of an Earth, Wind and Fire stage routine.

Before the bus monitor could think to speak Basil Sr. passed her and the bus driver a fifty dollar bill each and flashed a warm Colgate smile and calmly walked off the bus with his son. I guess that was enough to make sure they did not speak on the incident. The bus monitor stared at Fire and Jamaal with anger as the bus pulled off. Jamaal brushed off her dirty looks and pushed Fire towards the window so he could get a view of Basil and Basil Sr. He slightly envied Basil Jr. thinking to himself "Why can't I have a Dad like that?" He saw them turn down E.32nd Street and Avenue K, he was in awe. Jamaal turned to Fire with a suggestive look on his face.

Jamaal pondered, "They live in this good neighborhood where all the white people live. Look at all those nice houses. Basil must be cool. Yo Basil probably cool right?" Fire figured Jamaal had lost his mind. Fire fired back, "Fuck Blood Clot Basil and him fader!" Jamaal argued, "Shut up! Basil is cool man and his pops is rich." Fire sucks his teeth and asked, "How you know dat? Jamaal answered, "Cause look at the stop he got off at. He got off at the rich white people stop!"

"Word good fe dem but still me no like dem."

"Alright, Fire just chill man. Let's just hope we aint getting in trouble tomorrow."

Jamaal ended up telling Fire whatever he had to tell him to get him to shut up. Fire was a hot head, it always took him a while to cool off. Plus, all that "Black brother Africa stuff" Basil Sr. was saying kind of reminded Jamaal of Rita. All these cultural values seemed to attract Jamaal at a early age for some reason. Jamaal just stared out the window day dreaming. While Fire continued his ranting and raving about how much he hated Basil, but Jamaal just ignored him. All he wanted to do was stare out the window.

Basil Sr. gave his son a long speech that started when he got off the bus until they got home. "Basil, we are a proud Barbadian family. Jr., you are not performing at an acceptable level. Your behavior is poor and your grades have been below average (*Any time you get a 80% score it is considered poor by Basil Sr.*) What do you want to be when you grow up?" This was more of a demand than a question and Basil Jr. responded like a robot. "A lawyer Dad." Payne Sr. "Now, future lawyers don't fight on school buses do they etc……"

It played out in Basil's head like, "blah blah blah la la la." He heard it all so many times before how his father was the first architect in the family and Basil Jr. had to be the first lawyer or doctor of the family. Basil just said lawyer to impress grown ups but he didn't really know what doctors or lawyers did. He just knew he didn't want to spend his time around any sick people, so a doctor is was out of the question. Basil was not an abused child he was just very sheltered. Basil's parents grew up in St. Michaels, Barbados. They were disciplined God fearing Christians who had built their lives around living righteously. Payne Sr. went through a slight bout with alcoholism and violence in his earlier years but with the support of a loving family and wife he overcame it. He had been married for 12 years at the time and hadn't had a drink in 10.

The Paynes moved to New York for his first big job as one of few black architects. In the Bible it says that the sins of the father shall be the burdens of the son. This verse wrung loud in his head as Payne Sr. who was a manic depressant or bi-polar, but he learned to control it. His greatest fear was that his son would have the same medical condition and wouldn't be able to control it? Payne Sr. went out of his way to have his son's diagnosis swept under the rug. He didn't want to his son's life be stagnated by the medications which really do more harm than good, usually turning children into fat Zombies. Plus, any type of mental diagnosis at an early age can stunt a child's academic career. Basil Sr. refused to have this be his son's fate, so he worked with him day and night. Basil Jr. was able to read at the age of four. He may never have received a physical beating but he did get punished. Taking away toys, TV privileges or making him stand in the corner for hours. Payne Sr. always made his son respect the house rules.

All the time he spent disciplining Basil Jr. didn't go without its toll. Between Payne Jr. and his architectural work he hardly had any time for his wife Sofia. She was a very busy person herself always working overtime at Kings County hospital in Brooklyn as a Nurses Aide. They never cursed or yelled at each other, at least not in front of their son, but then again, they never hugged or kissed in front of him either. Sophia rarely intervened in Basil's school affairs. All she was concerned with was her home "Don't touch that!" were her favorite words. Picture this little red boned woman with almond eyes with a slight physique wrapped in a conservative dress. She possessed a high pitched voice that could break glass, when she yelled at clumsy Basil. Basil Jr. was a little concerned about what kind of punishment he would receive for his altercation on the bus. On the other hand, he was almost satisfied with the kicks he delivered to Jamaal's chest. He was contemplating another fight and figured he'd even the odds. So he brought one of his mother's steak knives to school with him just in case.

The next morning on the School Bus Jamaal and Fire got on the bus and sat down to continue their intense debate that spilled over from the previous day. It seems that Jamaal wanted to befriend Basil and make him part of their little crew. Of course, Fire being his usual self highly objected to being anything less than Basil's enemy for life.

Fire blurted, "Pure traitor business how ya wan be fren wit de Botty Bwoy Basil!"

"Man his pops be talking all that Africa stuff like ya moms man.", Jamaal shot back.

"So?" Jamaal kept on, "So if his pops talk like your Moms then he probably cool right?

"Maybe, still me no like dem."

Jamaal wouldn't budge, "Well, learn to cause I'm putting him down with our posse."

Fire freaked out, "Nah we can't!"

"We can and we are. Damn!"(*Jamaal noticed the bus getting closer to Basil's stop.*) "Now move over towards the window man, cause Basil's going to sit wit us."

Fire moved toward the window his body language clearly expressed his displeasure. The bus pulled into Basil's stop, Jamaal hovered over Fire, leaning on his shoulder to see out the window. Basil did not notice him but Basil Sr. did. They caught brief eye contact and he gave Jamaal a wink, Jamaal responded by winking back.

While Basil was walking to his seat Jamaal screamed from the back of the bus. "A! Yo! Basil!" Basil looked a little startled at first, but when he saw that it was Jamaal who called him, he kept walking. Jamaal could not understand why Basil did not acknowledge him. So he yelled out to him again, this time inviting him to the back of the bus. Basil took off his He-Man book bag unzipping it while walking directly towards Jamaal. Basil got a firm grip on the wooden handle of his mother's favorite steak knife and moving forward until he was right in front of Jamaal's face and in a bold manner asked Jamaal, "What do you want?"

Jamaal could sense Basil's discontent but he disregarded it because he understood. Jamaal replied, "I want to know if you want to sit with me and Fire. We got Chico sticks and Lemon heads, plus some Boston Baked Beans if you want some." Basil was somewhat confused but he quickly released his concealed weapon and closed his bag. Inside he thought to himself, "Yeah I'll go sit with them and eat up their candy but if they try anything I'll stab them to death." Jamaal sat between Basil and Fire like a referee and said, "Yo, you already met my homeboy. His name is Fire."

Basil busted out into laughter and Fire turned to him asking, "What's so funny?"

Basil was still giggling when he replied "My name is water."

Jamaal couldn't refrain from giggling a little. Fire shoots back at him "Well what kind of name is Basil? Sounds like sumtin me muder put ina foo!"

Jamaal quickly brought the ruckus to a halt knowing that Fire is usually getting very angry when his accent gets deep.

Jamaal passed Basil a box of Lemon Heads "Alright Ya'll chill, stop acting like girls, Yo Basil you got any toys with you?"

Basil starts to let down his guard, "Yeah, I brought some Transformers, with me. I got Optimus Prime, Star Screen and I brought this …."Basil pulled out the two toys passing them both to Fire and passing the knife to Jamaal. Jamaal spoke while admiring the knife, "Why you bring this to school? Man you crazy!"

"Nah! Somebody crazy if they mess with me, especially any big kid, I'll kill him! I don't care if he is as big as my dad. Nobody picks on me!"

Jamaal turned to Fire seeming to be a little impressed by Basil's mannerisms and whispered to him, "See he cool man. we going to put him down."

Fire says, "Yo Basil I like de knife tink all tree of us should do it" Jamaal agreed "Yeah you right."

Basil grew in confidence, "Yup For the stupid big kids".

Jamaal insisted out loud, "Yo, Basil you cool man. You down wit our posse now."

Right then Basil kind of took a liking to Jamaal. Plus, he had never been part of a crew before, he was always a loner. Besides, every body knew these guys were the toughest kids in the school, so it made perfect sense to join forces.

"Yeah I'll be in your posse. But what's the name? N what do we do?"

Fire interrupts, "We The Killas! Fuck wit us and we'll kill ya pussy clod!" Jamaal shakes his head in disapproval, "Shut the fuck up! That's a stupid name, I got a good name; C.M.K." Basil asked, "What that mean?" Fire chimed in, "Yeah what dat mean?" Jamaal spoke with pride, "Criminal Minded Kings! Sounds dope right?"

Basil agreed, "Yeah that sounds right." Fire gives Jamaal a "pound"(handshake], "Word! Yo, I like it you got it from that KRS-One song right?"

"I like that song and ya Moms always say we are Kings so that's the name of our posse. Now what's the first thing we going to do?" Jamaal inquired and Fire said, "We start wit some rules. Rule number one we must all bring a knife to school everyday." "What if we get caught." Jamaal asked. Fire

"Don't worry about that just keep it inna ya bag just in case a 6th or 7th grader wan fe mess wit we." Fire explained.

Jamaal was convinced, "Alright then, all C.M.K members carry a knife daily. Every body in C.M.K. must share food and money with each other. Nobody, I mean nobody picks on a C.M.K. member and we never let each other fight alone. If you fight one of us, then you have to fight all of us. Can every body deal with that?" Thus the union was formed, and to think, these three young men didn't realize what they had started.

The rest of the school day was spent showing Basil the ropes. Basil was taller than Jamaal (*though Jamaal would never admit it.*) and big boned, so he had some really flesh splitting punches. Fire was always used as the decoy because he loved to instigate shit. Basil and Jamaal were the clean up men who jumped you from behind when you thought your only opponent was going to be some scrawny little loud mouth kid. Together all three boys made the entire student body of P.S. 197 /Huddy Annex fear C.M.K. At the age of 10 these three basically controlled the school. There was no one who would stand up to them and it wasn't worth being a "tattle tail" for it only guaranteed you an ass whooping later. If you had problems with them, it was like the whole school turned on you. Of course they still got into plenty of trouble, especially Basil. He had a big mouth that he often put his foot in talking to the Dean. Basil was like the charming spokes person of the group who was very well kept and lucid. Basil's problem was he thought he could talk his way out of anything and he usually just buried himself deeper.

The Dean was Mr. Shandler, a short stumpy black man who resembled a brown gnome. The principal was Mr. Theapal a real Sean Connery look alike with bifocals that made his eyes appear larger than they were. These two men were on a non-stop campaign to have Basil put into special Ed classes, but his citywide exam scores were to high for them to remove him from the honors class. His father's hard work paid off because Basil maintained a 90 average while still causing more trouble than any kid in the school.

Basil's home was the "house of punishment". All he did at home was study and chores. "No play time Basil! All you do is play at school so all you will do is study at home! Go to your room and leave the door open. If I walk by your room and you not studying I'll make you stand up all night and study. Hear me? Basil Vaughn Payne Jr.?" Payne Sr. uttered these words every day and meant them with conviction. Basil had his own little trick. He would stash his Marvel Comic Books under his school books and listened carefully for his father's foot steps while enjoying the adventures of Spider Man. If he heard his dad coming he'd quickly throw the comics under his school books and act like he was studying.

Meanwhile Fire stayed clear of trouble, believe it or not he was usually the cause of the trouble that he always weaseled out of. No teacher believed this scrawny little kid could do so much harm, most teachers had sympathy for Fire because they all knew he would catch occasional sickle cell flare ups. It would start with diarrhea followed by some feverish chills, then his slanted little beady eyes would turn yellow. Then he would end up in Kings County Hospital for at least two days. He was a stubborn little kid and had a bad habit of trying to hide the symptoms when he was sick. Fire was unusually small for his age but a giant in his own right. No matter what your size he'd figure out a way to knock you down. At the early age of five, Fire learned that the way to respect is through fear and intimidation. Fire's Uncle Magnum would talk to him and Jamaal for hours telling them gangster stories and Fire looked up to Magnum and wanted to emulate him.

Magnum was much more vocal than his older brother. From the exterior they seemed like complete opposites. Bulla wore his long locks like a crown and never cared for extravagant clothing. Never one for much words either Bulla preferred beads to gold, and comfort over fashion. Magnum was a trendsetter he had every hair cut before it came out, the flat top, the Gumby, the Kwame. Magnum kept himself draped in jewelry with two huge 14kt gold Wonder Woman bracelets. For all the differences in these brothers there was one overwhelming similarity. They were both ruthless in every meaning of the word; Magnum was just the duo's part time mouth piece.

"Mafia!!Bumba clod botty bwoy afi dead! You hear mi Bula! We na let no Yankee bwoy rob we—mi trow fire pon dem bumba clod head!!!!!!"

Fire used to stay up late in his bed just to hear Magnum and his father talk. They were hit men with no remorse for human life and for some reason that style attracted Fire. Bulla, Fire's father hardly acknowledged him and practically resented him for being so weak in a world that devoured it's weak. Bulla knew all too well that there is no mercy for the poor, the weak or the underprivileged "third world people" as Bulla would say. Bulla felt that his son was cursed for all the people he had killed. It was as though Fire could sense his father's resentment and tried to prove himself by being tough. It's pitiful but it was as though Fire figured the only way to get his father's love was to be a gangster.

Bulla was never the same after all the atrocities he had committed in Trench Town. He'd done everything from burying men alive, to be-heading entire families. To Bulla, shooting someone was cowardice but America quickly made him adjust. It was a different place but the same rules applied. Bulla's mind was on business all the time so he hardly spoke but when he did it was powerful.

Bulla would say to his son, "Fire, listen, I know you sick n ya feel to die but dat a good ting. Pain let's you know your alive. Don't ever fear death, fear life, because that is what determines your judgment at death. Nuttin can't stop you because you have royal blood. Ya fader and ya fader's fader were all noble men dating back to Ethiopia. Ya understand jah bless you right now ya don't know but one day ya will."

Bulla was by no means a role model, but those were his truths and they became Fire's ideals. Bulla's mind was always on business and his business was murder so he didn't really concern himself with worldly things or "Babylon ting," as he would say it. Rita handled the bills and dealt with the cooking and cleaning of the apartment. She was the voice of diplomacy when they dealt with their landlord, or schoolteachers. Being Rastafarian while being a hit man on the side had its moral conflicts, which pushed Bulla further away mentally and emotionally. How could some one be loyal to an ideology that advocates peace, love and justice while being an angel of death at the same time? How could he tend to his wife and son when he was spending most of his time fighting the one thing he couldn't beat –himself? Fire was a mixture of his mother and father because he had her sorrow and his father's icy heart, but like both of them he adapted to a constant feeling of pain.

Jamaal noticed Fire was preoccupied, "Yo, Fire you alright man?" Fire simply ignored Jamaal and continued playing. "Yo, ya eyes is yellow!"

Fire groaned, "Mi feel a little sick so fuck wa?" Fire sucked his teeth and gave Jamaal a menacing look. It's was hard on Jamaal when Fire got sick because he really looked at Fire as his little brother. So he felt obligated to watch out for him. "Okay, stupid, you sick. Then I'm a gonna go upstairs and tell your Moms so she can take you to the doctor."

Fire pleaded while rubbing his arms to ease the sharp sensations he felt in his bones. "No mon mi hate de doctor. Mi gon make mi self betta." Jamaal protested, "What? Get the fuck out'a here! I'm'a tell ya moms."

Fire attacked, "Gon be an informer! Eh listen me don care if me live or dead, sometime I just wish me dead cause me body just hurt so much. I have fi take de pain, can't just walk round like some botty bwoy crying fi nothing every time. Ya understand?So if you gon and tell mi mader den we can't be frien."

"If that's how you want it, then fine, I won't tell your moms, but don't say nothing when you die." Jamaal respected his courage and agreed to Fire's terms.

For 12-year-old kids they had a somewhat distorted way of thinking. Fire was always the first of the three boys to march head first into a conflict. His toughness and aggression made him the enforcer of C.M.K. The size of his body had nothing to do with the size of his heart. Jamaal was the brains of the team; nothing went down without his approval. Jamaal with his ancient soul kept a more mature attitude than most kids but there was one thing he envied about the others and that was their families. Jamaal never felt like he had a family, as a matter of fact at the tender age of 5 years old he was accustomed to being home alone. His mother, Margy, would make it home at about 6a.m, just in time to get him ready for school. Jamaal managed to get decent grades but he was more concerned with survival. Sometimes he would have to eat a stick of margarine or drink large glasses of powdered milk to ease his hunger. Luckily, Rita would treat Jamaal like her own child, when Margy was out on her 3 or 4 day runs, Rita would make sure Jamaal had dinner. Jamaal's thirst for family is what created C.M.K.

Basil seemed to add the last element to the sinister adolescent movement C.M.K. He became the face and mouth of the group. You know, the negotiator, because Fire was lacking in diplomacy and Jamaal was never the most out going person being comfortable playing the back round. Basil felt that the entire world was a stage and he brought that attitude to every endeavor. This made him the front man for C.M.K.

As the boys grew older there posse turned into a gang and became more brutal and more advanced. Even Basil adapted and became even more rebellious; he was actually responsible for recruiting, he made their numbers multiply. Basil hated any form of authority and would deliberately sneak out of his house every day. At 12 years old this kid was riding his silver Huffy bike from East Flatbush to Bedford Avenue and Clarendon Road. It was like clock work. Everyday Basil was riding to the hood. Fire had a Mongoose bike and Jamaal, being a little less privileged than the other boys had to get his GT All Terrain bike from a robbery went well.

The C.M.K. boys would get on their bikes and tear Flatbush Avenue apart. The first stop was Jose's corner store. The owner was an older Puerto Rican fellow, he was so tired of chasing the boys he just gave them free goodies every day as a way of keeping them at bay. After their daily extortion, they would continue riding up to Flatbush Avenue to Tony's Pizzeria and Game Room. This was a "hot spot" for C.M.K. It was like a bar to the younger kids. Every one played video games like Street Fighter with the big buttons you had to thump on. They shared everything from slices of pizza to coins for games, and of course they shared the spoils of their conquests. The game room was fertile ground for innocent little kids who came just to have a good time but they usually ended up in a violent loosing situation. C.M.K. were the big fishes in the pond but there is always a bigger fish than you. They were guaranteed some easy robberies if Fat Pat wasn't there because he was a Shark.

Fat Pat was about 3 years older than them and he lived over on Flatbush. He hung out with a lot of older guys but he still found time to stop by The Game Room and bully a couple a kids out of their change. He was a fat, smelly, Haitian kid with a hell of a punch and an aggressive disposition. They despised him but couldn't beat him. He was just too huge to be phased by them. Fat Pat never tried to rob the C.M.K. boys, not because he couldn't, but because he knew they would be a very difficult fight. So instead, he subtlety robbed them by getting to the kids with money before them or intervening during the process of their robbery. He was just a lot more intimidating than them. Fire and Fat Pat had a deep loathing for one another. Fire had a special name for Pat always calling him, "Fat Pat the Haitian Booty Scratcher"! Pat was just waiting for the right moment to catch Fire alone and off guard to really punish him. In some strange way it seemed like Fat Pat feared Fire just off his reputation. If C.M.K. was feared then Fire caused sheer terror.

GROWING PAINS

"I aint have jack but a black hat and nap sack
War scars stolen cars and a black jack
Stop that now you want me to rap and give
Say something positive well positive aint where I live"
By: Treach from Naughty by Nature— Song: Every thing's gonna be alright

This was Jamaal's favorite song and he played it at full volume that Saturday morning. Margy wasn't home. She was on her normal weekend run, she'd be back Sunday night when she ran out of money. Jamaal and Fire sat at the table in the living room with two pounds of good yard weed, one pound of chocolate and one pound of light green skunk. Jamaal cracked the philly blunt and began to roll up a huge spliff. Fire was breaking down the weed and complaining as usual.

Fire ripped the buds apart picking out the stems and seeds. "Blood fire! Why de mon Basil always take so long at de store?" Jamaal responded, "You know that nigga don't go without fucking with some bitch!" Suddenly there was a loud knock at the door. Fire opened the door for Basil.

By now the boys were 14 years old and they were all in there freshman year at Arasma's High School. What started out as a grade school crew from back in the days, turned into a large gang. Long gone were the days of petty robberies. The three boys have become marijuana dealers and made that C.M.K.'s primary interest. Magnum supplied them with their first pound of weed on consignment and from there their business took off. They sold fat 2.0 gram nickel bags of chocolate and skunk weed around the clock and they gave wholesale prices to their soldiers. They were hard to compete with because they had superior product and they were always open. They rotated shifts daily but it usually turned out to be the three of them hustling together for hours, sometimes days. They split the profits evenly though Jamaal did most of the work. So he made the shift rule that Fire and Basil would be required to serve customers for a certain period of time daily. Jamaal was like a manager, he'd page them like crazy whenever they were late. If they did not move at least a pound and a half a day Jamaal was furious. You could always find at least two of them three sitting on the stoop of 2491 waiting for customers and if you couldn't find them, then you'd just knock on Jamaal's door, Apt 2B. They'd be there.

Jamaal and Basil decided to change the meanings C.M.K., now it stood for Cash Money Kings. Besides, it was all about the money right?! They were all growing tired of street brawls, strong arm robberies and adolescent activities that seemed to be more of a hindrance to their financial gain. Jamaal used their neighbor hood influence to convince the C.M.K. soldiers to make wholesale purchases and start weed spots provided they were at least two blocks away and only bought wholesale from Jamaal, Basil, or Fire. They were about business but occasionally they had little turf conflicts. They could stop any regular dude from selling weed within a five block radius by physical force, but there was no way you were going to stop the Dreads from selling their weed in Brooklyn. The only way to deal with them was to have superior product and Magnum made sure they had that. So this weed spot was their "pot of gold" and it was an ideal time to distribute cause most of the more ruthless older dealers were more interested in selling crack than weed. Basil pulls out the contents of his bags and places two 40oz Old English Beers, a box of Philly Blunts, a box of Newport cigarettes and about 20 packs of plastic bags. They always bought about 18 packs of Baggies, 8x12 Baggies and the sandwich bags for wholesale.

Fire "Yo! Basil why ya take so long nigga we got customers waiting, just pass me de 40!" Basil "Cause I was with a girl! Nigga." While passing Fire the beer. Jamaal while passing Basil the blunt. "Who?" Basil who has this irritating habit of playing with his butterfly knife all the time. "Chyna." Fire "Yeah she a sexy bitch too." Basil Forever the comedian. "Yeah but she sexy for me not your anorexic ass nigga!" Fire Responds in a very serious tone. "This anorexic nigga will kick your ass pussy!" Basil Laughs while still performing tricks with his butterfly knife. "You can't kick that high nigga." Fire Stands up and stares directly into Basil's irises. "So cum mi na scared a no knife business." Basil doesn't even budge he just flashes his Kodak smile. Every body was used to Fire's hostile tendencies, he really couldn't help himself, he was just miserable. Jamaal Finally intervenes "Y'all need to chill the fuck out we boys and y'all make C.M.K. look stupid! Ya done fought mad times already, how the fuck we got enemies and we gone be our own enemies too! Nah ya niggas need to chill, smoke this weed and get this money nigga."

Basil and Fire frequently found reasons to argue with each other. It was a conflict of personalities, Basil was a Joker and Fire demands to be taken seriously. So you can see where they would clash. Basil was well known for his style he only wore

Polo or Tommy Hilfiger. He was one of the first dudes with a Sherling lamb coat. Loving jewelry he had a long ten-karat gold Gucci link with a weed leaf medallion. He wore a 14 karat gold 3D wring that read C.M.K.. All three of them had that same ring, it was a symbol of what they started. It seemed like all the chicks on the block had a thing for Basil with his dimpled smile and tall bowlegged frame. Basil had game and that's what made him important, people always listened to him. Jamaal constantly would ask him "Why you wear all those colorful clothes like a black super hero or something." Basil's only reply was "It makes me sell more weed and get more hoes nigga. If you want to be rich you got to look rich first nigga." Jamaal "Well just don't blow up our spot."

Jamaal was never much of the flashy type. His usual dress code was Carhartt jackets, pants and timberland boots. He loved to wear army fatigues because he felt like he should carry himself like a soldier in this urban jungle. He possessed a very peculiarly calm demeanor for a 14 year old weed dealer. He always had this stressed out look in his eyes like he was never happy and always thinking about something. He was intimidating to most of the kids in his area, not because of his toughness but his cold hearted approach to situations, never one to cause a scene with idiotic arguments he'd rather just fuck you up quietly. Jamaal had more patience then the rest of the boys but only because he plans and calculates all his moves. Now Fire will be a hot head no matter what. Fire can be described in one phrase "Napoleon Complex." Fire always had something to prove even if it meant going to the hospital afterwards. They stuck together and there personality differences seemed to compliment each other. They became one of the more feared gangs in Arasma's High school which was the breeding ground of some of the most feared Brooklyn gangs in the late 1980s and early 1990s like Decepticons and The Lo Lifes. It was hard to live in their part of Brooklyn and not have any beef with some one. If it wasn't Basil attracting all the attention from the girls then it was Fire with his disrespectfulness. Jamaal was just hated for being the leader with a strong little gang and he was often mistaken for an older child. Today was their day to meet and settle a beef they were having. After the boys finished bagging up two pounds of weed. Jamaal began to roll up another Philly blunt this time he put some of his personal Hawaiian skunk weed in it. Jamaal put his Cypress Hill tape into his stereo system and said

"Now this shit is dope! Nigga!""Here is something you can't understand! How I could just kill a man!"

B-Real's and Sen Dog's lyrics ripped through the air, Jamaal looked ready for war. He wore the all camouflage army pull over hood and pants with all brown Timberlands and the covert action hat low over his forehead made him look dark and evil, it fit his mood. Earlier Jamaal had heard some news that angered him but he had to think, plan, then consult his boys before he moved. You could see the flame from the lighter reflect in his sad eyes as he lit the reefer. He took one deep inhale and began coughing while turning to Fire and Basil. Jamaal told them that Fat Pat has workers selling weed on Bedford and Clarendon.

Fat Pat grew up also but he'd been selling crack on Flatbush Ave and had a little reputation for hurting people. Why would he come all the way down the block to sell weed? He was 18 years old by now and moved with this huge crew of Haitians who are certified killers. Basil especially had a dis-taste for their fighting tactics, these guys would grab or punch your nuts, bite the meat of your hand or face, they were ruthless. That was one unique thing about them, they had no concept of boxing or wrestling their objective is to win by hurting you quickly.

Jamaal "Can you believe that fat greasy bastard is trying to steel our customers? We the one's that got mother fuckers coming to this block like crazy. You know if it was some other young nigga just trying to get some money I wouldn't be mad but this is a older nigga who got crack money being greedy trying to push us out of our weed spot. Nah kid this nigga got to be bugging the fuck out!" Fire "Fuck him let's roun up de bwoys n go up der ta Flatbush n rumble wit dem. Jook a couple dem Pussy clod." Basil "For once Fire is right, let's go step to them niggas." Jamaal "I knew ya'll would say that, but check this out , if we go to Flatbush we'll fuck around and get all of C.M.K. shot up. Them older Hatian niggas will try to kill us for bringing attention to their crack spots and you know police is going to come." Basil "Who told you that this nigga was doing all this shit anyway." Jamaal "Lil Reg told me, he thought the nigga worked for us, when he asked some lil nigga who he sell weed for the lil nigga said Fat Pat and I know Reg wouldn't just say that shit for no reason." Fire "Nuff respect, Reg always look out for we dat mi brethren. So how we gwon fix de problem."

Lil Reg was a older kid about 19 years old, he had a little crew a dudes that sold crack cocaine on Jamaal's block. Lil Reg got his respect for being a Knock Out King in the ghetto, he had the 52 hand block style without spending years in jail. He almost made it to The Golden Gloves but the streets engulfed him. His crack spot and Jamaal's weed spot co-existed on the same block with no hassle because they had a mutual respect for each other. In Lil Reg's exact words "I like them lil nigga's style." Plus Reg would occasionally need to get ounces of coke from Bula when he can't make it uptown. Every body knew

Jamaal's mother was a crack head but no one said anything and Reg would not allow any body on the block to sell to her, she would have to take walks to make her purchases and that was how Jamaal wanted it. Jamaal heard all the stories about her, every one knows the things that crack heads do, he just didn't want her doing it on their block. Reg offered Jamaal a high position but Jamaal refused mainly because he saw what it did to his mother and wanted no part of it. Weed never hurt any one, but crack makes you a living zombie and Jamaal's conscious wouldn't allow him sell it. Jamaal wanted to make money not enemies but this situation with Fat Pat had to be dealt with. He decided the best approach was to have a talk with Pat, see if they could work things out, but the only way was to get him to walk away from his crew where he would let some of his ego down. Basil volunteered to go up to Flatbush and talk to him, Fire insisted on going with him and Jamaal had to finish his shift (*That's the rule you can't go no where until you finish your shift*). Basil was a slick dude, he took a blunt with him so he could get Pat high to try and break the ice.

It was about ten o'clock on a breezy Saturday morning. They got up to Flatbush and the streets were alive with dancehall, Calypso and Soca music blaring from various store fronts and street level windows. All these different style's of music mixed into a tune that said "This is Brooklyn, the Melting Pot's Melting Pot" get it?! They scanned the block for Fat Pat who was standing in front of the Pizza Parlor wit two little workers next to him. Fat Pat noticed them immediately and wondered what were the doing around here, mainly Fire, he had a despised Fire; he always wanted to kick his pint size ass.

Basil threw his arms up in the air and yells "A! YO! Pat come here man!" Pat began jogging across the street to meet up with the two boys. Pat's no fool, he already knew they wanted to talk about his weed spot. He also figured they would come looking for a fight so he was on guard. Pat's husky jog came to a halt and he looked at Basil and said "What!?" implying that he was ready for anything. Basil Smiles "Chill out big man we aint got no beef." Pat "Oh alright." Fire " Ya get fatter and fatter every time mi see you." Pat"You get littler every time I see yo punk ass." Basil shot Fire a look that meant calm down. Basil convinced Pat to walk and smoke, they conversed about the neighbor hood gossip, about girls everybody knew Basil was fucking, Chyna and all the other's everybody wished they could. About 15 minutes into it Pat stopped walking. "Alright this is cool and all but ya niggas ain't never come all the way to Flatbush just to smoke with me! So fuck that, what ya'll niggas want?!" Basil "Wow this guy is a genius", okay listen, something has got to give we've been selling herb on Bedford and Clarendon for like a year and a half and it look like you trying to snatch our clientel." Pat "So, I was hustling way before ya'll little niggas, I sell whatever, wherever, to whoever, whenever the fuck I want. We aint kids no more nigga!" Basil "Damn chill kid you acting to hostile right now." Fire's Anger bubbles over. "Yo fuck that you can't sell der no more mon fa real. A we who make the weed gate strong n ya wan come snatch up we money ya must be bumba clod crazy!"

They were on Rogers Ave side a block away from Pat's boys. All three were squared up arm's length away from each other like the beginning of a two on one handicap death match. The anger coursed through Fire's veins like liquid lightning. He couldn't disregard this level of disrespect. Pat had respect for Reg he didn't try to move his crack operation to our block so why blatantly violate C.M.K. as though they were weak. They knew if they let this thing with him slide it would never end, the streets would smell blood and move in for the kill. If you're in that game and you set a standard as soon as you go below it your weak and will be looked at as food for the wolves. Basil looked at Pat and gave him a sinister grin before delivering a wind up sucker punch that looked like he was pitching a baseball. It only staggered Pat, Fire tried to get to him before he could recover but Fire's blows only annoyed him, Basil pulls out his butterfly knife and starts doing all his dazzle tricks but can't get a good stab in because Fire is in the way. Then suddenly in three devastating motions Pat lifts Fire up by his neck like a rag doll, using Fire's momentum to twist his hips and slam him to the concrete pavement head first. The Back of Fire's skull hitting the ground sounded like a coconut being cracked. Basil never really stabbed any body, none of them did, they sliced people, beat them to a coma but never punctured a lung or something. So Basil tried to pull him off of Fire kicking him, punching him but nothing worked. You could see the blood and saliva spewing from Fire's lips while blood leaked from his head, Pat's fat fist bounced his head off the street and Fire's eyes rolled into the back of his head.

Basil could see no other option he gripped the butter fly knife firmly, stood behind Pat and thrusting forward with the force of his body weight shoved the blade between the fold of fat in the back of Pat's neck, making the tip of the blade protrude through Pat's Adam's apple. He must have hit an artery because the dark burgundy blood shot out Pat's neck like a water gun. Pat fought for his life still mounted atop of Fire as though he was going to continue his thrashing; he was shaking, trembling, and choking on his own blood. Until the calmness came and his life left. He stopped shaking and just rolled over onto his side looking like a big aborted fetus. Basil was still in shock, he screamed out to Fire "Come on get up nigga let's go!" But Fire was not even conscious he just laid there bleeding. He wanted to run but couldn't leave Fire helpless. So Basil didn't really think he just acted. He sat on the floor next to him and lifted his head and cradled it in his arm. Basil cried like a battle scared warrior holding his fallen comrade. By now plenty of nosey on lookers stood by. Basil screamed "What the fuck you mother fuckers looking at? Call a fucking ambulance, my friend needs help!" You could hear the police sirens in the back round, two feet from Basil and unconscious Fire laid Fat Pat in a pool of his own blood resembling a freshly slaughtered cow. Basil didn't notice the paramedics strip Fire from his arms, he barely heard the police scream at him, the three glocks pointed at his face hardly made him widen his eyes. He ignored the racial slurs and physical abuse of the arresting officers who cuffed his wrists tightly. He was in a daze, his body was numb, his mind ridden with guilt. This all happened so fast it had to be a nightmare, but his eyes were wide open and wearing cold steel bracelets while sitting in the back of a cop car was a harsh reality check. He was froze with shock, though his mind yelled out to him "Run! Resist! Fight! Get out of Here!" his body just couldn't. In that moment young Basil realized that he has just drastically altered the course of his life.

A HOUR LATER BACK AT THE SPOT

Jamaal is pacing back and forth smoking a cigarette thinking out loud. Jamaal dialing Basil's beeper number. "How many times I got to beep these niggas. Shit I should have went with these niggas! Fuck is they doing?!" Jamaal slams the phone down and it starts ringing immediately. Jamaal answers "Yo who this?" His mother Margy is on the other end of the phone. "Oh, now you answer my phone like that." Jamaal "Sorry Ma." Margy "It's alright, listen baby, listen to me carefully I'm a need you to do exactly what I tell you." Jamaal loved his mother's voice it was something so tragically calm and peaceful about it. Jamaal "Mommy where are you? Margy "Upstate New York" Jamaal "You want me to come and get you?" Margy "No! I'm to far." Jamaal "So I got money I'll come and get you." That's when Margy's smooth calming tone switched to a crying tremble and every word seemed to quiver out her mouth. "Jamaal listen I got problems that I have to fix. I'm at a place called Veritas, they can help me with my addiction. Jamaal "So come home Ma you don't need them I can take care of you..." Margy "No you can't! I have to do this for me so I can be a real mother for you. You have to go and stay with your father for a while." Jamaal "No I'm not, I hate him, I might kill him for the things he did to us." Margy "That's the past, besides your father has a good job and a nice place. He could put you into a good high school and you can start fresh, beside you getting in to much trouble out in Brooklyn anyway." Jamaal disagreed with his mother's idea but respected her all the same. So instead of disputing her out right he began forming a plot to keep the apartment , maybe he could work something out with the land lord, besides he did bring in enough money to pay the rent. Jamaal "Ma will I ever see you again?" Margy "Yes Jamaal of course I will always be your mother. Now I need you to be a man and be strong for me okay baby." Jamaal "Okay Ma I love you." It took all of Jamaal's strength to hold back his tears but when he realized he might not ever see his mother again. Margy "Now get there by Monday, I'll be calling your father's house to see if you got there." They exchanged I love you's and good byes, Jamaal felt lost inside without her, despite her faults and short comings. He became accustomed to protecting her, she never abandoned him like his father did and she never beat him when he was younger like his father did. She just didn't take care of him. He easily overlooked that and loved her unconditionally, unjustly blaming his father for their problems.

Before he had a moment to reflect on his situation the door bell wrung. He walked to the door assuming it was a customer or his boys. When he flung the door open he was surprised to see Chyna, Basil's girl standing there. She stood there teary eyed and shaken with sorrow, describing the vivid bitter details of the fight between Basil, Fire, and Fat Pat. He interrogated her intensely to fully soak up all the information. They exchanged hugs and Jamaal slammed the door. This was hard for him to take, he doubted Chyna's story, she was rambling and emotional. So he called Lil Reg knowing he would know the news on the street and Reg confirmed her story. They say that bad events happen in threes well he lost three of the most important people in his life all in the same night. After hanging up the phone with Reg he felt like his whole world came crashing down. He grabbed his head, slid down the wall and sat on the floor rubbing his temples to ward off the thumping sensation in his brain. Jamaal felt like it was his fault entirely, Basil is definitely going to jail for a long time, Fire might not live, and his mother was gone. He experienced an internal conflict trying to re-write passed events in his head as if he could go back in time. His logical thoughts were not mature enough to tame his emotions as he watched his tears slide down his nose and tap the floor. The tears seemed to lift a piece of the burden from his shoulders because in his pain he found clarity. Brooklyn was not the place for him, there was nothing left there, maybe a change is exactly what he needs.

Jamaal spent the rest of the night selling off his weed and packing his clothes. The next morning he called Reg over to smoke a blunt with him. Reg arrived at Jamaal's apartment only to be shocked at the site he saw. Jamaal sat there in a all black Guess Jean suit, a red Jansport book bag, hat and three big garbage bags of clothes.

Reg "What up kid? Where you going? Jamaal mumbled "Uptown to live wit my Pops, my Moms broke out man. She in some drug program shit." Reg "Damn, so yesterday was just a fucked up day for you all around. I respect you kid, ya niggas stepped to Fat Pat and merc'd that nigga . It's fucked up what happened to your boys but at least they still alive. But Yo on some other shit, you going uptown and I got connects up there." Jamaal gets curious "What type of connects?" Reg "I got connects for coke, herb, acid, dust, heroin whatever! I know some Puerto Rican Papi's in the Bronx that got some heroin called D.O.A. kid, some other Dominican niggas in Harlem with mad coke, ready rock and all that."

Jamaal "You know I don't fuck with the crack and all that other shit. That shit fucked my Moms up, for that alone I won't even try to sell that shit so other black niggas could get fucked up too. Nah." Reg "Alright I understand all that shit, but here's the facts. First of all you aint got nobody, your Moms is gone, your whole crew is done cause even though you still got them other lil niggas I always looked at C.M.K. as you Fire and Basil. So now ya done and you got to move on. I mean be a man nigga, you the fucking brain kid. You a born hustler, I never seen nobody sell weed like you, I offered you a job cause I was worried you might become my competition, eventually I was ready to make you like second in command kid. I'm saying kid I know you seen my rides so you know this Coke shit gets you money. It's all about money, if you don't sell it somebody else will. Here nigga just take this kid Sopa's number, he my man, I re-up from him and his crew from time to time. If you need money call him I already told him about you kid, so when I tell him you moving up there he probably set you up nice kid trust me."

Jamaal reluctantly takes the number from Reg, he always figured Reg was a good honest dude, but sometimes foolish. He never planned to use the number but didn't want to hear Reg's mouth any more either. He let the marijuana clouds take his mind to another place, to Samaya. She lived across the street from his father, he used try to see her every time he visited him. He hasn't been to his father's house since he was 12 years old, by now she would be 17 years old, two years older than Jamaal. Samaya had this look that reminded him of his mother in her youth; being part of a strict Sunni Muslim family she had a sort of royal air about her. She was never fast and easy like the other girls. You catch her outside without her kiman on (*female Muslim head and body garments*), never spoke much and she mostly played with the kids in her family, but they'd get this occasional eye contact. Jamaal prayed that she didn't move or at least didn't change because she was special. He was in a zone where he was trying to adapt to a negative situation, and the thought of her helped. Jamaal had Reg give him a ride to Kings County hospital to see Fire before he drops him off in Harlem. When they arrived at the hospital on their way to Fire's room, you could hear Fire's mouth in the hallway. Apparently he was recovering pretty well he sure sounded like it. Fire "Mi understan wha you a say but No! Ya can't give me no damn needle!"

Reg and Jamaal walk in interrupting the dispute between Fire and the nurse. Reg "Yo Jamaal is this little nigga always mad? Nurse you want to give us a couple of minutes before you give him that needle." The nurse exits but not before stressing the purpose of an antibiotic and remind Fire that she will return.

Jamaal pulled up a chair next to his bed side, he was given a detailed account of how Pat was killed. Their conversation was a "Victorious Tragedy". They eliminated the enemy but lost everything in the process. Fire almost had tears in his eyes telling Jamaal that he was going to go back to Jamaica as soon as he leaves the hospital. For Rita those 300 stitches and fracture in the back of her sons head were enough to mandate his return home. Although the ghettos of Trench Town are ten times rougher than any American ghetto, there was a different moral standard shared by the citizens of Trench Town. This moral standard would definitely be instilled in him by his grandmother. Magnum would accompany him on his trip. There was nothing Fire could do to avoid his parent's ruling, and it broke his heart to tell Jamaal he was leaving. Fire was not the only one who had to bare some bad news. Jamaal told Fire of his plight while writing down his father's phone number and address. Fire told Jamaal to send his love to Basil through Chyna who definitely would be in contact with him. Jamaal and Fire's eyes were a little glossy as they exchanged a firm C.M.K. hand shake and good byes. Jamaal left Fire with a Jan sport book bag filled with 5 thousand dollars in twenty dollar bills it was his share of their stash. He promised to keep Basil's share and use it to take care of him during his time in jail.

Jamaal wanted to call Basil's house but he knew his parents would have no words for him, they despised him and Fire and blamed them for steering Basil down the wrong path. He always knew that Basil had an affinity for knives and cutting people but he never thought he would end someone's life. He felt partly remorseful but also felt that Pat would still be alive if he didn't try to infringe on there territory. Basically Jamaal felt he got what he deserved. Lil Reg had a real big mouth and couldn't stop talking about this Sopa guy like he was Pablo Escobar or something. All of Lil Reg's talk fell on deaf ears though, Jamaal seemed to be in complex dream state. He sat in the passenger seat of Reg's Acura Vigor staring out the window watching the streets pass buy. Everything he loved and trusted had been shattered in front of his face and there was nothing he could do to put the pieces back together. That's what aggravated him the most, the fact that he did not have control of the situation. When C.M.K died his adolescence died with it.

Lil Reg startles Jamaal "Yo nigga wake up, snap out of it, we here. You said it was 148th street and Amsterdam right." Jamaal snapped out of his daze. "Damn, sorry man I was just zoning out but yeah this is my fathers crib right here." Jamaal gets out the car and goes to the trunk to get his bags; he reaches inside to shake Reg's hand. Reg tells him to wait up and gives him a present, a nickel plated 38 Revolver with a pearl handle and a plastic bag of hollow slugs. Reg "Here nigga put that in your book bag. Look nigga I ain't never shot anybody with it but it got me out of some tight situations. Plus I'm about to get some bigger shit kid so take this and if one of these faggot ass uptown niggas front on you, let em know how Flatbush niggas get down." Jamaal looked sad as he told Reg "Thanks man I'll never forget this, I owe you a favor." Reg Replies while pulling off in his car. "Well do me a favor and call Sopa nigga." Jamaal watches Reg speed away and become smaller in the distance as if Reg represented the last little speckle of Jamaal's past fading in the distance. He hauled his bags of clothes towards his father home.

SUPREME

8 MONTHS LATER...........
LOCATION: SPOFFORD JUVENILE DETENTION CENTER.—Hunts Point BRONX

THIS is Basil's new home, he has been back and forth to court fighting his murder case. Spofford was a place where young boys had to learn to be men very fast. The walls were made of gray bricks which added to the gloomy feeling and they wear jumpers like adult prisoners. He dreaded waking up in this place, sometime he dreamt of home in his slumber. The letters and money he received from Jamaal and Chyna seemed to keep him going. He met a dude from South Side Jamaica Queens he was the only other 14 year old facing a murder charge in the entire facility. He went by the name of Justice, you could call him "Jus" if you was cool with him. His government name was Neil Hicks but even the facility staff called him Justice. Justice was Basil's enlightener, he inducted Basil into the Five Percent Nation of Gods and Earths as his student. At this time in New York there were a lot of gangs all through the inner city neighbor hoods and the correctional facilities (*By the way the ghetto and jail have always seemed to be directly connected to each other.*) The older black gangs like Lo-Lifes and Decepticons seemed to be fading fast while the number of Latino gang members increased in groups like the Latin Kings, Netas, and

La Familia. The Five Percent exists as neither a gang nor a religion but a positive way of life, but this did not stop some of them from indulging in street activities. There was a on setting war between The Five Percent and The Latin Kings. Ironically both groups share very similar ideals, even their flags share the same colors. Any jail could be the perfect breeding ground for testing and obtaining new recruits.

Basil took three months to memorize the 120 lessons of The Nation of N.G.E (*which are very similar to the teachings of Elijah Muhammad*). The lessons deal with numerology as well as different principles of Islam and science. To obtain "knowledge of self" is an honor – and every one in the nation has their attribute which is name reflecting your true self instead of the name you inherited from your fore father's slave master. Justice decided that Supreme Justice Allah would be Basil's attribute. He refused to be called Basil any more and Chyna and Jamaal witnessed his change through letters and in visiting rooms. He stopped eating pork and locked his hair to start growing dread locks. In 8 months he became a more mature intelligent person; the strict teachings helped broaden his mind as well as disciplined his mind to prepare for his legal woes. If you ask Basil who we will now call Supreme will tell you that the three principles of N.G.E Knowledge, Wisdom, and Understanding saved his sanity. In a way Supreme became a worse individual as his knowledge grew, he was the most violent inmate in the Spofford facility. He finally found a solution for all the violence he had to deal with, he decided to become it.

His parents put up 35,000 dollars initially for defense attorney Ira P. Goldberg. Supreme just calls him Bullshit Goldberg. Supreme hated the fact that all these devils had control of his life. Every time he went to court he can feel the judges hate for him as he sits up high on his pedestal. His face was old, wrinkled, and very pale. You could see the veins around his eyes which were a cold bright grey and his black robe only made Basil say he resembled The Grim Reaper. The Grim Reaper, Bullshit Goldberg, and last but not least The Prosecutor; the name says it all. She always wore the same navy blue women's business suit and these thick glasses. Every time she'd glance at Supreme it was as though she were examining a science project of some sort rather than a human being. At times in court he'd watch Goldberg, The Prosecutor, and the judge speak to each other with such mutual respect while they looked down at him and spoke to him in a condescending manner. It was as though he had no true allies in this legal system, like he was a pawn in a big game where he is the only looser. Goldberg was trying to get Supreme the lowest possible sentence and have him trialed as a juvenile. The Prosecutor wants Supreme to face the maximum sentence and she wants him trialed as an adult. He felt like a caged animal it was difficult facing the possibility of spending the rest of your natural life in prison starting at the age of 14. It made him a colder person, the fear morphed into anger and that anger turned into a constant state of rage.

His parents tried to be supportive of him but they could not hide their shame and disappointment. Basil sr. swore to disown his only son. Supreme utilized his newly found "way of life" to find mental stability in the chaos that is his life.

Today Supreme is going to have a very important visit from Goldberg to prepare his upcoming court date.12:00 pm the visiting room packed with round plastic tables and chairs. Supreme was always required to have two security escorts when ever he was in a unsecured area, with ankle and wrist shackles just in case. Goldberg was a funny looking guy, he reminded you of the actor Billy Bob Thornton with a hunched back dressed in cheap polyester suits with worn out rubber sole shoes to match. Goldberg noticed Supreme and gave him a fake smile, Supreme answered with a cold stare that could only mean "fuck you" before he takes a seat across the table.

Mr. Goldberg "How are you today Mr. Payne?" Supreme "Look just tell me whatever the fuck you got to tell me cause we both know you don't give a fuck how I'm doing." Goldberg ignores Supreme's comments. "Good that must mean your doing great. Well I have some important things to tell you. First of all the Prosecutor is no longer pushing for the life sentence." Supreme "Shit bitch could of fooled me." Goldberg "She is willing to negotiate if you plea guilty to involuntary manslaughter, which carries a sentence of 5 to 15 years. You'll be eligible for parole in about three or four more years, if you stay out of trouble." Supreme gives his famous smile that insinuates anger more than pleasure. "Listen man I'm not stupid if I get a 5 to 15 I'm going to have to do like damn near 8 years before I see daylight, that's some bullshit. This was fucking self defense and I keep telling you man fucking self defense. I'm supposed to be doing a year man that's it! Goldberg "Well you know what Mr. Payne in a perfect world you would probably get a year. Unfortunately we have no witnesses to support your testimony, in fact every witness says they saw you and your friend attack Pat. Then you have your so-called friend, this Fire character whose testimony would help you but he is all the way in Jamaica right now. I've spoken to your parents about all the options and they agree the involuntary manslaughter charge is your best chance. If we go to trial they will pick you apart they will gather information from your juvenile record and use it against you. Now I may be able to get this case adjourned a little while longer but you are going to have to make a decision soon. Now I have an urgent 2 o'clock appointment so I have to go, just take some time to think things over." Goldberg pats Supreme on the shoulder and leaves. Supreme stares at Goldberg for along time thinking to himself how much he would love to choke him to death. He had his freedom, he did not know the feeling of being trapped with no control over your life. He still can see Pat's fat face in his head, it is the haunting feeling of regret. Wondering why did his whole life had to change in just one moment and why he does not have the power to change it back. He fought back his tears as the officer grabbed him by his shackled arm and led him back through the corridor to a secured area.

"UPTOWN BABE!"

"148th street between Amsterdam and Broadway." Harlem where some of the greatest hustlers have lived. Jamaal thought he would hate it up there but it was becoming more of a home to him daily. He really liked the way Harlem dudes hustled; it was more organized than Brooklyn. The Dominicans on Broadway controlled the coke and the Jamaicans down the hill on St. Nicholas had the weed on lock, the American Blacks were left with the scraps they sold the crack. Harlem was like a narcotic ecosystem. The hustlers fed off each other, you could purchase any drug at whole sale price –cook package it and sell it all within a five block radius and dido for heroin or weed. This was damn near any where in Harlem. It was drawing closer to the end of David N. Dinkins's reign as Mayor of New York City. The 90's had the fading spark of the 80's multiplied by the solar beginnings of Hip-Hop's second golden age. New

York was still "The Hustler's Heaven" and Harlem-Washington Heights was documented by the authorities for supplying the entire North East of America.

Jamaal made his money up there working with his uncle Hashish. Hashish was a lot older than him but was just a nickel and dime hustler, Jamaal stuck around him because he let Jamaal rent a room in his apartment for 75 dollars a week. Jamaal's re-union with his father didn't turn out so good, it only took a couple of days before a dispute led to a fist fight that Jamaal lost, in turn he held his father at gun point while packing his bags. That day they drew the line as men and it was obvious he could not live there, not with all the animosity he harbored towards his father. Like his father says "He's man enough to fight his own father then he is man enough to be on his own."

Jamaal completely lost contact with his mother, he figured she was better off where ever she was. He got like one letter from Fire and that was it. He only corresponded with Supreme through letters he refused to go visit him and Supreme understood why. Jamaal considered jail a place that you should avoid and a person in his profession should never go there voluntarily. So sending Chyna to visit him as a mule for weed and money would be his way of showing his support. Jamaal started a small spot with his uncle but it never flourished to the magnitude of the old one in Brooklyn. The money was coming in slowly because there was just too much competition. Who is going to purchase a bag for five dollars when they can go down the block and get a ounce of the same stuff for fifty dollars. At best he'd get the younger after school kid traffic but he missed the money he got from distributing weight. He still felt there was something in Harlem for him beside Samaya, he just didn't find it yet. Jamaal was barely making a living and was finally considering making a career change.

Jamaal met Samaya at a time in his life when he was searching for some kind of faith or perhaps even companionship. They needed each other, she kept him grounded while he gave her a chance to let her hair down and experience life. Just as she made Jamaal embrace her world she embraced his. She was well aware of what he does to make "end's meet" and would even bag up his product for him on occasion.

They fell in love despite her family's ill feelings. Samaya's family did not want her involved with someone they considered a street thug. So you could imagine how disappointed they were to find out she wasn't just involved with him for a year but she was pregnant with his child. Since they do not believe in abortions the only feasible choice was for Jamaal to take his Shahadah (*Islamic declaration of the belief that Allah is God and Mohammed is his prophet. The pledge should be recited in front of two Muslim witnesses for the candidate to become a Muslim-the equivalent to a Christian baptism.*) and marry Samaya. Jamaal felt surrounded by the Islamic faith, his father was Muslim and Supreme wasn't Muslim but his new way of life dealt with some of the same principles. So Jamaal's conversion seemed inevitable, Samaya taught Jamaal most of his Hadiths, prayers and the Koran. It was traditional for the men to teach the men and women vice versa, but he was comfortable as her student. Jamaal loved Samaya and though he was a young man he made an oath to himself; to never abuse or abandon Samaya or his child. He didn't want his child to grow up the way he did, and he didn't want to be anything like his father. He wasn't sure if he was old enough to be married he just felt it was the right thing to do.

Jamaal was in need of extra money, with Samaya's

pregnancy he was getting desperate. He tried his hand working for Kentucky Fried Chicken on 148th street and Broadway but minimum wage just couldn't cut it. He quit in his second week after he received a $75 dollar pay check. He was tempted to call Reg's friend Sopa but he figured he could do it on his own plus he never liked the idea of working for somebody. Samaya had aspirations of attending a business school but he couldn't even afford that or an apartment for his family. He wasn't in a rush to be a family, he was in a rush to have a family.

Frustrated and tired off "short money" he turned to his last option. He decided to use his uncle Hashish to help him get in "The Crack Game". Hashish had first hand knowledge of the game, he was one of the first guys in Harlem selling crack back in the early 80's. He soon quit hustling due to the cut throat and violent nature that came with the genocidal evolution of the drug business. Hashish was a person that said things but never did them. He was always talking shit about how he used to hang around with Alpo and Rich Porter. Jamaal would always ask himself "If Hashish was such a big time gangster back in the day then why doesn't he have any money?" Hashish did little handyman jobs here and there but his main source of income was to mooch off of friends and family. He does have one particular talent though, he can talk his ass off. Hashish can give you details and facts about any subject, it's like he was a human encyclopedia.

Hashish warned Jamaal of what he might be getting into, he told him numerous tales and accounts of murder and deceit to discourage him. Jamaal gave his uncle's tall tales much thought .He knew that crack was the same demon that possessed his mother he even questioned if maybe it was coming for him to. He prayed that Allah would forgive him for his sins and understand that he is only doing this to take care of his family. Malcolm X's Autobiography was one of Jamaal's favorite books, Samaya convinced him to read a little bit of it and he never put it down. There was a phrase in the book that stood out so much that Jamaal adopted it as his personal motto. "By any means necessary." Even though the importance of one young man's street dreams could in no way compare to the civil rights movement, the phrase still fits Jamaal's cause.

Hashish connected Jamaal with this Dominican kid named Allahandro .He had some fish scale butter beige coke for like 20 dollars a gram. You could find him on 148th and Broadway right in front of La Casa Restaurant every day. He was tall and slender with a fast accent and a witty mouth. The pretty boy type wit a curly fade-hair cut and some high cheek bones to match his feminine face. Jamaal didn't necessarily like him because he knew Allahandro had a fork tongue. No one would know Jamaal was half Dominican unless he told you, he could under stand Spanish he just couldn't speak it fluently. He used this to his advantage in order to always know Allahandro's true intentions. Jamaal never revealed his advantages until it's time to strike. Allahandro and his peoples were known for having some of the best coke in Harlem so Jamaal tolerated Allahandro's sly bilingual sarcasm.

Crack fed the strong, starved the weak and raped the ghetto of its purity. Jamaal knew he was doing wrong but discarded his guilt by justifying his actions. "Sometimes you have to do the wrong thing to come out right." He kept a little weed around but now it was all about that crack. Hashish taught him the basics of cooking coke properly, with baking soda and water. Jamaal took it to the next level, he chose to use the black top vials to package his product. So customers could differentiate between him and the spot up the block; Jacob and his older brother Alshaun used the yellow tops and they were right on 148th street towards Broadway. Jamaal looked at them as two dusty niggas, and considered them no competition at all, besides he had knocked Jacob out a couple of months ago for disrespecting Samaya. Jamaal had those eyes that see into souls and it wasn't hard for him know a coward when he saw one.

Jamaal kept a business sense and implemented a 24 hour shift rotation between him and Hashish where he would work nights, Hashish worked the days. He broke his product into 10 dollar jumbo vials and two for 5 dollar vials. He had no marketing scheme he just stuck to a basic concept, quantity plus quality equals satisfied customers. While other young dealers dilute their product to make more money Jamaal focused on keeping it as pure as possible. He managed his finance, sales and merchandise by splitting his week Monday – Wednesdays was rent days – that's when he got together re-up (*remerchandising*) money, and Hashish's pay—Thursday – Saturday – is his personal money . He made up to 3 to 5 thousand a day and completely closes shop on Sundays. Jamaal bought Samaya a used Audi to help them get around. He would have bought it for himself but he knew that a black boy his age driving around in a sports car would cause too much attention. She appreciated his many expensive gifts but wanted nothing more than for him to go to school and become a regular "working stiff", yet she felt that she had to be supportive. After all he wasn't cheating on her or mistreating her he was just doing something illegal to make sure he can do something for his family. She has gone through long mind probing discussions with Jamaal, she knows his life and the things he's been through. She feels that only Allah can judge her man—and she rebukes any one that speaks negatively of him. Jamaal had a very humble demeanor maturing way beyond his C.M.K. days. He kept his building in order by showing the neighbors courtesy. As you know it's usually the nosey neighbors that call the cops, you can't really get mad at them because they are law abiding citizens. So if they feel like you are disrupting the quality of life in their area then of course they will try to remove you. So Jamaal made sure he made the residents in his building feel comfortable. He didn't allow people to smoke weed in front of the building and crack heads were not allowed to smoke in any building on his block. Except a few dumb crack heads in lobbies and alleyways and they were beat to a pulp as examples. Taking a bunch of the neighborhood kids to the store for candy was a usual thing for Jamaaal. He won the approval of the community and his business was running great except for one weak link-Hashish.

Hashish had a knack for talking shit, everyone said he should have been a comedian, but his problem was he ran his mouth to much and he was addicted to spending his money on women. Hashish was stealing from the business to support his addiction; he would make up false excuses like claiming he got robbed in front of the Cineplex Odeon Movie Theater. The more he stole the more outlandish his story would be. Jamaal turned a blind eye to his uncle's insubordinate moves as long as Hashish doesn't take to much money. Plus he felt he could never stomp out his own uncle like some regular worker.

Even Alshaun and Jacob eventually started working for Jamaal because he took over the block. With the extra workers now he could get traffic from both sides of the block and take some responsibility away from the forever irresponsible Hashish. Usually after Jamaal re-ups he makes two stops, first he stops at Alshaun's house to cook, chop and bag his crack, then he goes to his house and repeats the process. Jamaal and his crew had a sensational four month run before the unexpected happen. Allahandro gave him some bad coke; he didn't get his estimated comeback. Allahandro already raised the price on the ounces and grams and now he was trying to skim off the top. It didn't make sense especially after Jamaal has been such a faithful customer. Jamaal was starting to get a name uptown so he could not let this slide but he did not have the man power or fire power to take on Allahandro's crew.

So he figured exercising diplomacy would be the best approach, this was one of those days he wished he still had Fire and Basil around. He walked down the block to La Casa Restaurant as soon as you hit Broadway you can hear the meringue music hitting you from all angles. He had his box cutter in his pocket although he did not think he would need it. He had a look of determination in his eyes and he wore an all beige army fatigue suit with the Vazquez Gortex boots, his choice of gear matched his militant stride. Allahandro spotted him before he had a chance to walk inside the Restaurant. Allahandro's called out to him while sitting inside an all black Acura Legend. Jamaal walks up to the car …….. Alahandro "Meda Blacko What's up? What joo need?" Jamaal "I need to talk to you man." Allahandro "Okay so get in the back seat." Jamaal was always leery about getting into other peoples cars especially when the tints are so dark you can't see who might be sitting in there. Jamaal "Nah that's alright, let's talk out here." Now Allahandro could obviously sense the tension, he got out the car mumbling all types of derogatory statements in Spanish calling Jamaal every name in the book. Jamaal knew exactly what Allahandro was saying but ignored it. Now they stood in front of the restaurant. Jamaal "Listen B you shorting me on my ounces. I ain't never ask you for nothing on consignment, my money never been short. So you going to have to reimburse me for the last two ounces cause that shit was garbage." Allahandro was a very arrogant person and it showed in everything he does. Allahandro "Listen Blacko, every time I give you coke, de coke iz goo, thas it, I no give you nothing, sorry!" Before Jamaal had a chance to realize how angry he was getting, he was stunned by a sneaky hay maker punch from Allahandro. Jamaal's bottom lip opened up and started to bleed profusely. Jamaal retaliated with raw anger and bull charged him scooping him of his feet, slamming him to the ground. Jamaal didn't get off more than two punches before Allahandro's security "Stud" jumps out the passenger seat of the Acura. He pulled Jamaal off him and put him a strangling choke hold. Stud stood a hulking 6ft 3in 310 lbs of pure muscle. Jamaal gagged and spit his own blood wrestling to get out of Stud's grasp. Allahandro rose to his feet and treated Jamaal's midsection like a human punching bag. Sometimes the best defense is just maintaining your composure, which Jamaal did. He managed to reach into his pocket and retrieve his box cutter and cut a huge slice out of Stud's arm forcing him to release him. Instinctively he tried to pounce on Allahandro but before Jamaal could attack him the entire block descended upon him like a swarm of locust out of a biblical plague. At least 20 Dominican guys were damn near fighting each other just to get a stomp in on him. Jamaal curled in to a fetal position trying to protect his face. At this point he could not even feel the blows; it was as though his body was a shell and he could hear the multiple strikes hitting his shell.

When a warrior is engaged in battle and discovers he is loosing it changes the stakes often causing the warrior to stress survival. Now most if not all will do some sort of dishonorable act to insure survival like retreating. Some how he gathered his wits, jumped to his feet and charged through the crowd while being knocked from left to right. He managed to break through and run up the block to Hashish's apartment. He entered the door looking sweaty and disheveled. Hashish was not home but Samaya was and when she saw her husband bleeding from his face she started crying and screaming. Samaya "What the fuck happen to you?!" Jamaal ignores her and walks straight into their bed room and grabs his 38. revolver from under his mattress. She runs behind him and blocks the door way exit.

Samaya "Jamaal I'm fucking talking to you put that fucking gun down and tell me what happened!!" Even though she is screaming at the top of her lungs his expression is blank and motionless as though he were in a daze of revenge. Retaliation was all he could think of and once again he was inside his shell. He could hear her knocking but couldn't answer. While hysterical with the fear of Jamaal dying or killing someone, she slaps him . Samaya "Wake up stupid ass, stop acting fucking crazy, please Jamaal think about your seed inside me, I love you please don't do this, please, think first."

His eyes were still blank but he does focus on her, before he could utter a word she snatches the gun from his hand and presses her lips against his. As their lips locked she could taste his blood, the salt from her sweaty tear drenched face stung his wounds. She drops the gun on the floor, hugs him tightly as if she were trying to over power his anger with her love. Then Samaya pushes Jamaal on to the bed proceeding to pull off his ripped up army pants stained by blood and dirt. Samaya was three months pregnant she had gained a little weight but she was still beautiful. She quickly went to the bathroom to retrieve a wash cloth and soak it with hot water, black soap and rubbing alcohol. So she could wipe Jamaal's body down and nurse his wounds. Samaya was used to him having fights but she never pictured him loosing until now. After wiping him down she slid her panties off and raised her night gown (*which was any over sized T-shirt she took from Jamaal*).

She closed there bedroom door, put the gun under the mattress and laid next to him naked. Jamaal was not even erect he was still numb with rage. So she pulled his arm to make him hold her. She seductively gyrated her waste rubbing her plump buttocks against his penis reminding him of one of the many reasons she was his wife. That was all it took to get him ready she was already moist inside, she placed his manhood inside her throbbing pink vagina. He started to move and she stopped him – Samaya "It's okay baby I know you tired, don't move, just go to sleep we'll talk when you wake. I just want to fall asleep with you inside me." He submitted to her will while she got on top of him and rode him until the shared orgasmic bliss and fell asleep with him inside of her just like she wanted.

A couple of hours passed before the couple woke up. They were startled by a loud knock at the bedroom door. Jamaal jumped up, thinking inside that maybe it was just an intense nightmare but his sore body and swollen lip reminded him it was all reality. Jamaal threw on his grey Champion sweat pants and pulled the blanket over Samaya's body. When he opened the bedroom door it was Hashish "Yo what happen B I heard the platanos jumped you?" Jamaal "What the fuck you think happened, look at my face, but fuck them niggas I'm alright." Hashish "So what we gonna do B?" Jamaal "Nothing, we going to finish off this package then we going to chill with this crack shit." Hashish "So that's it, we just going to stop selling? We aint going to get those niggas back?" Jamaal "Did I say we wasn't going to get them back, no! I said we going to chill and lay low for a while! This shit is deep B and we aint going to talk around my wife, so just do me a favor B roll up a blunt, I'll be out in a second." He turns to Samaya as he shuts the bedroom door. He told Samaya he needed her to stay up the block at her parent's apartment for a couple of weeks. Samaya didn't like the idea but she was familiar with the Islamic term Jihad and knew that war is no place for a woman. He was a stubborn young man and he would never allow some one to get the best of him without avenging himself. His determination and discipline was so attractive to her but those same traits made him a thug. She entered the relationship feeling that she could push his power in a positive direction. She held back her tears to hide her sorrow because she knew what Jamaal planned on doing. He reached under the bed and pulled out his shoe box stash and pulled out four rubber band rolls of money a thousand dollars each and passed them to Samaya. He gave her strict instructions to stay in the house as much as possible. He didn't want to meet outside anymore, only indoors. He was just being cautious, he wanted the streets to forget about him for a while and he didn't want his enemies to associate Samaya with him or else she might become a target.

Once he got Samaya out the way and sent her to her mother's house he called Jacob and Alshaun and told them to sell off there packages and keep the entire profit. He gave the block to them, and they were quick to oblige him. With every one out of the way he was free to plan his revenge.

First he put 3/4 tints on every window of Samaya's Audi. He was planning to murder Allahandro but he knew they had the upper hand so he had to see exactly how they operate before going to war. For two weeks he parked across the street from

La Casa Restaurant. On Monday through Thursday he would park up and watch them from about 8:00 am to like 6:00pm and Friday through Sunday he would do it from 7:00pm to 2:00am.

One thing he noticed was that Stud was like the enforcer of the group, all he did was fuck people up for not doing their jobs properly, but he never arrived until about 1 o'clock everyday. His presence seemed to make every one nervous when he was around though. He would lash out unpredictably at Allahandro or any other worker. They had a lot of salesman but Allahandro was by far the most ambitious. Jamaal noticed all types of expensive cars with out of town license plates coming to see Allahandro for coke. All the major deals seemed to go on inside with Stud and Allahandro present. Stud was also the pick up man for the big boss, because every day around 10 am Allahandro would come out of the restaurant with a huge garbage bag and put it in the trunk of this broken down Chevrolet on the corner. Stud would arrive much later retrieve the keys from Allahandro drive away only to return about 30 minutes later. The dudes outside the restaurant kept their weapons strategically positioned on the ground near them concealed in garbage bags camouflaged by the usual littered Harlem pavement. Stud always wore all black but the bulge in his back insinuated that he always had a weapon present.

It took a short amount of time for Jamaal to gather the information he needed and he figured the less he tells Hashish the better. He would attack when they were most vulnerable, the morning. Allahandro was always alone when he comes out to put the bags in that car, there is usually little or no soldiers around to help him at that time.

That morning Jamaal gave Reg a call for the first time in about 10 months and requested a real big favor. He gave Reg a specific time to meet him by the east 125th street FDR highway entrance. Reg had no idea why this was such a big deal but he knew Jamaal wouldn't ask for a favor unless really needed it. It was an early Monday morning and kids were on their way to school when Jamaal woke Hashish to drive him up the block. Jamaal had on all black army suit on, his hat pulled low and a black bandana around his neck. He had his 38 revolver filled with hollow slugs on his waste with his book bag on filled with a bottle of liter fluid and a navy blue Champion sweat suit.

When Jamaal and Hashish were parked across the street from La Casa Restaurant at about 9:45 a.m Hashish started asking a lot of questions. Jamaal gave him the answers while putting on his gloves and pulling his gun from his waste.

Jamaal "Nigga I'm going to kill Allahadro what the fuck you think I was planning for?!." Hashish "Yeah but in broad daylight man? Are you sure about this? I ain't never killed nobody before B." Jamaal "Me neither but fuck that, I'm going to kill this motherfucker." Hashish "Man you aint serious is you? Can't we just fuck the nigga up or something?" Jamaal stares through the tinted glass at the restaurant across the street and reflects on his objective. Jamaal "Man I'm younger than you, why you acting pussy?! You told me this was a dirty game right. So if I'm in it I'm playing to win. Anyway you ain't got to do shit after I shoot this nigga, I'm taking that car right there, trust me it will be sweet. You play look out, honk your horn if you see Five-O coming. After I drive off you drive off slow and normal, park the car, go to my girl's crib and give her the car keys. Just do ya regular shit during the day and act normal. I'll come back to the crib a little later B. Don't let me down, I'm counting on you." Hashish is nervous and asks Jamaal if he is sure. At that moment Jamaal watches Allahandro walk out of the restaurant. Jamaal says "Yeah I'm sure" and pulls his bandana over his lips and nose. Like a hungry jaguar stalking its prey he carefully gives Allahandro enough time to put the bag in the trunk. That's when Jamaal opens the car door and sprints across the street towards his unsuspecting victim. Allahandro is awoken from his casual stroll with the feeling of car keys being ripped from his hand and a cold gun barrel pressed firmly against his fore head. Allahandro's mouth was wide open he was frozen with fear as though he couldn't even blink. A second becomes an eternity and there is a moment of silence, Jamaal heard nothing but the click of the gun's hammer like the snare in his hearts drum beat. His index finger contorted around the trigger as he squeezed. A spark spews from the nozzle of his weapon, the hollow slug entered Allahandro's head and exploded. Shards of metal tore through the various regions of his brain cracking his skull. At that very moment you could see his spirit exiting his mouth with his final breath like a brief puff of smoke in the cold winter air. The sound is what Jamaal would never forget, it was a cold low whisper that meant death. The blood didn't even spray out of Allahandro head like you would imagine. It just sort of poured out of his ears, nose, mouth and eyes like chunky reddish black mud as he fell to the floor. Allahandro's head swelled up, his eye sockets were so bloody that he resembled something demonic and Jamaal was pleased that he had vanquished him. He wished he read Allahandro's mind to know what it feels like to die as he watched a puddle of blood form around Allahandro's head growing rapidly as though it was the demons final attempt at consuming him. Jamaal felt if the blood touched him it would damn him to hell.

A voice in his head demanded that he run and he shook

of his state of shock and responded. He ran to the Chevrolet and sped off with the tires screeching. Hashish began to pull off slowly still frightened by what he witnessed. Hashish under stood Jamaal all too clearly now, he was something that Hashish claimed to be but never was. His nephew was a killer and a gangster and for the first time he felt afraid of Jamaal. As Jamaal twisted and turned down different blocks and avenues to get to his destination he felt a chill all over his body, his hair's stood up like Allahandro's ghost was following him. With one hand on the steering wheel he searched his book bag for his bottle of lighter fluid. He removed his sweat suit and began putting lighter fluid all over the back seat. He reached Reg within minutes and pulled up along side him. Reg "What's going on with you nigga?" He did not even respond he jumped out of the car and stood between the Chevy and Reg's Acura. Jamaal changed into his blue Champion sweat suit like Clark Kent in a telephone booth. He threw his army suit into the car window and emptied the remainder of the lighter onto his clothing. He grabbed the garbage bag out the trunk and set the car a blaze with a couple of matches. Jamaal threw the bag in to Reg's backseat and jumped into the passenger seat all the while Reg stares at him in awe. Reg speeds off and jumps on the highway.

Reg "Yo what the fuck did you do kid?" Jamaal's heart was racing but he was shockingly calm. Jamaal "I just murdered a nigga now let's hurry up and get to Brooklyn."

The rest of the ride was spent in silence Reg hadn't seen or heard from Jamaal in a while but he never thought Jamaal would turn out like this. Reg was in his early twenties and was heavy into the crack game since it started. So he has met enough murderers to know what a killer's eyes looked like, Jamaal had those killer eyes. It was a cold hearted peacefulness as though murdering some one didn't bother him at all. He grinned at the sight of his old neighbor hood Jamaal forgot how much he missed Brooklyn, things seemed a little simpler there. Jamaal almost broke a sweat dragging the garbage bag up the steps to Reg's place. When they got inside they emptied the bag's contents on to his coffee table. There a bunch of shredded news paper and 10 stacks of one hundred 100 dollars bills each, that's 100 thousand dollars. It wasn't hard to count because it was so neatly packed. Jamaal refused to get into details with Reg about how he got the money Jamaal felt like he already gave Reg to much information. Neither one of them ever saw this much money at once.

Reg "Damn kid you a bad motherfucker. What you going to do with all this money?" Jamaal could sense him scheming but had no worries because he knew he would kill Reg if he had to. Jamaal "I'm going to give you 20 thousand and I'm stashing the rest." Reg "Thanks kid but where are you going to stash 80 thousand, and who you going to trust with that much money?" Jamaal was loosing trust for Reg at a rapid pace. Jamaaal knew he planned on leaving the money with Samaya and no one could know that. Jamaal "Now it wouldn't be a stash if I told you where it was at." Jamaal felt a funny vibe from Reg, he was to inquisitive for a street nigga who just got 20,000 for doing next to nothing. He should be grateful but instead he's probing for information and Jamaal didn't like him probing.

Reg could feel the tension as he rushed to call Jamaal a cab. The cab arrives downstairs and honks his horn until Reg sticks his head out the window. Jamaal extends his hand to Reg and thanks him once again and runs downstairs to make his way back uptown. He sat in the cab and sparked a blunt before the cab driver could even think to complain he was handed 2 hundred dollar bills. The driver turned on the radio and one of Jamaal's favorite songs came on "*Some might say take a chill B\ But fuck that shit there's a nigga trying to kill me\I'm poppin in the clip when the wind blows\Every twenty seconds got me peepin out my window\ Investigatin the joint for traps\Checkin my telephone for taps\I'm starin at the woman on the corner\It's fucked up when your mind is playin tricks on ya." By --Scarface and The Ghetto Boys song-My mind's playing tricks on me.*

The song some how fit Jamaal's mood and it served as a theme song for his current state of mind. Jamaal was in a state of utter paranoia but he was not disillusioned. In fact he did not know how accurate his feeling were. As soon as he left Reg's apartment Reg got on the phone and called his friend Sopa to do some of his own investigating. Reg did not know who Allahandro was but he knew that if any one lost 100,000 dollars uptown one way or another Sopa had to know about it. As a matter of fact Sopa knew exactly who Allahandro was, that was one of his best sales men. Reg turned out to be a belly sliding snake, he begged him not to kill Jamaal, Sopa agreed. Sopa told Reg to keep the 20 thousand, and never tell Jamaal he called him.

Sopa had been giving Reg coke on consignment for a while, Reg was always kissing his ass trying to find a way to get a permanent spot in Sopa's organization. With the betrayal of Jamaal he just might have found the perfect opportunity. Reg was curious about exactly what Sopa was going to do Jamaal. Sopa told Reg nothing except these last words in his "spang-lish" accent. Sopa "I'm going to teach him a lesson, but don't ever tell him you called me when you speak to him again okay! Trust me everything is going to be alright, you showed loyalty that I thought you didn't have so you'll be rewarded. Oh and keep the money don't worry about it, just wait for my call." Sopa hangs up the phone. Reg held the guilt of someone who has just traded a friend's life for personal gain.

SOPA

JAMAAL gave the Hindu cab driver a generous tip for letting him smoke weed in the back of the cab. He still felt a little nervous killing his own lungs by chain-smoking cigarettes between blunts. Something just wasn't right, he couldn't quite put his finger on it but he knew there had to be more to it. It seemed too easy and that made him uneasy so he had the cab driver drop him off up the block at Samaya's Umi's (*mother*) building.

He ran up the stairs instead of waiting for the elevator, he wrung her door bell and to his surprise Samaya had a lovely smile on her face greeting him with a huge hug. He couldn't imagine what would have her feeling so ecstatic especially since she was going on 4 months pregnant and she's been a little bitchy lately. Samaya showed Jamaal a huge bouquet of dark pink roses and a card, she described some big guy named Stud who helped her mother up the stairs with her groceries. While he stood at the door he gave Samaya the flowers and said he was a very good friend of Jamaal's and questioned his whereabouts. Looking disappointed that Jamaal wasn't present he left about thirty minutes ago. Jamaal's face turned pale when he contemplated what Stud could have done to Samaya, her mother, and his unborn child. She was in tune with his feelings though he tried to hide them.

Now Jamaal understood that funny feeling he was getting,

those Dominican guys were on the attack and they knew he killed Allahandro. Apparently that was just a taste of what they know. His first objective is to get Samaya out of harms way. He gave her the book bag filled with 80,000 dollars, made her pack her clothes and drive the Audi to her aunt's house in Jamaica Queens. He loaded his 38 revolver and begged Allah's protection in prayer; they brought this conflict to this level now some how he must take it to the next level. His second priority was to go check Hashish at his place, he quietly speed walks up the block.

He entered Hashish's building and as usual the front lobby door was open. He pulled out his gun and crept down the hallway as silent as possible. Delicately slid his key into the door and opened it. He whispered Hashish's name and extended his gun arm forward while scanning the wall for a light switch with the other hand. He began to squint attempting to gather some type of night vision while he walked through the dark apartment. Suddenly he was startled by what didn't feel like a light switch but a person. Jamaal fired one shot out of sheer panic and fear. A sharp pain jolted through the back of his skull as some sort of blunt object crashed across his head. Blurring his already distorted vision he began to see little sparkles of light and he heard the faint voices that were clearly of Hispanic origin. He struggled to remain conscious as he was beat on repeatedly until he passed out unconscious and his vision faded to black............................

...........Some where in what appears to be a basement with all gray cylinder block walls. The floor is made of raw concrete and this place was faintly lit by over head hanging light bulbs. Three blue nose pit bulls are chained up in the far corner barking ferociously. One pit bull stands out more than the rest, his name is "Trouble", the father of the other two smaller pit bulls. He is all white and blind in his left eye as a result of a previous battle. Trouble is so vicious that he doesn't even bark he just growls before he strikes. This place carries the peculiar aroma of blood, liquor and dog shit. This is where they brought Jamaal to torture him until he gives up the money. Jamaal is still unconscious his hands are cuffed together behind his back while his feet are bound to his chair with duct tape. His body was propped up on a raggedy wooden chair; there was a steady trickle of blood flowing from a huge knot in the back of his head. He had swelled up and a purple bluish discoloration from his left eye to his cheek bone. The drops of blood seem to hit the damp cement in slow torturous pattern, the sounds seemed to irritate the dogs. Hashish was also battered and bound to a chair about 12 feet from Jamaal but there was one difference. Hashish's mouth was bound with silver tape to prevent him from screaming. Well at least his mouth couldn't scream but his eyes did with tears as they raced from side to side as though he were attempting to warn Jamaal. Finally two men entered the basement through the steel reinforced door. One was Stud, the other was a short stocky fellow named "Modelo". Stud's usual uniform was all black suits but today he was dressed for work with black slacks and tank top, garnishing an apron around his waist and wearing long latex gloves like some sort of cryptic butcher.

You could tell the dogs were very familiar with Stud because their barking ceased upon his entrance. Hashish's eyes read fear in capital red letters when he saw Stud because they had been beating on him for a while. The shorter man Modelo was dressed like Stud except he wore shades and carried a 45. caliber hand gun equipped with a silencer, he held an open bottle of Brugal (*Dominican Rum*) in his other hand. The two men walk towards Jamaal; Stud looks at Modelo and says. "This is the one who killed little Allahandro, I want to kill this fucking little black piece of shit but Sopa wants him alive, he wants to talk to him." Modelo looks a little frustrated and has a itchy trigger finger but did not want to disobey Sopa. Modelo lifts his bottle of Brugal and takes a good swig of rum then he pours the remainder of the bottle all over Jamaal's face. Startled by the burning sensation Jamaal wakes up gagging and coughing. At first he squints his eyes because the rum is irritating them, but it doesn't take long for him to gather his senses and realize what has happened. There is concern in his face when he sees Hashish bound and gagged in the corner. Jamaal looks at Stud and regrets that he hadn't killed him along with Allahandro. Stud "Good morning sleepy head, you had a goo rest bitch? I want you to know I would have choked you to death with my bare hands but the boss wants to talk to you." Jamaal can barely muster enough strength to speak. "Fuck you!! Ain't shit to talk about, kill me you Platino mother fucker!" Modelo moves toward Jamaal as if he would like to oblige his request. Modelo firmly presses the nozzle of his silencer tipped 45. caliber against Jamaal's forehead. This didn't silence his mouth it only angered Jamaal because he felt like begging for his life would be cowardice when he was surely about to die, in away he welcomed death. Jamaal "Come on just shoot me you bitch ass mother fucker!!" Blood and saliva shoots from his mouth giving emphasis to every word he screams riling the dogs up. Hashish cringes in horror feeling as though Jamaal is destroying any chance they might have at survival. Modelo raises his gun above his head and whips it across Jamaal's face resulting in yet another huge gash on the side of his cheek bone.

Jamaal in an angry rage instinctively attempts to retaliate by lunging at both men, which only resulted in Jamaal and his chair falling to the ground. Stud and Modelo repeatedly kicked him in his ribs and abdominal area until he was practically coughing up blood. A fifth person enters the basement speaking with a soft yet powerful voice, he says "Stop". He stood about 5'8 with a slender frame, in his late 40's, wearing a cream colored Guahaberra shirt with linen pants. His Panama hat shadowed his face, only the haunting vision of his cold heavy eyes and salt and pepper goatee were distinguishable. He doesn't wear any jewelry except a immaculate wedding band and multi colored rosary beads that hung from his neck. He is the top boss of a Dominican crime syndicate that controls a good portion of all Cocaine distribution in New York, the tri-state, and north eastern U.S. This was the infamous "Sopa". Stud and Modelo quickly ceased beating on Jamaal and raised his chair up so that Sopa may have a word with him.

The room was spinning from Jamaal's point of view but he could still read Sopa's aura, it emitted a power and wisdom that only a true kingpin could have. Sopa told Stud and Modelo to leave him alone with Hashish and Jamaal but not before he took Modelo's 45. millimeter hand gun with the silencer on it from him. As Stud left the room he says "call if you need us Sopa." Jamaal ears rose like a startled dog's, he knew that name Sopa sounded all too familiar. It came to him swiftly; this was the guy that Reg was telling him to call a bout a year ago. At first he thought about mentioning his friendship with Reg, but changed his mind fearing it would only result in Reg getting killed. Jamaal did not want to involve another person and have Reg's life on his conscious so he kept his mouth shut. Jamaal never once thought that Reg might have betrayed him.

Sopa glances at Hashish for a brief second then moves towards Jamaal. As though Hashish is insignificant and Jamaal was Sopa's true prey.

Sopa "So what's your name and where you from?" Jamaal "Just shoot me!" Sopa erupts with laughter and replies. Sopa "You know what I like you already not like that piece shit over there." *(He uses the handgun to point at Hashish)* Sopa begins pacing back and forth while lecturing Jamaal. Sopa "Since you won't tell me who you are I will tell you who you are. Your name is Jamaal and your from Flatbush, you're a friend of Reg's but your stupid ass didn't call me when he told you to, now look at the mess your in. Trust me if I find out Reg had something to do with this I'll kill him too! It's funny, I would never have been able to find you if it wasn't for your uncle here, your own uncle gave you up. Oh and I forgot to tell you that your beautiful pregnant girl friend Samaya is safe at her aunt's house in Queens. She's on 168th street and Hillside, right?! I have two black Lincoln town cars full of soldiers parked up the block awaiting my instructions. Now learn to speak to Sopa."

Jamaal "But how the fuck you know all that shit? Sopa "Because of who I am, I could have the fucking Mayor killed if I want comprende. Now you stole 100,000 pesos from me and you killed one of my best salesmen so you actually owe me way more than that. Why did you kill Allahandro?" Jamaal "I made him a lot of money and he played me you know what I'm saying?! We was doing straight business, that nigga ain't need to short me on no product you know. Sopa "So it wasn't the money ...." Jamaal interrupts him "No it was the principle" Sopa only laughs. It is eerie the way he wields the gun so casually as though it was a prosthetic hand. Looking slightly confused he rubs his own fore head with the silencers nozzle. Sopa "Never the less it was a sloppy kill, I was much better at your age but you got heart and you'll get better." Sopa only pauses to glance at Hashish whose eyes are still screaming out behind the duct tape. "You know your uncle is a fucking traitor, all we had to do was put a gun to his face and he told us everything, I'd kill him if I were you. Any way let's cut the bullshit, you owe me big time and you owe me at least fifty thousand dollars in cash and about 1mil worth of work. You can keep fifty thousand dollars of the money you stole just to get started. Oh and these are not requests, these are demands. You have two alternatives, you can work for me and get filthy rich or I kill you, but not before I cut Samaya's belly open and stomp on your unborn fetus in front of you. I love nothing, I feel nothing, I know La Compania, I know La Familia and I have power and money which are the two things I do love. You will work for me until you repay your debt understand." Jamaal met a lot of crazy street dudes in his life but he never met anyone who he was afraid of until Sopa. Jamaal "Yes I understand." He felt like he sold his soul to the devil with those three words.

Sopa "You know that old cliché; "an eye for an eye" well don't take this personal okay." Sopa walks over to Hashish and rest the silencer on top of his head and empties out 7 bullets into his head. (*Well two into his head and five into the sloppy mess on his neck*) All while keeping direct eye contact with Jamaal. Jamaal's eyes well with tears until they rained down his face. His body went numb as he stared into Sopa's eyes and all Jamaal could see was death staring back at him. A hot splash of Hashish's blood trickled down their faces and they spoke telepathically. Sopa' eyes said "I own you" and Jamaal's said "I will kill you one day". Sopa just chuckled again a little amused by Jamaal's brave yet foolish anger, it was like toying with a lion cub.

Sopa "Now I've taken a life from you and we are even in principle, but there is still a financial debt. I can give you the world but you must pledge your loyalty. Remember you owe me your life, don't be like Allahandro, he was a fucking serpiente! Motherfucker was stealing that's why he shorted you, and Hashish's a fucking dead traitor, "La Compania" is your new family now. Stud's going to take you to my private doctor get you stitched up after you rest for a week or so I'll send for you." Sopa exits the room as Stud and Modelo enter.

They un-cuffed Jamaal's hands and feet, he sat still limp and motionless. The image of Hashish's dead corpse was something he would never forget. Hashish face was distorted it almost looked blue with globs of blood pouring from his nostrils and eye sockets. It reminded him of Allahandro in a way. Stud and Modelo threw a blind fold over his eyes and ushered him to his feet. Jamaal was still in a trance, behind the dark veil of the blind fold his eyes are left with nothing but the faces of the dead. He tenses up for a moment until he realizes that Stud and La Compania really aren't going to kill him. As Jamaal was led out of the basement he was greeted by the sound of people in jubilee clapping and whistling as though a celebrity has arrived.

Stud tells Jamaal "You're not the first kid to be recruited this way Papa, that's why they clapping for you because you one of us now "La Compania" Allahandro got what he deserved for doing bad business. Sopa would have had me kill him anyway. We had to blind fold you because we have to make sure we can trust you before we let you in on everything. But trust this lot of La Compania member know you now and will be watching. Meda negrito this is your new familia."

By now they were outside walking to the car, Jamaal is still blind folded but he can feel the suns rays on his face. Stud eases him into the car. While in the back seat Jamaal begins to speak. Jamaal "So when you gonna take off the blindfold." Stud "When we get to Doctor Milagros house and private practice." Jamaal "Who is Doctor Milagros.?" Stud "He is La Compania's private doctor, hopefully you won't ever need him again, he handles all our injuries in the line of duty if you know what I mean." When they finally arrived Stud removed Jamaal's blindfold. Then he gets out of the drivers seat and jogs up to the doorway of this old fashion brownstone. Jamaal peers out the window, he recognizes this area as the Whitestone section of the Bronx, the nice area for the middle class and semi rich. An old Dominican man in his late 50's wearing a lab coat comes to the door Stud hands him a vanilla envelope and gestures for Jamaal to come in. Jamaal gets out the car and limps over to them in pain. Stud introduces Jamaal to Dr. Milagros as the new guy. The doctor looks Jamaal up and down and asks "I hope you're not scared of needles because you're going to need some stitches. Go inside, my nurses will tend to you." Despite its humble exterior the inside of the house was a "state of the art" medical facility, he was greeted by two beautiful nurses. They escorted him down the hallway into the examination room. He was given Percocet a powerful pain killer and a glass of water. He was at a point where he felt totally confused and disillusioned; he swallowed the pills and lay back against his better judgment. Within a few moments the effects of the pain killer put him to sleep. He slept hard because he was physically exhausted and in desperate need of rest. I guess it took the pain killers to give him some peace. A peace he can never find on his own. Jamaal was at peace for about 72 hours.

When he woke up his head had about eight stitches in the back and apparently they cut a bald spot into his fro. He also had a couple of stitches over his right eye where Modelo had pistol whipped him a day ago. He looked down at his body, he had on a hospital gown with a catheter attached to his penis. Jamaal never saw anything like this in his life. He started flipping, screaming for the nurse. The nurse seemed a little amused, when she entered she helped him remove the catheter and gave him a bundle of clothes and a set of car keys. His face became distraught with confusion, that's when the nurse told him that everything was compliments of Sopa. Jamaal gets dressed and takes the car keys from her. He made sure to thank the doctor before he exited. There was a black Nissan Maxima in the drive way for him. When Jamaal sat down in the drivers seat he noticed a Motorola beeper and a envelope – he opened the envelope and there was a set of house keys, 200 dollars and a note, it had an address on 190th street and Wadsworth Terrace in Washington Heights with one sentiment "This is courtesy of La Compania, we will send for you."

Jamaal's first thought was to find them and kill them all but he couldn't after he signed that deadly contract with Sopa, he couldn't renege. Going on the run with no money wasn't an option but he had to avenge himself and Hashish even if Hashish was a traitor. Then he had a revelation why not learn from Sopa gather his strength then move in for the kill. It was time's like this that made him really miss Fire and Supreme *(Basil)*, but even with them present he would still have to plan and strategize because Sopa is not some one you can just murder and expect to get away with it. Sopa had an army and the fact is you can't go up against an army without money or your own army or better yet both.

Samaya was the only person Jamaal really trusted and right now he had to see her, she was probably worried sick about him. He hits the Whitestone Bridge at 75mph rushing to Queens hoping Samaya has been safe. He reached Samaya and told her a bunch of lies so that she wouldn't fear for his life, Samaya knew something terrible happened, she just turned a blind eye to it. She couldn't ignore the stitches on his face he told her he had a bad fight, but she knew it had to be more than just a fight. He stayed at Samaya's aunt's house for a couple of hours before he left to drive back to Harlem to Hashish's place and check his mail box for letters from Supreme.

When he arrived on his block he noticed a dark blue Ford Taurus double parked in front of Hashish's building. These had to be detectives –"What are they doing? Why are they here?" he asked himself while he parked his Maxima around the corner he gave one of the local kids 100 dollars to pop open Hashish's mail box, retrieve the mail and find out what the detectives were doing. The little boy sped around the block on his bike determined to earn his cash. He returned with his mail and some interesting information, apparently the two white detectives were asking if any one saw Hashish. Jamaal gave him a extra 50 dollar bill and drove off. Jamaal decide that calling Samaya and telling her to take the Audi and meet him Wadsworth terrace wouldn't make sense. Plus he had to check the place out first and make sure it was safe. He finally reached the apt on Wadsworth Terrance up the block from the 190th street A Train station across the street from a Cambrini High school, an all female catholic school. It was a pretty nice neighbor hood, it overlooks the rougher area Inwood separated by Fort Tryon Park. (*It is weird but it seems that historically all the ghetto areas of New York are separated from the upper class financial areas by huge parks, and shopping districts.*) The building was good, quiet, no crack heads in the hall way, no graphitti on the wall but the inside of his apartment was the icing on the cake.

He couldn't believe how nice this place was, the whole place was a dark burgundy with all black leather furniture, a television, a sound system in the living room and bedroom. The whole place seemed the follow the black and burgundy theme, the place was immaculate, this was the highest level of luxury he had ever experienced. He sat on the couch, a strong feeling of guilt over Hashish's death engulfed him, his head was flooded with conflicting images. He had to question Sopa's motives; it just didn't make sense for him to let Jamaal live and recruit him to. What is Sopa's real reason and did Hashish really betray him or did Sopa kill him for another reason. This was all to strange but he was in a bind and it was made very clear that he has to work for La Compania or they will find him and kill him. At the age of 16 he was in over his head and the only way out was to learn his enemy. He sat back on his brand new leather couch and checked through his mail for a letter from Supreme. Luckily for him there was one, he lit up a cigarette to find comfort and clairvoyance in the N.G.E (Nations of Gods Earths) lessons Supreme has sent him.

La Compania

JAMAAL enjoyed settling into the new apartment and so did Samaya even though she doesn't know what Jamaal went through to obtain it. Thirty thousand dollars was more than enough money to accommodate their material and financial needs for a couple of weeks. Sometime had passed and Jamaal's Motorola beeper never went off unless it was Samaya. He healed up and Dr. Milagros removed his stitches but he was left with a thick slim scar across his right eye brow and another in the back of his head. He felt ready to put in work for Sopa and hopefully repay his debt and acquire enough money to leave with Samaya, after he destroyed Sopa's structure from the inside.

He got deeper into the knowledge he received from Supreme's letters. It caused some debate with Samaya who stressed that Jamaal was Muslim and shouldn't stray from the Koran and traditional beliefs. Samaya would always say the 5% was some type of gang/cult and tease Jamaal by saying "If you are God then make a fly" while giggling. His stern reply was "I'm a God because I'm the original man whose ancestral history precedes earth. On this planet black men and women are the supreme beings". That usually ended the argument, Jamaal wasn't one for much words. He was determined to to master the teachings of the N.G.E, the 5% lessons known as "120". Jamaal wanted knowledge of self and was looking forward to getting his "attribute" (*righteous nam*e) from Supreme. This particular morning he was just relaxing with his wife rubbing her belly when his phone began to ring, Samaya answered assuming it was her family. She quickly passed the phone to Jamaal and goes into the living room.

Operator "Rikers Island Correctional Facility do you except?" Jamaal "Yes" Supreme "Peace God, I'm go get sentenced tomorrow they giving me a 5 to 15. I'm just going to take that cause if I go to trial they'll kill me. I already bin locked for 18 months so I'll probably be on the island for a while before they send me up north. After about 3 years more years I'll be eligible for payroll." Jamaal "Damn that's the fucked up God you going to be gone for a while but I got your back B." Supreme "Yeah thanks for the equality with those packages an all that." Jamaal "No doubt God I'll give Chyna some shit to bring to the Island, just make sure you stay out of trouble and come home god I need you to be out here you hear me?" Supreme "No doubt God that's peace how's your earth and your seed?" Jamaal "They doing good it's just she get more and more moody as her belly grows ha ha ha (*laughte*r)." Supreme "ha ha ha ha (*laughter)* you a funny nigga God let me call Chyna man peace God write me a letter and next time we on the phone you better be ready to recite all the lessons from memory." Jamaal "No doubt I'll build with you later." They both hang up the phone.

A little while later his Motorola beeper goes off, Sopa is the only one with the number. Jamaal grabs his navy blue flight jacket and his Yankees fitted cap and goes towards the door. Samaya questions him, he only answers with the word "business" as he left. Samaya sat on the couch feeling like her 3 week fantasy had come to and end. She just hoped that Jamaal would come home alive. He jogged downstairs and went to the pay phone. When he called the unfamiliar number he was greeted by Sopa's voice "Hola negrito, I like your style not calling from your home phone, never call me from your home phone. Now come to the pool hall on 193rd street and Broadway" and hung up. Jamaal jumped into his black Maxima and went to his meeting.

The Billiards on the corner was flooded with Dominican dudes but half these guys really look black. The older guys in their late 20's wore pointy shoes and colorful shirts with these funny looking jherri curl partial mo-hawks. The guys Jamaal's age who were first generation Americans would adhere to the 90's dress code. You know Carhartts, Guess, Polo etc… it was hard to tell some of them weren't American black until you spoke to them. Then there was the older guys who dressed like Sopa, very plain .there eyes were cold like his to. Jamaal parked his car and noticed Stud and Modelo waiting in front. Some of La Compania who were there the day they kidnapped Jamaal seemed to recognize him and gave reassuring nods as though they were approving his safe passage into the pool hall. Stud gave him a firm hand shake and led him into the pool hall through all the loud Brugal drinking pool players, the meringue classics bumped out the juke box in a small back room with a separate exit. Sopa sat there reading a book called *The Prince* by Niccolo Machiavelli smoking a joint of exotic weed. He stood up and gave Jamaal a handshake while pulling him closer for a brotherly hug. Sopa tells Stud and Modelo to exit the room then asked Jamaal to sit down.

Sopa "I know a lot has happened in the past weeks but I need you to be ready to go to the next level. I have a bunch of perico (*Cocaine*) spots in Harlem and up here but I'm getting robbed. First the fucking American chocolos and now the fucking Jamaicans trying to move in on my business. They're getting perico from the Columbians and snatching my out of state customers." Jamaal "Okay so what's that got to do with me?" Sopa "I want to give you "Black Harlem". I want you to collect all the money in Harlem and I want you to control the blacks for me." Jamaal "This shit sounds stupid! So what? So I'm supposed to go against my own people for you?!" Sopa interrupts "Do you think I don't know your mother is Dominican? Motherfucker we all black, you couldn't tell some of them stupid motherfuckers outside that, but I know that. I would never tell you to betray your people, I'm just trying to bring order to chaos. There are to many little gangs trying to move in on La Compania so I have been recruiting soldiers but I have got a special assignment for you. Nobody in upper Harlem can sell crack unless they're buying weight from you or working for you. That's every body from 145th and Broadway to the 135th street. I need the fucking Jamaicans wiped out and you're going to help me. The average hit pays about 10 thousand but mine are special so you get 15 for every hit. It is not going to be an overnight process but trust me you can own the world. I can see you have the fire inside you that it takes to be successful." Jamaal "I don't know if I can do this, I'm not a killer." Sopa "No one wants to be a killer and only a chosen few truly love killing but in life you have your "necessary evils" and killing is one of them. The streets are paved with blood, I want it to end but every other day there is war. That's why you are a part of La Compania. Listen, because this is the last time I'm going to tell you this shit. I see something in you, I know that you are a true warrior who is loyal so I'm going to help you, give you a family to lean on. You are one of us now, your going to start working with Stud and Modelo, so for now look at them as trainers. After you work with them for a while then you'll be doing jobs alone. We'll get you some key locations in Harlem to distribute weight, but let's not get a head of ourselves, we've got some cleaning up to do first. So, are you ready for this?" Jamaal doesn't take a moment to answer "Yeah, I'm ready" even though he would rather say "no" it was just something inside compelling him to take this chance even though it was wrong.

Jamaal was never a bad kid he just never had a home or a normal life so to him this was natural progression. There was one part of him that was somewhat fascinated by La Compania, despite their ill first impression they had been somewhat hospitable. Every time he began to have even a little trust for them the image of Hashish's blue face oozing blood flashes before him as if it happened all over again and reminded him of his hidden hatred. He rationalized it all with his desire to be on top, he had to learn how to be a boss. He decided to gear his entire life towards being in control . To Jamaal it seemed the best way to avoid being a victim is to be a victimizer.

Sopa "Oh do you have that 50 thousand for me?" Jamaal "Yeah it's in the car." Sopa "Well keep it consider it an advance on your first three jobs." Jamaal "What about my debt?" Sopa "Oh don't worry you'll pay it, now go outside, Stud and Modelo are waiting for you and remember they are your brothers now."

Jamaal was instructed to tailgate behind Stud and Modelo in their navy blue Acura legend up Broadway towards Dyckman Street. They made a left at the junction, bringing them into a labyrinth of roads that lead to parking by the Cloisters Museum. Stud and Modelo got out and began walking towards the museum's exit road. As Jamaal followed them along the driven trail he noticed them jump into the back of what appears to be a raggedy abandoned white Chevrolet van. Modelo and Stud were silent as they changed into baggy all white maintenance jump suits and caps to match. Stud passed Jamaal his suit while Modelo squeezed passed Stud to get in the driver's seat. Jamaal turned his nose up at the suit which smells and looks like it's been used a million times. Modelo passed Jamaal a 45. caliber berretta. He wondered if it was the same one used on Hashish. Stud and Modelo carried tool boxes to conceal their guns while Jamaal kept his in his pants. Jamaal was amazed by their level of cold hearted professionalism and he knew he had to be the same way to survive. He had to be more coldhearted than them if he ever wanted to have power over them. They drove to 4523 165th street and Edgecombe Ave. Jamaal recalled coming here before but couldn't remember when. They parked in front of the building and were granted entry by an older black woman who clearly thought they were repair men. All three of them jog up the stairs to the 4th floor apartment 4K.

Modelo pulls his gun out and wrings the door bell. A young lady behind the door asks who it is. Modelo says "Gonzalez Plumbing we come for your annual pipe cleaning." Modelo turns towards Stud and Jamaal and winks as though his lie was ingenious. All the while Jamaal is saying to himself "There is no way anybody is stupid enough to believe that." This tall chocolate Amazon with long black extensions wearing a man's Guess T-shirt opened the door exposing her lush braless breasts and long strong thick legs even though her face left much to be desired, her body more than overcompensated for her features. Modelo gave her a smile and put the tip of his gun in her face and his index finger over her lips signaling for her to be silent. He pulls her into his arms and wraps one hand around her mouth and keeps the gun on her head with the other. Modelo whispers in her ear "where is he bitch?" She answers with a whimpering whisper telling them he is in the bedroom.

Modelo kept the woman in his grasp while signaling Stud and Jamaal to move forward. Stud quietly locks the door while Jamaal moves forward with his fire arm extended in front of him. As Jamaal brushes past Modelo and the woman, he pities her feeling her fear. She seems to recognize Jamaal and whispers "Jamaal why are you doing this?" Modelo reduces what little breathing room he was giving her and tightened his grasp over her mouth to the point of almost choking her. Jamaal takes a closer glance at her and remembers her, she was one of Hashish's girlfriends, but there was no time for reminiscing, he had a job to do. As soon as he refocuses on the bedroom at the end of the hall a deep voice bellows from inside the room. "Yo who the fuck was that at the door bitch?" Whoever was in the bedroom was blasting DJ Ralph Mc Daniel's Video Music Box on the television. Modelo covered the girl's mouth with his palm so tightly that her tears were forced to roll over his knuckles. Jamaal was right outside the room when the voice bellowed again "Yo Bitch, you ain't hear me, who the fuck was at the door?!" Whoever this guy was he didn't seem to be to smart but eventually his instincts must have kicked in cause the next thing Jamaal heard was the sound of a hand gun chambering a bullet. Jamaal thought fast and crouched down low pointing his gun in an upward angle, guessing that the man would come standing upright, that would give Jamaal a split second advantage. This guy had to be about Stud's size, he came out the room in his boxers with his gun down by his thigh yelling like he expected to be greeted by some silly ghetto chick. He didn't stand a chance as Jamaal unloaded four 45. caliber bullets that ripped through his heart and burst out his upper back. The impact threw the man's back to the wall like a swatted fly and he collapsed to the floor leaving a long streak blood stain on the wall that followed the pattern of his fall. Jamaal wasn't sure the guy was dead so he stood over this man's twitching body and look into this dying man's eyes before he put one more shot between his eyes to stop the twitching. Jamaal learned a lesson that day when your instincts tell you something is wrong always come out with your gun up. Expect the unexpected and be ready to shoot or you'll end up like this unsuspecting victim. Jamaal was startled by the sound of one more gunshot that came from behind him. He turned around to see chunks of the woman's brain mixed with blood and bone splattered against the wall. Jamaal gives Modelo a long cold stare, he felt they didn't have to kill her. As he drops her limp dead body to the floor and wipes her blood off his face. Modelo only giggles at Jamaal and says "Come on papa she knew your name she had to go."

Everyone heard the shots that went off but paid no attention to the maintenance workers coming out the building. They took the white van to the Cloisters museum exit trail and removed there maintenance suits. Stud torched the van and they quickly walked to their cars. Modelo was responsible for getting rid of the guns so Stud hitched a ride with Jamaal while Modelo drove off the other way. Jamaal didn't feel particularly comfortable having Stud in the car with him even if they just pulled off a hit together. Stud could feel the tension and decided to start up conversation. Stud "Jamaal you did good back there papa, you know Sopa was right about you, he said you was a warrior, that's the same shit he said about me and Modelo, soon he'll be sending you on jobs by yourself." Jamaal sarcastically replies "Oh yeah, I can't wait, I always wanted to kill people for Sopa." Stud just smirked at him "You know what's funny; no body chooses this life it chooses them that's just how it is." Jamaal "Word B you right though but where you going anyway." Stud "oh yeah papa my fault, I got this freak on 173rd and Audubon Ave, I'm a go and fuck with her for a while." The guys kick small talk back and forth for the rest of the ride. Jamaal drops Stud off and heads home.

He spent the following months doing hits for Sopa, and it didn't take long for Jamaal start working alone. Jamaal was able to adapt to the killing and assimilated into La Compania. After a while he almost forgot about Hashish's dying face it's as though it was lost in the shuffle of Allahandro's and the others. Sopa and La Compania provided him with the product and soldiers necessary to push out the competitors. Jamaal lived up to Sopa's expectations mobilizing a team consisting of Reg, Jacob and Alshaun—with Reg as his lieutenant his team helped him manage all his various newly acquired crack spots through out Harlem. Jamaal was really making a name for himself in a very short time and winning Sopa's favor. What impressed Sopa most about him was his cold calculated style of aggression, he reminded Sopa of him self at a young age. Jamaal never spoke of his affiliation with La Compania and did not permit Reg to reveal it either. He used deception to keep enemies off balance and made Sopa's enemies his own. Through Jamaal La Compania gained a strong hold on upper Harlem but there was still one last problem; the Jamaicans and the black Americans that aligned themselves with them. Multiplying like roaches they had their hands in everything coke, weed, and heroin. They weren't as strong as La Compania because they lacked in numbers, but what they lacked in numbers they made up for with pure brutality and ruthlessness. That's part of what made this beef a personal one, the Jamaicans had no respect for any one they encountered. It was a kamikaze style of hustling, they have robbed and murdered Columbians and Mobsters with no fear of repercussions. If they couldn't extort you then they would wipe you out and if they can't beat you they won't retreat.

La Casa Restaurant had been robbed at gun point on two occasions so Sopa changed up his pattern and placed Modelo there as head of security from open to close. It didn't take longer than a week for the Jamaicans to hit them again, and this time they kidnapped Modelo and a voluptuous waitress. The next morning there was a large gift box in front of the billiards pool hall on 193rd street addressed to La Compania with Modelo and the waitress's head's inside, with the frozen look of horror on their faces.

Killing was something Jamaal was able to do exceptionally well. He medicated his own emotions with Hennessey, weed and occasionally a little angel dust. With Jamaal being in control of his own situation he then turned his focus on crushing the Jamaicans. Jamaal proved to be a very formidable opponent with his innovative style of performing hits. Jamaal would use different disguises dressing up like a woman or a homeless person and he was always patient with his work insisting on watching his victims learning there patterns before striking. He learned to move like a ghost, all of his movements were in and out and everybody knew his name but only a third of them knew what he looked like. Jamaal learned from Sopa that you must avoid the public eye in this business, it's good to be faceless and only be festive amongst your inner circle. So he never went out to party like Reg, Alshaun, and Jacob did. Instead you would only see Jamaal when he is picking up money or dropping off product. He was real cautious and with good reason, the Jamaicans had 40 thousand dollars on his head.

ROBO-COP AND MR. BALDWIN

X-FACTOR is the missing piece to a puzzle or the unpredictable mishaps that may occur whether they turn up by chance or by the work of the devil or karmic law. There is one thing for sure, every man's mishap is another man's good luck and no one can predict them. For some one like Jamaal who is a beast of logic determining the X-factor before it determines you can be a nerve racking struggle to become a master of preparation. (*This is literally impossible unless you're a psychic.*)

Detective Shultz and Detective O'Neil were hot on Jamaal's trail. These were the same Detectives who were questioning Hashish's were bout's, His family reported him missing and the person he's usually with is Jamaal who hasn't been able to face his family yet. There is no way he'd tell them the truth but just lying to every one would hurt. Schultz and O'Neil were investigating Jamaal feeling like he had to know why Hashish has disappeared. The streets were a little envious of Jamaal, there were a lot of angry dudes out there who were put out of business or hurt by Jamaal, most of them didn't have the strength or resources to go war with him. So it wasn't difficult for The Detectives to get basic information from these disgruntled disenfranchised dealers. To their shock the detectives discovered that Jamaal was a drug lord in the making with a big hand in about 50% of the murders in their district, with control over everything from 135th street to 155th, they were already aware of the Jamaicans and La Compania, but Jamaal and his Cash Money Click seemed to be a new upstart. *(Even though Jamaal took his third of Harlem from the blacks and Jamaicans the Detectives still didn't make the connection between him and La Compania.)* They knew of Jamaal and figured he would follow in his uncle's foot steps and be a lower level hustler, now with their newly found information they've come to know that Jamaal rose to power in just 6 or seven months. Judging by his means of rising to power they felt he was the type who would kill his own uncle. They were still faced with one last dilemma: none of the informants agreed to testify or commit to a written statement. So the Detectives decided it was time to find a real "rat" that was close to Jamaal so they could apply some pressure, see if he bursts.

Just for your info; Detective Schultz and O'Neil hail from the thirteenth precinct also known as "The Dirty Thirty" which controlled 151st up to the thirty forth precinct on 180thst and Broadway : here existed some of the most corrupt officers in New York City. Some of them like Schultz and O'Neil were obliged to receive or take pay-offs and they would even carry out hits or set-ups if the price was right.

Det. Schultz worked for narcotics, he was of Irish decent with a love for beer and brawls. Towering at 6foot 4inches weighing 290 pounds with about 10 percent body fat, he looked like Goldberg the pro wrestler. Violent methods and random jump out extortion tactics along with his bulky appearance wearing a vest garnered him the nick name "Robo-Cop". Then you have Det. O'Neil who is a short, clean cut cunning fellow who could easily pass for one of the Baldwin brothers *(actors)*. Working for the homicide unit O'Neil talked the Captain into allowing him and Schultz to partner up. In Harlem drugs and homicide are like husband and wife.

The Detectives were determined to hit Jamaal's main spot first: 519 apt 1B 148thst west. Jacob spent most of his time there. Alshaun and Reg were like Rovers handling deliveries and distribution of "Ready Rock" or pure Coke. Jamaal was his own enforcer he kept Reg as second in command not to say that he trusted Reg fully but he was the best candidate. He took Reg on two execution style hits with him but it was obvious he did not have the stomach for it. Alshaun sort of worked as Reg's assistant, while his little brother Jacob worked the spot you couldn't trust Jacob with to much responsibility.

Early the next mornings the Detectives were on 148th staking Jamaal's drug base. It was late November and it was time to get ready for the first of the month. Jamaal was on his way at about 8:00 a.m to drop off a package for mass distribution, but was set back by the sight of a familiar navy blue Ford Taurus. He reversed backwards up the block and drove a couple of blocks away and called Reg at the spot from a pay phone and told him the Detectives were watching. He ordered Reg and Jacob to close up shop stash every thing, leave and to beep him on his pager when they are done.

Reg and Jacob were on there way out the door when Jacob was met by a sweeping kick to his ankles and a jaw cracking right hook that floored him instantly. He looked up from the pavement and he was staring up the barrel of Robo-Cop's 45. caliber Smith & Wesson hand gun. Reg took off down the block like Carl Lewis in the 200 meter dash. O'Neil made a futile attempt to grab him but was flung to the side like a mere rag doll. O'Neil was to stunned to give chase and Schultz was already cuffing Jacob, Schultz told O'Neil to forget about Reg and open the car door. At that time he shoved Jacob into the back seat Jacob screams "Fuck you! Why you fucking with me? I aint do shit! I know my rights!" Jacob continues to ramble on while Schultz goes into the building 519 and kicks in the door of apartment 1B regardless of the fact he has no search warrant. O'Neil sits in the driver's seat and waits for Schultz while dispersing the small crowd that had gathered. Shultz emerged from the building with two large garbage bags, the contents goes as follows: 1 fully loaded 38. Lorcin automatic, 15 thousand dollars, 10 thousand worth of half pure coke and half broke down in crack vials, a triple beam scale for weighing drugs and other drug paraphernalia. Schultz displayed a sarcastic grin while victoriously placing the bags in the trunk. O'Neil read his partner's body language and knew they hit the jack pot. Mean while else where Jamaal has received a 911 beep from Reg, as soon as Jamaal learns of Jacob's predicament he scrambles for his bail money. Now it was just a matter of waiting for Jacob to go through the system so he could get bail.

O'Neil and Schultz had Jacob sitting in a cell alone for about 6 hours before they brought him into the interrogation room.

O'Neil "Here have a seat my man are you okay?" Jacob "Yeah I'm alright but could you loosen these cuffs? And you got a cigarette?" Schultz interrupts them slamming both his hands onto the desk. Schultz "Where the fuck you think you at, the fucking Hilton hotel? You can't have a cigarette you little black bitch. All you can have is some fucking jail time, with some big guerilla shoving his cock up your ass!" Jacob "Fuck you I know you ain't have no search warrant." Schultz empties out the contents of both bags onto the table. Schultz "Do you think judge Rothwax is going to give a fuck whether or not I had a fucking warrant once he sees all this shit! This shit can get you a lot of fucking time and personally I don't give a shit, I like to see little fucks like you in jail." Jacob's eyes get a little watery with tears that seem to just well up at the tip of his eye lashes. Schultz ferociously slaps the tears off Jacob's eye lids and grabs his neck lifting him from the chair and slamming him against the wall. Just when you would think that Schultz was about to pulverize Jacob, O'Neil jumps in. O'Neil "Hold on, give him a chance, I think he can work with us he seems like a good kid." Schultz let him go and steps back while O'Neil continues speaking in a calm tone seeming to be Schultz's total opposite. O'Neil "Listen kid I like you and I know you're really a good kid. *(By Now Jacob is wide eyed and his head is still buzzing from Robo-Cop's iron palm)* Frankly I don't want to see you go down for something that ain't yours, that gun was used in a murder, I know it isn't yours it's Jamaal's isn't it? Jacob "No it ain't his." Schultz lifts Jacob from his feet and through him on the ground showing him the same 45 caliber hand gun from earlier but this time he shoved the barrel in Jacob's mouth. Schultz "You know what, I'm going to put your face all over this floor if you don't tell us who this shit belongs to! Who are you more scared of him or me!" O'Neil makes one last futile attempt at saving the kid's life only to be shut down by the enraged Schultz who had a bullet in the chamber. Schultz "But out of this O'Neil your not going to save him!" Jacob begins talking even with gun in his mouth Schultz walks away from him giving O'Neil an alright "we got him" wink as he passes. Jacob "It's all Jamaal's, I just work for him." As he passes Jacob a pen and pad. O'Neil "Have a seat young man and relax I'm on your side, now I'm going to need you to write down every thing you know about Jamaal and what he does . Don't hold any thing back, write it all down. Don't worry about Jamaal we'll take care of him, he won't know it was you until trial, and he'll be locked up by then." O'Neil gives Jacob a cigarette and lights it for him as though it were some type of mystic preparation but this was no holy ritual it was simply the tragic act of betrayal. A detailed two page statement that would make you question why Jacob dropped out of school. It has details about a great deal of Jamaal's drug transactions and speculations of different murders –except Jacob never knew of Jamaal's affiliation with La Compania.

Jacob didn't know too much about the murders but his drug info was enough. His testimony would be the enough to get Jamaal about 10 or 15 years in prison. The crooked Detective released Jacob with a misdemeanor trespassing ticket, and instructed him to lay low until Jamaal was in police custody. Jacob returned home and did exactly what he was told, he lied and told his brother that the crooked cops merely kept all the drugs and money leaving him with a ticket. Jacob gave everyone that same lie and told Jamaal that he was not going to hustle anymore. Jamaal knew something was wrong with Jacob's story, but couldn't find the time to really have a one on one with him. Jamaal could feel something amiss but didn't want to jump to conclusions and murder Jacob for no reason. Alshaun, the more resilient of the two brothers still continued to work for Jamaal but was kept at arm's distance. One thing was for sure, Jamaal had to close up shop on 148th and switch his main location around. When Jamaal informed Sopa of his current troubles, Sopa told him he would contact a couple of his connections at the 30th precinct and find out what really happened with Jacob, but he also wanted Jamaal to lay low until the smoke cleared. Schultz and O'Neil did their home work and knew that Jamaal would probably be keeping low for a while but they knew he would come by 148th street eventually because Samaya's family lived there- so it basically became a waiting game. The Detectives took one more little precaution and changed cars leery that Jamaal might be aware of their usual vehicle.

Like clock work Jamaal showed up with Samaya who was already eight months pregnant. Jamaal hadn't been around 148th street in weeks, he was waiting for Sopa's feed back. He wanted to step out and run some errands with Reg, he didn't want to leave Samaya in the house alone so close to her due date so he was dropping her off at her mother's place. The Detectives had been waiting for this moment.

Like two predatory reptiles the Detectives ran up on the side of the car with their guns drawn, they showed their weapons against both the driver's side and passenger's side windows ordering Jamaal out of the car. Samaya began to curse and carry on as though she were wiling to fight the cops. Jamaal sat there for a moment unshaken by the event just angry at himself for coming to this area "How could I be this stupid" he thought. A spectacle that riled up the entire block began as the detectives yelled at Jamaal through the tinted windows as he attempted to gather his thoughts. It was as though the Detectives thought he was refusing to get out of the car. Jamaal tells Samaya in a very plain voice to calm down and get out the car. (*Making this statement with no eye contact*) Samaya jumped out of the car and lunged at detective O'Neil who dodged her, before she could turn around and lunge at him again she was restrained by her mother who had just joined the on looking crowd. Jamaal saw his father standing across the street with a look of shame in his eye's and returned his glance with a look of hatred. Jamaal sticks his hands out the car door and starts to get out but not before Schultz pulled him out of the car and slammed him against it. Jamaal instinctively returns the favor by throwing a wild punch at Schultz that grazed him and hit O'Neil square on the chin dropping him for a moment. Though Schultz was a little Dazed by the graze he still had the advantage with Jamaal's back turned to him. Schultz put Jamaal in a choke hold, wrestled him to the ground and leaned on Jamaal's back with his knee. It still took some help from O'Neil to get Jamaal's hands cuffed together. Jamaal's black leather jacket with tassels hung off the end of his cuffed hands. The burning sensation in his back from Schultz knee and the dry icy feeling of his chest pressed against the cold concrete were numbed by the engulfing flame of Jamaal's rage. Jamaal knew that one day he would have a run in with the law but he didn't expect it to be like this. The neighbors and on lookers screamed police brutality but it was in vain. They were just being nosey. No one, not even Al Sharpton is going to really protest for an inner city drug dealer who has been physically abused by an officer. They can basically beat you to a near dead bloody pulp and get away with it unless it's on tape or they kill you or commit such a horrendous act that it must be addressed, even then you still might not see justice. When you get killed or go to jail the "ghetto" might remember you for a day or two but when you're gone it's back to business.

Jamaal attempted to offer Samaya some comfort while being shoved into the car "I'll be out soon babe, I'll be okay!" Jamaal sat in the back of the cop car and saw two important faces, his eyes darted form Samaya to his father and back again. It was the present and past- and like some type of apocalyptic omen the back of this detective car was his future. The car seemed to sit still while the street buildings and blocks passed it which created a panoramic collage of freedom, Jamaal watched as it was stripped away.

Only now could Jamaal truly understand Basil's letters the way he described feeling like a slave and police officers were just plantation overseers, whose only goal in life is to try and break the black man. Jamaal went into his comfort zone, a quiet little place in his mind where he buries his pain- he was numb to Schultz' brutal tactics. Inside the very same interrogation room that he was betrayed in, Jamaal was cuffed and beaten by Schultz who met every blow he inflicted upon Jamaal with a menacing stare. Jamaal made a mental note adding the detectives to his "hit list". Despite Schultz methods Jamaal refused to snitch, matter of fact, he did not speak a word. Jamaal was given a strict code from Magnum (*Fire's uncle*) and he stuck to it. *#1. Never speak to the police, they will try to manipulate your words and use them against you. #2. Never stitch –a snitch is considered the lowest of criminals, far below a pocket book snatcher and rivaled only by rapist. #3. If you must speak then request a lawyer and a phone call.* Schultz grew tired and frustrated of trying to beat any info out of Jamaal. His last words to Jamaal before he sent him down town for processing "You think you're a real tough guy hugh? Well listen tough guy your going to be convicted of at least 3 homicides, assaulting an office while resisting arrest, possession and distribution of drugs motherfucker you'll never see ya kid till he grows up and meets you in jail you piece of shit." Jamaal still refused to acknowledge him, the words couldn't bother him, he already knew that he was a nigger in cops eye's, this white detective re-assured him of that. The whole fiasco was somewhat amusing to Jamaal, how two cowards would beat on a defenseless person in hand cuffs and still believe they're tuff.

Jamaal still felt an uneasy feeling as he lined up to get on the bus and embark on a prisoner's journey.

The prisoners were being transported to "The Tombs" (*Manhattan Central Bookings*) where Manhattan's criminal offenders are temporarily held for court dates or transports between long term correctional facilities. The ghetto calls it The Tombs because you could definitely get lost in it's maze of dirty grey cells with metal benches and shitty toilets that don't flush. The tombs can leave you for dead in some far off cell filled with enemy predators, where the corrections officer's can't hear your screams.

Jamaal did not have many words for Samaya when he called, he just reassured her that everything was fine, he wanted her to stay at her mother's place for the time being and to stay strong. After convincing Samaya that he would be out in a couple of days he gave Reg a call. Reg was to keep running business as usual; Reg gave him a message from Sopa saying that he will take care of the snitch and that his bail and lawyer fees will be covered. Jamaal was surprised and gained a newly found respect for Sopa as his comrade. This still did not remove his undaunted plan to eventually murder him.

Jamaal was never locked up before but he always had a slight case of claustrophobia and a deep hatred for crowds of people which attributes to why he always tried to stay away from social gatherings. The main holding cell is where prisoners wait to be finger printed and then wait about 8 hours to see the judge at which time, they are either released or they must wait another 8 hours to be transferred to Rikers Island Correctional facility. Some prisoners stay longer in the Manhattan holding facility for misdemeanor sentences or to be expedited by other facets of Law Enforcement. Jamaal was surrounded by every aspect of the street inside the main cell. There were homeless people, drug addicts, homeless drug addicts, drug dealers, well known killers, all types of criminals down to young guys who simply were caught smoking weed. The cell smelt like a huge garbage dump, grotesque to say the least. Jamaal sat in the corner rocking back and forth growing impatient with this long process. He kept the hood of his champion sweater over his head in a futile attempt to ignore his environment.

Jamaal felt a presence and noticed some one staring at him from across the room. It was one of the Jamaicans he had a beef with, his name was Agony. Agony had this hard jet black leather face that seemed to be naturally frozen into a scowl and a head full of stringy disproportioned dread locks. He was a special kind of ugly his face appeared impervious to physical damage and his natural expression brings new meaning to the expression "If looks could kill." Jamaal remembered Supreme's words "When you behind bars you have to become a caged animal in some sense because your mind must be sharp and alert while your reactions must be instinctive or the other animals will devour you." Jamaal did his best to ignore Agony's stares but it was becoming harder and harder to ignore him. Agony hollers from across the cell "A Yankee bwoy ya don know me now eh? Lickle pussy clod ya gwon get dead trust me." Jamaal only glanced at him enough to size him up for attack all the while playing possum. Agony was the same height as Jamaal but was a lot more muscular. Jamaal had to figure a way to immobilize this guy fast because after the pounding that Schultz gave him he didn't have much strength to really tussle. The way Jamaal pretended to ignore Agony made him believe Jamaal was weak, motivating Agony to be bolder while antagonizing him. The correctional officers opened the cell and had the prisoners line up for "cop out sandwiches" these were no frills bologna sandwiches and welfare cheese with hard flaky bread that fell apart before it reached your mouth. The meal was complimented with this red juice that tastes just like flat "Tropical Fantasy" fifty cent soda. Jamaal sat in the corner staring forward in a zone refusing to eat the infamous sandwiches while surveying Agony through his peripherals. Agony took a break from looking at Jamaal to get on the chow line (*food line*). Agony was relaxed and must have really underestimated his adversary when he turned his back. Jamaal exploded off the bench with a jolt of speed, Agony turned to late and Jamaal grabbed his dreads and used his own momentum to slam Agony's head into the hard cell bars repeatedly. Three correction officers rush in and pull Jamaal off him. Agony had a big gash in his fore head bleeding profusely His body fell limp and he fell to the floor dazed and bloody though still attempting to get up like a punch drunk boxer who misses the count. The corrections officers were the first Jamaal has met of their kind, they almost seemed okay. Apparently, they observed Agony's hostile, antagonizing behavior earlier and felt he got what was coming to him, so they let Jamaal off with a warning, put him in a single person cell and transferred Agony to the medical unit. Jamaal found a brief moment off peace within the solitude of those walls until the momentum of self hatred tore it apart. Sometimes being alone in a cell can drive you mad but the truth is the cell can also help you learn to control your own incessantly wondering emotional mind. Some say the toughest thing in life to conquer is one's self and conquering one's self is a life time war. For a lot of us the worst battles are fought when we are completely alone. Every body's got there own personal demons they fight to suppress right?

THE ANIMAL, LA BESTIA

CORRECTIONAL Officer "Jamaal Seifullah time for court!" Jamaal did not even notice that he slept so long, he woke up startled. His face was bruised up and his back and ribs were throbbing. Lying on that frozen steel bench all night did not help much either. His Levis jeans hung down to his hips because the correctional officers took his belt. Jamaal threw on his tasseled leather and held up his pants with his right hand as his left was cuffed to another prisoner. They were led in line towards the court cell block where you meet with your lawyer before you go to arraignment, the chain gang went passed the main holding pens. Agony returned from the hospital but his paper work was pushed back in his absence. Agony made whimsical attempt at slicing Jamaal from behind the bars, but his arm was restricted by the limited space and Agony's big mouth projected the attack. All this helped Jamaal weave the attack and follow up by spitting lumps of mucous and saliva that landed on Agony's face. Agony tried to re-act but Jamaal was already to far from the cell. Pride can often make a man deny when he's been beaten even when it's written in front of your face or in Agony's case: written on his forehead in big gashes. Jamaal and about 8 pairs of cuffed prisoners followed the officer through the twisted tunnel like hallways of the tombs, unlocking different gates as though they were in the inner chambers of a dungeon. The prisoners were packed into this large cell that was equipped with 6 private visiting windows where you can talk to your lawyer. All the prisoners stood around talking "jail house law" some guys discussing bail, and their charges just to pass the time waiting for the lawyers. There is always that one guy that thinks he knows everything about the law and can fix every bodies case, but the truth is if he knew so much about the law then why is he in jail?! Jamaal was his own man, he had no need to socialize with the rest of those guys; he thought they were fools for being so comfortable in captivity. Most of the prisoners if not all of them had legal aids that have no true concern for them as clients. They are not being paid by the client but are getting paid by the same establishment that is attempting to convict the client. How can a defense attorney defend you if the defense and prosecution have the same boss? In any other system that would be considered a conflict of interests, but of course it's okay within the American legal system. Legal aids are put in place as a front, they do not offer any real help and most inner city ghetto civilians can't afford to pay for quality legal representation so they settle for these "Welfare lawyers" (*that's what I call them*) who lead them like lambs to the slaughter. 90% of the time they are trying to convince you to plea guilty.

It was funny how no one bothered Jamaal and he knew it was due to the way he dealt with Agony earlier that earned him some respect. Unfortunately one thing Jamaal could count on was that he would have plenty more altercations the longer he's there. Jamaal was the first inmate called to see his lawyer. Jon Muita was a slick talking flashy short white guy wearing a tailored made Armani grey wool 3-button suit with flat-front trousers with a pair of tan Roberto Cavalli pointed tipped shoes. Mr. Muita was sent by Sopa and Jamaal could tell this was a pro from the moment he met this guy through the glass that separates clients and lawyers.

Muita "Don't worry about anything your going to be out soon just not today because you have a cancer in your group, Sopa has the cure. When the cancer is cured it has to look like you had nothing to do with it so you have to stay hear for a while."

The defense attorney Jon Muita had Jamaal's case adjourned, judge Rothwax was on duty. He was an evil old guy who was well known through out Manhattan for his vicious sentencing and he denied Jamaal bail for the safety of the "confidential informant". The court date was adjourned for three months to provide the police more time for further investigation. Jamaal didn't like the situation but had no choice but to deal with it, leaving him to wait and wonder if Sopa would fulfill his promise and there would be a positive outcome for Jamaal.

He thought it would only take a few hours but it turned into forever. The prison transportation bus took 5 hours to arrive. Him and about 19 other inmates were finally packed in the bus. Basically all of them were cuffed to a guy they never met before in their life. This feeling can only be compared to slavery. The windows were gated, the bus seats were made of hard plastic and were to small for anyone to sit on comfortably. He looked out the window and said good bye to his freedom. He pondered the wild Rikers Island stories he heard about; would some one try to rob or kill him, he figured at least one out of two would take place. So he prepared his mind for the necessary animalistic metamorphosis that was about to take place inside him. He pulled his hood over his head and rested his head against the window trying to relax himself and zone out to the sound of the raggedy bus shaking over every bump.

Jamaal's moment of peace was crudely interrupted by the buses immediate stop. Some how he must have fell asleep along the ride. Suddenly a Dominican guy jumps up with a look of shock and fear written all over his face. He was slashed with a razor by another inmate so quickly that the cut didn't even start to bleed yet. What turned out to be a deadly slashing looked like a mere right jab at first. The cutter was this dark skin dude with a red bandana over his forehead laughing hysterically as though it was hilarious to him. The victim stood paralyzed like a deer frozen by a car's headlights holding his face with his uncuffed hand as facetious comments spewed from his adversary's lips "Some body get this man a napkin!! Don't you go and rat now cause their all going to laugh at you and don't scream cause you'll bleed more!!!" He seemed sinister and hadn't an ounce of remorse for his victim continuing to mock him even as the corrections officers opened the security gates and made their way to the back of the bus. Jamaal has murdered people but it was always silent. He never heard a man scream for help, cowering in fear. The cut opened like sliced rubber exposing the white flesh and just like the hysterically laughing cutter told his Dominican victim, the more he screamed the more he bled. Jamaal learned an important lesson as soon as he arrived at Rikers Island, that anything can happen and it's never safe to sleep. What surprised Jamaal most about the cutting was that there was no prior signs of aggression from either party. It was as though the guy got cut for just looking weak. He watched as the bleeding victim was rushed off the bus and the cutter was beaten senseless by the corrections officers while they dragged him off the bus, still laughing as though cutting someone had given him a euphoric high. Another inmate says "welcome to Rikers Island" on cue as though it had been rehearsed for a moment like this, his words couldn't have been more appropriate, because they were entering a young man's war zone.

If the dramatic end to this bus ride wasn't enough, Jamaal would have to encounter a couple more dehumanizing experiences before he would rest his head for the night. Every one on the bus was stripped searched and forced to put his clothing through a metal detector. After which they were required to stand in front of a male officer, squat down, spread their butt cheeks and cough to prove they did not have any type of weapons in their anal cavities. All inmates then were made to take showers in front of each other in what could only be described as filthy gym showers. After seeing the facility nurse and being checked for everything from tuberculosis, lice to gonorrhea, (*which takes hours*) the weary prisoners are escorted to different sectors of the prison according to their classification. Although Jamaal was facing serious charges and being held without bail for the safety of a witness, it was still his first arrest so he had a low classification. He was brought to C74- Mod #4 which was a military style dormitory setting divided in two half's. The entry and exit to Mod 4 was what they call "the bubble", that's where the corrections officers sat in the middle of the dorm. Each side had about 60 beds with lockers for private storage right next to each bed and a day room with a bunch of plastic chairs. The day room was where inmates socialize during the day, playing cards, watching television, reading etc. The bathroom had about eight shower heads and six toilets lined up separated by stalls. There was only one sink and aluminum mirror right above it, the bathroom also moonlights as a boxing ring for settling personal disputes. Last but not least was the most important thing to most prisoners, the phone. Each dorm had at least two to three phones on each side. Phones were an inmate's direct connection with the outside world. This connection with the outside world is the most precious thing in jail. It is a source of power in jail if you can control the most valuable privilege allowed. Then you have the will to move men, the strength to strike fear into a man's heart to the point where he is a prisoner's prisoner. One thing is for sure, whoever controlled the phones controlled the house (*dorm*). Phones were usually between the Blacks and Latinos or The Gods and The Latin Kings or The Bloods and Netas etc. The circumstances of who controlled the phones varied with each house. So wars and rivalries over power were bound to happen.

Jail is similar to the rats in a maze experiment where some scientist took a bunch of mice and confined them to small limited living quarters where they were over crowded. The results of the experiment were grueling, the rats started to attack each other and eat each other devouring their own. Some even showed abnormal behavior by trying to mate with rats of the same gender. There is no way you could compare humans to rats but let's be honest if a human was exposed to those same conditions his reactions would be similar. Then there is that degree of separation between animals and humans, the highest power has graced us with the ability to overcome extreme social conditions and mental strain. We are way more mentally advanced than animals yet we are still bound by the same physical laws. You would think that man would be more civilized than animals but animals kill to eat and man kills for sport. As a matter of fact we as man kind are responsible for the most death and destruction of earth's people and natural resources.

So in conclusion when they performed the same

experiments with humans it wasn't just similar it was far worse. Look at the jails, projects, group homes and ghettos all over, but like all undesirable living conditions we manage to find a way to make it home.

THE RE-UNION

AFTER being supplied with a towel, a green cup, a tooth brush, wool blanket and a bar of Carcraft soap which is toxic for brown skin but works wonders for white clothes. Before new inmates get to their beds they are required to go to the day room and be debriefed on "the house rules." Prison, like everything else has its own peculiar political infrastructure. The corrections officers rely on certain prisoners to help control other prisoners. In every jail house there is always a group of inmates who seem to manage the others, they maintain peace and order in exchange for little favors or privileges if you will. This position is considered a place of stature for inmates who are ignorant, not realizing that this position is for "thugged out Uncle Toms." Ironically they call them the "suicides". Suicides are allowed to break the rules they enforce and officers will always favor them in any conflict.

Jamaal was escorted to the dorm with about ten other inmates most of them looked scared except for Jamaal and this short wiry kid named Mo from Park Hill Staten Island. Jail is centered on control, they control how you eat and sleep etc. Stripping you of the many things that are assets to a man's soul. So in turn inmates seek comfort in other forms, to fill the void a few inmates will go inside of themselves and elevate their minds through books, art, religion, or the discipline of exercise. Others will seek to reclaim the precious control that was stripped from them by dominating other inmates through violence and intimidation. New inmates are prime meat for the predators. The predators were already scheming on Jamaal's footwear and jacket and Mo was short with a big mouth and an over sized Pelle Pelle jacket. As a new inmate you could feel the heat emitting rays from the predators' eyes beaming at you from every direction. Once inside the day room it is time to meet the four "Suicides" and their "House Gang" who were the suicide's dodgiers or lackeys. The head suicide who ran Mod4 north side was from "Crown Heights", Brooklyn. He always kept a real serious face with deep set eyes and a wide protruding forehead that seemed to push his eye brows out further magnifying his cold stare. He wasn't a big muscular guy, he was a medium sized dude, a lot shorter than Jamaal but his demeanor said he was not to be taken lightly. Next was "Mell Murda" a blood general from Brownsville, he was a tall lanky light skinned dude with a wild knotty afro and a scar under his cheek bone. Then you have "Dominica" this Latin King kid from Washington Heights who had a real stocky build like he had been working out for years. Last but not least was "Gargamelle" this real short chunky ugly dude from Bedford Stuyvesant Brooklyn with a black du-rag over his fat head. They all stood in a line and Krown Heights was the first to speak. "Alright this is how it goes at 6:00am every body gets up for shit, shave, and shower- breakfast is 7:00 a.m, every body stands up in front of their bed at 6:45am for the morning count. 12:30 is lunch and at 5:30 is dinner. When it comes to the phone you'll get five minutes twice a day. There are two phones; the black and the Spanish phone and nobody gets more than five minutes. (*Mo sucks his teeth and mumbles "yeah alright". Crown Heights takes note of him and continues speaking*) "We don't need police, we police ourselves and there is rules. No sneak thieving and no fighting unless you consult one of us first. Any problem you consult with the house gang. If any of you become a problem we will take care of you. Now Gargamelle will show you your beds so you could get settled." He finished of his statement giving Mo direct eye contact.

Jamaal was blown away by the whole scenario, he couldn't believe that Crown Heights actually controlled the other inmates and realized he would eventually bump heads with him. Jamaal's bed was right next to Mo's, the two made a silent allegiance as they sat on their beds playing chess, while the other inmates were scattered through out the dorm's day room. If you have never been through a war then being a soldier will be foreign to you, but a man who hath endured the trenches can always recognize a warrior of similar background. In the middle of his game with Mo Jamaal became a little thirsty and got up to get some water out the bathroom. When Jamaal walked into the bathroom Dominica was taking a shower. Jamaal looked away from him because he was naked. Dominica "Yo blacko what you going to do for those Jordans?" Jamaal would have rather ignored him because he did not want any problems but he had to reply to such a bold comment. Jamaal "Anything I have to do." Jamaal was calm and he came to expect this type of altercation to occur. Dominica "You got to give those up Papa!" Jamaal's first thought was how arrogant and cocky could a person be to challenge him while he was naked Dominica clearly had the disadvantage. It was times like these moments before striking when Jamaal could tell if he had a sure victory. He would measure the urgency of his battle by his own internal meter: his own heart beat when it was rapid and fast he is unsure of the outcome but when it is calm and normal he is always victorious. Jamaal decided to make Dominica pay for his stupidity and amateur intimidation methods. Dominica made the fatal mistake of underestimating some one he knows nothing about. Jamaal noticed a mop and bucket in the corner of the bathroom he walks toward it while Dominica tries to quickly dry off with his towel. Jamaal quickly grabs the mop and swings it at Dominica's ankles sweeping him clear off his feet. He then began to thrash him continuously making Dominica bleed from various parts of his body. It was still mid day in Mod 4 and the day to day hustle and bustle shielded everyone's ears from the commotion in the bathroom except for Mo and Crown Heights who both kept their eyes on the bathroom for two different reasons. They both got up and went into to the bathroom, only to find Dominica curled up like a newborn baby naked, wet and bloody. Dominica wasn't unconscious but he was to hurt to even move and apparently some of the mops sharp edges have punctured his flesh. Jamaal was calmly putting the mop and bucket in order as though nothing had took place. Jamaal gave Crown Heights a very plane look and bluntly said "He wanted to know what I would do for my Jordans so I showed him." Crown Heights knew that Jamaal would be a problem but now wasn't the time to settle this problem. Crown Heights "Ya niggas just go about ya'll business like nothing happen we'll settle this later."

Mo held a sarcastic grin as Jamaal sat on the opposite bed explaining the little altercation while the medical unit came to transfer Dominica to the medical facility. Jamaal had drawn the line and by Mo sticking so close to Jamaal he was considered a problem as well. Word spread through the dorm at light speed and although the correctional officers had no idea of who assaulted Dominica every inmate knew what happened. At the time Mod 4 was a mostly black house but the Latin Kings were still a force to be reckoned with and they definitely wanted revenge. Soon it was time for dinner or "chow" everyone had to line up and march to the "mess hall" (*dinning area*). When Mod 4 entered the mess hall you saw all the other dorms. Every body who had neighborhood allies or other gang members would use this time to speak and relate to each other from across the cafeteria. Some Brooklyn dudes from mod 5 showed Mo some love. One of them passed by and gave Mo a quick hand shake and passed something to him wrapped in a napkin, the pass off was so quick that Jamaal barely noticed it. There were a couple of Harlem dudes that recognized Jamaal but did not know him well enough to say anything or approach him. Who would want to approach a ruthless killer if he were not your friend?

There was something awfully familiar about one of the inmates serving food, Jamaal and the inmate shared slight eye contact until he made it to the front of the "chow" line. Jamaal stood in front of this taller inmate who stood about 6'3 with short dreads that hung chin length, and in that moment Jamaal remembered where he knew this dude from. It was Supreme (*Basil*) his child hood friend. Supreme put extra food and chocolate milks on Jamaal's tray while saying "Peace God good to see you but bad to see you in here." Jamaal "Man it's a lot a shit we got to build (*constructive communication*) about, a lot of shit been happening God." Supreme "I understand God, trust me I be hearing about what's going on in the streets in here. I got shit on lock, watch, I'm going to get you transferred to my house. Just maintain and stay away from them Germans (*Spanish gangs*) and 85ers. (*uncivilized people*) I'll hook up with you at wreck." Jamaal takes his tray and sat down to eat next to Mo. The Mod 4 house gang seemed to keep an eye on those two (*Mo & Jamaal*) wondering what their story was and why they were so known. This dude from Mod 5 empties his tray and while passing Jamaal says "Peace, this is from Supreme, travel in harmony God" while giving Jamaal a hand shake and quickly shoving something in his jacket pocket. All this activity going on around Mo and Jamaal made Gargamelle, Krown Hieghts and Murda Mell nervous. They could tell that their adversaries were armed or about to be. Later on that day the two comrades sat on their adjacent beds while revealing their newly obtained gifts to each other. Jamaal was given two butter knife sized metal shanks and a handful of cigarettes while Mo was granted a pack of Newport cigarettes and a gem star razor. They made a silent oath to watch each others backs.

It was late in the evening and the suicides had finally called Jamaal's name for his five minutes on the phone. Jamal missed his freedom but he missed Samaya even more so he had to call her house, the phone seemed like it must have wrung a thousand times before Umi (*Samaya's mother*) picked up the phone. This was good luck for Jamaal because she was the only person in her family that liked Jamaal besides Samaya.

Umi "As-salaam Alaikum" Jamaal "Walaikum salamu" Umi "Is this Jamaal?" Jamaal "yes"

Umi was a shrewd old woman but she was very nice—Jamaal compared her brand of wisdom to that of Fire's mother. Jamaal always showed her the up most respect. Umi "You know we are mad at you right?!" Jamaal "Why I ain't do nothing?" Umi "Yes you did! (*Raising her voice to a level of anger that Jamaal never heard from her*) You go and make these devils lock you up and you missed your own daughter's birth! That's right Samaya had a beautiful little girl this morning!" Jamaal ignores every thing negative about her statement and asks "Are you serious, did she name her yet?" Umi "Of course we did her name is Rain

Jamellah Seifullah." Jamaal "that is a beautiful name." Umi "Of course it is and that little angle is a blessing from Allah, now I suggest you re-think your goals in life and change: if not for yourself then at least change for your family. I don't hate you Jamaal, in fact I love you as though you were my own son but I hate the things you do. What kind of future will your daughter have with a father who is dead or in jail like every other black man? As a matter of fact I'm glad you are in there because now you have time to think before things really get bad. You need to use this time to study Islam, to prepare to return home and lead your family like a real Muslim man. Samaya and Rain will be coming home tomorrow night so call back for her then. As-salaam Alaikum." Jamaal "Walaikum salamu." She hung up the phone before Jamaal could think of anything to say. Jamaaal stood there for five more minutes with the phone in his hand feeling angry and guilty for his own faults yet happy as well filled with the feeling of having a new born child. Umi's words touched him deeply because she was right; making him cry while rubbing the phone against his temple as though it could some how relieve the great tension shooting through his brain. As the tear drops hugged his sculpted cheek bones he reflected on his life and the lives he has taken, briefly contemplated getting out of "the game", until he was interrupted. Crown Heights kept his eyes on Jamaal and figured he was on the phone way to long. In light of what happen to Dominica earlier Crown Heights felt as though he had to assert himself before Jamaal thought he could run the house. Crown Heights says "Aight nigga it's time to get off the jack." While disrespectfully tapping him on the shoulder, Jamaal lifted his head and turned around with eyes blood shot red, teary and glossy. Crown Height's mannerism attracted Mo and Gargamelle's attention. He must have mistaken Jamaal's teary eyes as a sign of weakness but sometimes emotional vulnerability does not equal mental or physical weakness. Crown Heights "Word to my mother I knew you was type sweet but you can't be crying on my phone kid. (*Mockingly*) What's wrong can't handle this jail shit that's why you crying like a bitch?" That's what lit Jamaal's fuse and set him to explode. He turned away from Krown Heights as though he were going to ignore him, and in that millisecond Jamaal slammed the phone's receiver into his forehead ripping the cord out the phone with the form of a drunken boxer delivering a wild right hook. Jamaal continued to bash in Crown Heights face making blood gush from his head. Crown Heights made futile attempts at retaliation but his eyes were blinded by his own blood. The attack was a spontaneous persistent flurry of blows, the momentum threw both men over a bed landing with Jamaal on top still trying to mutilate Crown Heights face. Gargamelle jumped off his bed to rush to his comrade's aid, but Mo was already racing towards him. Mo was wiry and fast he quickly dodged Gargamelle's blows and raked his newly acquired Gem Star razor across Gargamelle's face, giving him a horrible cut that went from his cheek across his nose. Mo followed up with consecutive slices across any part of Gargamelle that was in his path. The commotion was to much to handle for the limited number of correctional officers present. That one little conflict snow balled into a mini riot before they could calm down the ruckus. Jamaal and Mo swiftly annihilated their adversaries but in the fever of battle they began to take on whatever house gang members or corrections officers who joined the fight. The Latin Kings took this moment to seek Dominica's revenge, while every one else in the dorm decided this was the opportunistic time stab or hurt their enemies. Melle Murda whose loyalties were only to himself aligned himself and his soldiers with Jamaal but not because he had any admiration for him in the least. Melle Murda simply loathed the Latin Kings and never hesitated to go to war with them. If not for Mell and his Bloods Jamaal and Mo surely would have been swamped by the Latin Kings. The entire dorm was in frenzy and the corrections officers on duty were out numbered and beaten to near death, but not without having a chance to radio for "The Turtles"(*Officers in riot gear*) to come intervene and save them.

The situation was reaching the point of a small scale riot until "The Turtles" arrived. It was actually the Department of Corrections Emergency Task Force- but they were called "The Turtles" by all Riker Island inmates. Just picture a platoon worth of guys at least 6 foot 200 pounds each padded up with puncture resistant gear looking like new millennium hockey players, strapped with black Billy clubs and pepper spray or mace. They were trained to do one thing and that was pummel you to the point of complete submission using various judo and freestyle methods. They rushed the dorm in military strike formation. Most inmates automatically acknowledge these masters of police brutality and cease all activity. The only way to ensure that they don't crack your ribs and crack your head open is to immediately put your head against a wall while clasping your hands together spreading your legs and putting your elbows against the wall. Any one who doesn't comply will be subdued by severe and calculated violence. The messed up part is that you still might be subject to a hit or two for just being there.

The whole dorm was put on lock down, Mo took notice of The Turtles but could not snap Jamaal out of his berserker like rage so he chose to run and assume the position against the wall. Jamaal was still pounding an adversary into unconsciousness and still unaware of the imminent danger. The oncoming Turtles were tearing through every inmate cracking ribs and shattering jaws wielding there large black Billy clubs like medieval swords. Jamaal was in black out mode, when a fighters opponent has no identity and his own soul becomes momentarily intoxicated by the electric adrenaline of battle. As soon as the Billy clubs crashed across Jamaal's cranium causing him to reel forward he turned around and reeled back with a rising uppercut that struck his attacker in the groin. The blow did not do much damage dulled by the protective gear but it gave Jamaal enough time to scoop the Turtle off his feet by the back of his knees, throwing him off balance and awkwardly slamming him on his back. The Turtles descended on Jamaal like a pack off killer ants. Jamaal drunk with warriors venom fought as much as he could, until his vision went from blurry to black, from black to pitch black and from pitch black to sleep. Jamaal and a couple of other inmates were dragged out like cattle after a slaughter.

THE - UNION

JAMAAL woke up naked the next day in a small cell with his clothing loosely scattered throughout the cell with the exception of his jacket and sweater which seemed to be missing. Jamaal's body ached and he could taste his own dry blood on his lips. The cell was empty except one nasty toilet bowl that reeked of feces and wouldn't flush. The room was absent of light except for a small barred window to high above to see through. This cell had no bars instead it had a light blue solid metal door with one slot at eye level so a tray of food can be slid to the enclosed inmate. This cell block is un-fondly known by most inmates and ex-convicts as "the hole." Inmates in "the hole" are locked up 23 hours a day and allowed to come out of their cell to shower and go to the yard for "wreck". Any time they aren't in their cells they are shackled from wrist to ankle. When an inmate is sentenced to be in "the hole" for disciplinary action they are usually sentenced in intervals of 30 to 60 days, 60 to 90 etc. Even though every correctional facility will insist that "the box" or "the hole" helps and is a good way to punish a prisoner, "the hole" only proves to hinder an inmate from reforming and actually pushes them towards a state of insanity. Many inmates have come extremely close or have gone insane in those dark hell holes.

Else where on Riker's Island word got back to Supreme that Jamaal started a mini- riot in Mod 4. Figuring Jamaal would be some where in "the Bing" (*the hole)* being in charge of the kitchen was an asset. He automatically had himself switched from the food serving line to food delivery where he would be required to serve food to the Mental Observation unit, the Medical unit, and Solitary Confinement (*the hole*).

All these events took place and Jamaal hadn't been on Riker's Island for more than three days. Jamaal just sat in his miserable eight by eight cell thinking about Samaya and his daughter Rain. He felt so guilty for missing the divine moment of his daughter's birth and felt he unintentionally, almost indirectly abandoned his family. His braids were disheveled, he sunk his finger nails into the new growth and scratched and dug into the skin causing flakes of dandruff to fly from his scalp. The jet black shine of his hair turned a dark jail grey. Jamalal dusted himself off as though he could shake out the internal angels and demons that clashed within the arena of his mind. He wanted to beat his fists against the light blue steel doors but knew it would have been senseless. At the moment when he was almost completely lost in the abyss of insanity a beacon of light beckoned to him and guided him out the abyss. It was a loud knock on the cell door accompanied by the familiar voice of a friend. Supreme "Get up for chow!" Jamaal jumped off the floor and rushed to the door and opened the food slot recognizing the voice instantly. Supreme cautiously slides an open pack of Newport cigarettes through the slot. The open pack had a little bonus: two marijuana joints rolled up in Bible paper. Then he slides a book through the slot called *The Art of War* by Sun Tzu with his tray of food and cup of juice. Supreme whispered through the slot "Yo god you probably be here for like 60 days but I'm going to hold you down every time it's chow and I come to your cell just let me know what you need. I'm trying to see if I can pull some strings and get you sent to my house when you done here, tomorrow I'll bring you some of the lessons(the lessons of the 5% nation) aight peace God." Jamaal "Peace" Then Supreme continued his duties.

Jamaal's stay in "the hole" (the bing) went from 60 to 90 days, when he was forced to defend himself against one of Crown Height's boys who happened to be in "the hole" and had to go to Manhattan court,(*The Tombs*) need I say more?! He absorbed the 5% lessons as a way of life to elevate his logical and critical thinking while *The Art of War* was Jamaal's guide to battle and The *Autobiography of Malcolm X* became his inspiration. He imprinted the wisdom of these texts on his soul, and swore to apply those principles to his own empire. He began to mature within the bracket of his 90 day stint in "the hole."

Jamaal was transferred to "4 Upper" upon his release from the hole. Supreme ran this house, he even had a couple of the correctional officers under his influence. The heavy amounts of money Jamaal sent him through Chyna forged with his killer instinct mad Supreme virtually invincible in prison. Supreme was also "juggling" that was what they called it but it was sort of a jail house loan sharking operation. Inmates who were down on there luck would receive anything they needed from commissary to drugs and cigarettes "on the juggle". The inmates would be required to pay back their debt with interest. Of course there is a drastic penalty for anyone who accumulates a debt they cannot pay and with Jamaal's assistance Supreme's business became even more profitable. They were in complete control of 4Upper they had certain officers whom they paid for special services like bringing them Chinese food. Officer Lovell was their favorite. Lovell always let Jamaal and Supreme smoke weed while he was on night duty.

They were smoking so many joints in Bible paper that they started smoking the pages with words on them. Every night they would sit in the bathroom exchanging war stories bringing each other up to speed on the events in their lives. Jamaal spoke of all those he had shot and Supreme spoke of his numerous stabbings. Once Jamaal had showed Supreme that he mastered the "knowledge 120" meaning Jamall completely memorized the 5%'s lessons, Supreme gave him, his attribute *(true name)*. "Freedom" was his attribute as it was what he desired most plus he had the thirst for knowledge the ultimate freedom of knowing. Freedom defined in the 5% lessons is - To free your dome (mind) from of triple stages of darkness (*deafness, dumbness and blindness and usher in the triple stages of light (the knowledge which sets the mind free*) knowledge, wisdom, and understanding. Supreme called him Freedom from that day on and every other inmate followed suit. Freedom (*Jamaal*) promised Supreme second in command of his drug spots when he gets out of prison. When Freedom spoke of Sopa and the events leading to him becoming La Compania's head hit man Supreme had an automatic disdain for Sopa and did not trust him. See when you're in prison you spend a lot of time thinking and plotting, therefore Supremes mind grew sharper and there were certain revelations that Supreme helped bring to Freedom's attention. It came to pass that they figured out the truth to Hashish's death. It had to be Reg that betrayed him that day of Allahandro's murder and Reg was probably spying on him for Sopa all this time. Retracing the events Freedom remembered certain factors that he ignored at first. The whole time Hashish and Freedom were being beaten by Sopa's minion no one took the duct tape off Hashish's mouth. Freedom could remember his uncle's horrified eyes screaming at him from beyond the grave as testament of his innocence....... Sopa went through great lengths to control Freedom. Supreme's wise advice made it very evident that he would definitely have to murder Reg and eventually Sopa because they were snakes in the grass and would lead Freedom to his demise. Though Freedom was intent on the destruction of Sopa he still had a certain degree of love for Sopa. Sopa handled all of Freedom's legal fees and he was the driving force behind Freedom's rise to power in Harlem, so he did have certain loyalties to Sopa, but the spirit of revenge overrides Freedom's love for his mentor. Supreme was Freedom's only true ally and they decreed that when Supreme comes home he will aid Freedom as an invisible sword for weeding out the snakes in his midst.

ADULTEROUS HOME COMING

It took about 11 months but the Manhattan District Attorney finally dropped Jamaal's case. Since the key witness was the foundation of evidence and he died in a strange coincidental apartment fire that consumed Alshaun, his brother Jacob and their mother so it was pointless to pursue prosecuting Freedom. Freedom himself still being locked up at the time of their death couldn't have had a hand in this hidden act of arson only Sopa could employ the type of skill it would take to make the fire look accidental. Freedom was released from Manhattan court with time served for a lesser charge just in time for him to celebrate his 18th birthday. Sopa planned a splendid coming home/birthday party him. Rain's first birthday was coming up soon too and freedom was happy he would be a free man for that occasion. Supreme was soon transferred up north to Water Town Correctional Facility then Comstock where he would serve the minimum jail time of his sentence if he gets into a program, schooling, stays away from trouble and gets parole. Jamaal was happy to get home and see his daughter but he was anxious to get back to business and lay the foundation for Supreme's arrival.

Freedom's big bash was at club 2000 in upper Harlem courtesy of Sopa. Freedom hardly ever dressed up but he did for his home coming. He threw on an all black Armani suit that Samaya purchased him for special occasions. With a pair of black leather Salvatore Ferragamo shoes that the lawyer Jon Muita suggested he purchase. His side burns were freshly lined up and his braids were done for the first time in 11 months. Having his hair done by an inmate was definitely not an option for him. His braids hung down to his collar bone, Samaya was a little jealous watching her handsome husband leaving their place while Rain waddled in her walker and speaks in baby sounds.

When Freedom walks into Club 2000 all eyes were on him. He recognized all the security and was at ease, this was definitely a La Compania party. Every member and trusted affiliate was present to pay homage to Freedom . The laser lit dance floor was paved multi colored blinking squares with an abundance of barely clothed women of many nationalities. Freedom felt like a star. Method Man's classic "M.E.T.H.O.D. Man" shook the entire club while Freedom walked towards the bar exchanging handshakes with numerous members before he could reach into his pocket and order a drink – the bartender handed him a bottle of Moet and a bottle of Hennessey Privilege. He walked over to Sopa's table where Stud sat with him. Sopa stood up to greet Freedom offering his hand and Stud pulled him in for a brotherly hug, highly uncommon of Stud and Freedom internally questioned his motives. Stud

"Good to have you back primo!" Sopa also stands and gives Freedom a hug afterward he put his hand on the back of Freedom's head reminiscent of a father and son he locks eye contact with him. Sopa "Have fun tonight Negrito, this is your coming home party!" They all sat at the table and discussed recent events. Freedom told them of his partner Supreme who'd he like to bring into the organization. Sopa praised him for keeping his mouth closed and surviving in prison without using the La Compania name to get respect, instead he took it on his own. Sopa spoke between shots of Brugal and drags of his joint. "I got a higher position for you in our organization, you have proven yourself over and over, now, I trust you like a son." Freedom already knew what was taking place because you hear things even in jail. The war with the Jamaicans was getting out of control and Sopa secretly feared for his own life so he wanted his best killers around. Apparently since Freedom's been locked up the Jamaicans have been dominating the war even when they tried to form a truce in the name of good business the Jamaicans always broke the truce. Even the Italian Mob could not deal with these renegades. They had no rules, no code of ethics, if you were doing business with them there was always a 9 out of 10 chance that they would rob you. The fact was that they were selling enough cocaine to compete with La Compania but they weren't getting there product by bargain and trade, they were getting it by extorting the Tri-State's most well known drug organizations. They earned the rite to be feared by the common underworld and in this time of war Freedom was definitely an asset to his organization. Freedom sat at the table and felt a sense of unity between him Sopa and Stud similar to the brother hood he had with the original C.M.K. members but there was a big difference, he never plotted on killing them. Reg walked over to the table and rudely interrupted them. "Aye nigga I know you ain't going to spend the whole night huddled up with Sopa, let me introduce you to some bitches." Freedom can see that Reg was Sopa's pawn and he pondered the thought as he got up and walked over to a group of girls Reg had been entertaining. All of them were drop dead gorgeous but the one who stood out was Sopa's niece Mercedes. Her complexion was a light red caramel, her eyes were gray and the club rainbow laser lights danced in her gaze. She was thick but not fat. Mercedes had the body proportions of a full figured stripper and it was all natural. Her hair was a curly light brown her legs were hard thick and firm and her butt seemed to sit up right like two basketballs. Freedom's eyes were focused on hers and time paused for a brief moment. She majored in accounting at Boricua College and her dream was to open up a Traveling Agency. Her family had been butchered in a political gang war with dirty police involved back in the Dominican Republic. Sopa took her in as his daughter years ago because her deceased father was his trusted friend. Freedom and Mercedes were inseparable for the remainder of the night, drinking and laughing together even though he never dances she was still able to get him to dance to Mary J. Blige's song "Real Love." There was an intense sexual tension between them that could not be ignored. Sopa watched them from afar without the slightest emotional change. Yes, she was his little girl but she was a part of La Compania so her and Freedom together might work to Sopa's advantage. It was a beautiful night, DJ Kid Capri served up an unbelievable mixture of Hip-Hop, R&B, Dance Hall Reggae, Roots and Culture Reggae, Meringue, and Salsa. All you could see was packs of drunk Dominicans, Blacks, and Puerto Ricans stumbling out of the club. Mercedes agreed to let Freedom drive her home but he insisted on getting Sopa's approval. Freedom was a little drunk and his body wasn't used to getting so intoxicated but he held his composure. At 4:15 am everyone exited Club 2000. Stud and this young dude named Pistola stayed arm to arm with Sopa. Pistola must have been the youngest killer recruited. Freedom walked up to Sopa and threw his arm over his shoulder before he could even speak Sopa interrupted him, and says with a sarcastic grin. "You and Mercedes have a good night but I'm glad you tried to ask me cause if you didn't I would have killed you. Now keep me company until Stud gets my car." Freedom knows that Sopa was joking but still felt that the threat rolled off his tongue to easily as though it were a subliminal message saying "I will kill you." He gave Mercedes a nod to let her know everything was good as he continued to stand next to Sopa while Stud jogged around the corner for the car. Now Freedom started to get that bubbly feeling in his stomach and he didn't like the crowd that had assembled outside the club and the way so many members were exposed out in the open at one time. He was correct for feeling leery because right at that moment an all black Honda Civic began racing up the street. He noticed the car out of his left peripheral, Pistola pulled a 45. caliber hand gun and Freedom pulled out his nine millimeter and shouted to make everyone aware "It's a Hit!!!!!" Sopa was also armed with a steel 38. caliber revolver with a red wood handle. The Honda made an abrupt stop and two masked men jumped out with Uzi's and started spraying the front of the club at random. Most club patrons dispersed while some were touched by strays while Sopa's soldiers drew their weapons. Freedom made Sopa get on the ground for cover and took his 38. revolver from him and covered his body by standing in front of him, slightly leaning on Sopa to brace himself while he emptied the barrel of the 38. revolver. It was a real fire fight, he hit one of the gunmen dead in the face with a hollow 38. caliber slug. Another identical black Honda civic pulled up right behind the first and two more gun men emerged wearing masks and shooting AK-47 assault rifles. There wasn't much Freedom could do but take cover, the La Compania soldiers were equipped with hand guns and weren't prepared for this-and were running out of bullets fast so most of them took off running. Freedom watched as many members were picked off by the AK-47's tumbling bullets. Freedom ducked down and came back up firing his nine hitting yet another of the masked assault men. He looked over his shoulder and felt invigorated by Pistola who apparently had not ceased shooting and reloading as though he were on the front line of attacking military unit. Pistola lived up to his name and was one of the few who came prepared with plenty of extra clips. There were only two gun men left, the one with Uzi must have run out of ammo because he jumped back into his bullet riddled Honda and tried to abandon the fight and sped off. Before he drove off Freedom made eye contact with the fleeing gunman and it was as though they recognized each other. There is one thing for sure in the middle of this dirty game of guns, things happen in spontaneous moments that escape the memory in detail but you can always be sure to remember the eyes of the enemy. All the remaining La Compania members were at the gunmen's mercy all they could do was take cover while AK47 bullets the size of index fingers ripped through the air, cars, flesh and concrete to ricochet and shred through anything in their path. Like an avenging angel rushing to their aid Stud was speeding up the block doing at least 90 miles per hour in an Acura Legend and side swiped the gunmen making the gunfire cease with one big thump. Stud then put the car in reverse and drove over the gunmen's body one more time for precaution, you could hear the crackling snap of bones breaking. Stud stopped the car and yelled out the window "Vamano Viejo!" Sopa rose to his feet with Freedom's help, strangely enough Sopa did not appear visibly shaken by the whole ordeal. Just then Mercedes ran over to them with a smoking automatic 38. caliber Lorcin in her hand and says "Are you okay Papa? You know I couldn't live if something happen to you!" Sopa replies "Everything is okay Jamaal and Pistola were ready, now take her home Jamaal I'll page you tomorrow morning for a meeting." Pistola and Sopa quickly got into the car. Freedom was a little surprised to find that Mercedes was shooting at the gun men and not hiding. Police were definitely on their way, so everyone drove away from the scene leaving the carnage behind of at least 9 dead bodies and wounded stragglers.

Freedom was still a little tipsy and couldn't really focus while driving with Mercedes looking so sexy in the passenger seat. She sat in the car as calmly as she could but still had her adrenaline pumping she twisted and turned in her seat making it appear as though her legs were ready to burst out of her dress. A slit on the side of her dress made it look like black champagne dripping down her thigh. Her lips were voluptuous pink and wet while she seductively licked and rolled a blunt of hydroponic weed to perfection. She instructed him to take the West Side Highway and get off at 59th street: her place was on 54th 11th Avenue. Clinton Towers was a very expensive high rise apartment building with 38 floors. Freedom brought her to the lobby door and gave her a kiss on the cheek. Mercedes looked deep into his eyes and laughed at him. Freedom

"What so funny?" Mercedes "You act like you scared of me." Freedom "No" He was still trying to ignore his testosterone screaming for lustful intercourse while his conscious was telling him to get home to Samaya and Rain. Mercedes seemed like a mind reader because she knew exactly what to say. "Listen Papa I know you got a baby mother and I know you in love with her, I know you don't want to hurt her. I would never try to be the type of bitch to come between that but we could at least be close friends." She gently grasps Jamaal right hand and places it on her hip while passing him the blunt with the other. Freedom "Yeah, I guess we could be friends." Mercedes digs into her Lui Vuitton pocket book, moves her gun to the side and pulls out a set of keys. Mercedes "Mirar, these are the keys to my apartment, veinte ocho, I'll be upstairs waiting, don't worry about the door man, I'll let him know you're coming up." Freedom jumped back into his Maxima and drove around the block looking for parking, wondering why he wanted this girl so bad. He loved Samaya's purity but there was something that intrigued him about Mercedes' impurities. He stopped for a second to contemplate just leaving without going up stairs but decided that one night wouldn't hurt, besides, he owed it to himself since it was his home coming. He parked the Maxima and went to Mercedes' place. You could smell the apartment in the hallway, it was the scent of Vanilla and Jasmin and it grew stronger as he reached her door. The sweet aroma captivated him. Upon entry Mercedes greeted him wrapped in a towel, she was fresh out the shower. She resembled a Caribbean-Indigenous Queen in her basic garb. She to be more of a temptress than anything, she instructed Freedom to take off his shoes and offered him a glass "Morirse sonado"(*well known Puerto Rican and Dominican drink that combines sweet milk, milk and orange juice as the main ingredients*) and she already had a blunt pre-rolled. She held his hand and guided him on a little tour of the place; she had sun doors in her living room that led to a balcony over looking the sky-scrapers in mid town Manhattan and a clear view of the Hudson River. Her kitchen had Granite counter tops and top of the line appliances. She brought him into her bedroom and she exited the room to finish putting on her pajamas. Freedom relaxed and smoked while drinking the "Morirse sonado", she had a lovely bedroom with oil burners and organic scented candles in every corner. Her room had a sort of Asian theme, a bright red silk goose down comforter with embroidery of the Asian Zodiacs adorned her king size bed. It was like her place was a mini palace. Mercedes also seemed to have a fetish for ancient weapons because she had swords of every culture, from Cuban machetes to Samurai swords to African spears all mounted on her walls as decoration. Her collection must have totaled to at least 17 different weapons. Freedom loved her collection, especially the samurai swords she kept in her bedroom. He fell in love with her fascination with weapons of destruction and a feeling of kinship warmed his heart because he realized that she is also locked into a deadly romance with death. When murder is a part of your daily thought pattern it manifests itself in many different ways. The red light bulb only added to the nostalgic aurora of her room, the candle light flickered off the swords' blades. She called him into her bathroom and asked him "Aren't you going to join me?"

This was all very new for him, he had never been seduced by such a beautiful woman before. Freedom stripped down to his bare skin in front of her while still taking tokes of weed. She admired his dark reddish brown skin and thin yet chiseled physique, as he admired her nude supple body. Standing there bare of his garments he couldn't hide his erection. He joined her in her shower which was huge enough to include 4 people. Mercedes lathered her body with apricot & mango soap from Bed, Bath & Beyond and began to gently do the same to him, all over, beginning with his shoulders, down to the tips of his fingers, then all the way down to his ankles. Mercedes got on her knees and looked up at him with her bright eyes as though she were about to perform oral sex on him, but instead she just teased him. She lathered up his balls with soap and gradually stroked his penis while playing with his balls in a massaging motion. The moment she noticed that he was deriving some pleasure from it she got out the shower. Freedom grew tired of her games and got out of the shower right after her as she scurried into her room like a Lioness avoiding a male in heat. She was lying on her stomach displaying her plump caramel buttocks; he smelled her neck and mounted her back pressing his throbbing manhood against her. He licked and sucked her neck and back as though she were human candy while she purred like a pleasured kitten, but this kitten can be ferocious. She rebelliously turned around and begins to violently bite Freedom between soft sensual kisses. She tightly wrapped her thick legs around his naked body pulling his face forward and shoving her tongue down his throat then teasingly biting his lips. This strange display of masochism is their strange bond as they both derive some sort of pleasure from pain. Samaya wasn't the type of girl that Freedom would just have sex with, he makes love to her in a gentle and romantic fashion. He would never even ask her to give him oral sex out of respect, but Mercedes was different she had no sexual inhibitions.

He lifted her off the bed and slammed her back down to

get a better bearings on her, he aggressively pushed himself inside of her vagina. It was so sweet, wet and tight that it squeaked like a freshly washed porcelain plate. Once inside it was a perfect fit and the two aggressive animals began a sexual battle of slow grinding and primal lust. He turned her over and grabbed her curly locks and slammed her face into the pillow while propping her ass up in the air. Grabbing each huge cheek and spread her ass to improve his view before he jammed his meat into her vaginal cavity. As he slammed his hips against her "bubblicous" butt she pushed back demanding all of him. They were pounding to a steady rhythm making a sound like moist hands clapping together. Mercedes turned around and pushed Freedom back mounting him like he was a wild Bull. She bent her knees and had her ass slapping his balls while she move up and down, she whispered in his ear "Freedom please cum in me Papa I'm yours!" She pulled his waste forward and rode him harder and faster while whining and screaming "Aye Papa I'm cumming, Please cum in me Papa give me all of it!" She looked dead into his eyes with tears trickling from her gray crystal irises. Freedom answered her plea with a Neanderthal like grunt as he exploded inside her. Mercedes made her vagina muscles contract and expand tickling him as his remaining semen seeped out of him into her. She cuddled him like a newborn child and stroked his fore head until they fell asleep like two battle scarred soldiers exhausted from combat.

10am The Next Morning, Freedom awoke with a critical hangover and started rushing to put on his clothes realizing that Samaya must be worried sick and his beeper has 12 missed pages which were definitely from her. He would have called her back immediately but could not think of a decent lie to tell her, plus calling his home phone from Mercedes house might be risky. Mercedes was in the kitchen cooking up breakfast. Jamaal ignored the succulent smell of food and focused on getting home. Mercedes was butt naked with a plate of beef bacon, eggs and plantinos when she walked back into the bed room "Break fast is done Papa.... Damn you leaving hugh?" Jamaal "I wish I could stay but I got shit to do." Mercedes put his plate on her dresser and laid down back in bed inviting him to stay with her eyes. Freedom leans over and gives her a big hug and kiss "Later sweet heart". He pauses for a second and gets her apartment keys out of his pocket to return them. She refuses to take them "Oh no papa those are yours, you're going to need them." He puts the keys back in his pocket with a confused look on his face as he exits her place and locks the door. He rushed uptown to have a meeting with Sopa about last night but not before he went home to change clothes and deal with his family.

THE DEADLY LION POSSE

THE Deadly Lion Posse was a vicious gang of killers and drug lords that hailed out of Kingston Jamaica. Extortion, racketeering and Drug dealing was just a few of their many ways of getting money. In the late 80's and early 90's they were all but eliminated in Jamaica so to secure their strength and numbers they moved on to more fertile areas. They invaded the United States by boat, by plane with fake visas, or real visas, as passengers or stowaways, or via the Florida peninsula. They are well known through out the underworld for their terrorist style business. They introduced a new brand of urban guerilla warfare that was otherwise unheard of in the United States. Rumors about their gang seemed to become urban folklore, all types of stories about them circulated through the street. Some people say they chop up their victims and drink there blood because they believe the blood gives them strength. Whether these rumors were true or not the Deadly Lion Posse still left an imprint of legendary fear wherever they went. They were all over Miami Florida and the five boroughs of New York, especially Brooklyn, Harlem, The Bronx, and Queens.

Harlem was a new ghetto for them to colonize and they didn't have too many solid competitors until they bumped up against La Compania. In the beginning D.L.P (*Deadly Lion Posse*) was loosing the battle for territory and sales but while Freedom was locked up they flourished by absorbing the drug spots

Freedom left unattended. Freedom's problem was that he alone had to be the boss, the enforcer, and the bank of his operation along with working as an enforcer/salesmen for Sopa. Working for Sopa meant Freedom had access to La Compania enforcers like Stud, Pistola etc but it was only for temporary help and he needed soldiers for everyday, 24/7 work. The immediate leader of the D.L.P New York chapter was an evil old Rasta man named "Star" who was on the run from Jamaican authorities and the Department of Immigration. Star was a like a fire hydrant, short and stout with 7 huge thick dread locks that resembled withering tree branches that just seemed to lean down the side of his head. His beard hung to his Adam's apple and it knotted up at the tip. He walked with a terrible bowlegged limp as a result of being shot 7 times at point blank range.

"Screw Face" is what they call those mean faced "bad-bwoys" from Jamaica and even now in the ghetto's of New York it is ever present in our slang. If you come out to NY giving niggas the "screw face" your going to get hurt. Let's explore the term "Screw Face" some people just walk around looking all mad for no reason. Some just wear a "screw face" because they are really scared in the ghetto. The true definition of screw face comes from the truest men and women in every ghetto everywhere. For them it isn't a defense, they aren't scared for themselves, it is a state of mind, an adaptation to the constant state of war. "The screw face" is the face of the poor and impoverished. Dark brown glossy reddish eyes with bags under them. These eyes are ancient and have seen every mortal atrocity that man is capable of. A "screw face" is the face of the wretched "Field Nigger" who can remember being snatched from his majestic abode to be held as an abused captive. Who has seen his daughters, wives, sisters, and mothers, raped, his father whipped and hung. He loathes his slave master, he plots his slave masters death. A "screw face" is the face of bare-foot malnourished children in third world countries, who know more about AK-47 assault rifles than they know about toys and games. These children were bred in war and poverty and for generations our children have been born with bags under their eyes because they bare the burden of their ancestor's pain. They to will adopt the screw face as they walk through a place where every abomination is possible and this was the face of Star.

Star was an aging gargoyle of a man who had seen many things, mainly death. He was well versed in handling matters of life & death with astute calculated planning. Star was void of emotions and the thought of murdering entire families down to the infant children bothered his conscious less than urinating in the street. He was playing chess with Sopa but Sopa's knight-(*Freedom*) is an on setting threat. Freedom came home from jail and immediately began to reclaim the other half of his territory no matter who he had to run through. Agony (*who Freedom battered in jail*) was a trusted friend of Star's so Star had a special hatred for Freedom and has figured out that he works for Sopa. Just as La Compania seemed weaker without Freedom now they had a new invigorated strength with him back. Star has put hits on Freedom but the attempts were unsuccessful, he was to elusive to hunt. Freedom never let some one live after making an attempt on his life. Star was losing too much ground and in this 4 year struggle for power Freedom almost completely eliminated them by moving in on all their surrounding territory. It was getting to a point where Star had to contact "The Committee" which was the elected core of the "The Deadly Lion Posse". "The Committee" consisted of 9 members of which Bulla (*Fire's father*), Magnum (*Fire's uncle*), and Star were a third. The remaining 6 were spread through out Florida and Jamaica securing a strong hold at every location. The D.L.P. could be found all over the east, south east and north east of the United States. Star had to appeal to "The Committee" for access to a select choice of elite hit men knowing that even their employment is a sign of weakness or lack of control. But the use of the elite hit men was approved by The Committee. After all it was "all in the family."

There was Cry Baby, Dex, Magnum and Fire. Cry Baby was Star's only son- Star's wife was slaughtered in Spanish Town, Jamaica by a rival gang right in front of Cry Baby who was spared. He was only ten years old when he learned how to truly hate, starting his hit man career at the tender age of 12. The murder of his family was an attempt to lure Star back to the Jamaica but it only resulted in Dex (*Star's little brothe*r) and Cry Baby going on a vengeful killing spree ending with a body count of 25 men all slain execution style. Cry Baby and Dex moved to Miami when Cry Baby was in his early twenties and they have been running things out there ever since.

Now Magnum and Fire are two individuals you may be familiar with. Fire was actually sent back home to live a normal life with his grand mother after Fat Pat's death, Magnum escorted him on his trip. That was seven years ago and to Rita's (*Fire's mother*) great disdain Fire lived anything but a normal life in Jamaica. Fire resented his mother's decision and started to rebel as soon as he got there. Despite his small flimsy frame he learned to wield high caliber guns with ease and his family ties gave him access to everything. He was feared due to his father's reputation but he quickly earned one of his own as a vicious assassin. He collected thousands from the extortion of Trench town's drug dealers and small business owners, he earned the moniker: "Baby face killer" because he had a strikingly young appearance but was a deadly man. Magnum sort of mentored him citing that Fire would do it on his own any way Magnum found that the best way to protect his nephew was to teach him. Yet there was no controlling Fire, he had no regard for human life, not even his own. He continued with his child hood habit of disregarding his medical condition and as a result he frequented the hospital. High grade marijuana and alcohol was his medication of choice for his sickle cell flare ups. His parents kept tabs on him from afar because he had an open hatred for them and convicting abandonment issues. Fire's scorn for his mother and father spilled over into his parents' relationship; Rita blamed Bulla for Fire following in his footsteps. Magnum and his nephew were infamous through out Jamaica and the authorities were beginning to smell their scent. Star made them an offer for some decent money and a chance to return to the U.S. Magnum knew that the sporadic Fire needed a break from Jamaica after 7 years of murder and plunder; he needed a change of pace before some one killed him. Star offered the perfect opportunity to get away from Jamaica, Magnum accepted the offer with strategic plots in mind while Fire took the offer just for the hell of it.

"SEE DE SEE DE HIT MON A COM"

LYRICS FROM THE SONG ---LIMB BY LIMB-BY CUTTY RANKS

LOCATION: 145th street and St. Nicholas Avenue—the bar on the corner nick named "the dungeon" is the local D.L.P. hang out. "Nuh Bwoy caan play dolly house wid mi gal/-Mi wi step inna him face, inna him face/-Nuh care if a sergeant or general/-Mi wi step inna yuh face, inna yuh face/-A bwoy try dis mi wi play di ginal/-An step inna yuh face, inna yuh face" Song: Dolly House—by Spragga Benz is playing at full blast with the exaggerated bass line seems to vibrate the entire bar. There is the distinct scent in the air, jerk chicken and weed competing with the aroma of fried fish from the restaurant Famous Fish next door. Famous Fish always had a line that damn near went around the corner. Together the two bustling businesses kept this particular corner packed like Grand Central Station. That very same corner was a haven for delicious food but moon lights as a narcotic mini market. They had nickels, dimes, ounces, pounds and kilos of any drug you could possibly need. Harlem hustlers almost had a guerilla style of salesmanship, you couldn't walk down Broadway with out some

Dominican kid offering you something and you couldn't get off the D train at 145th street without having some Jamaican dude offer you something.

Magnum and Fire took a yellow cab from the airport, Magnum was an Original Gangster, you could tell by the look of him. He traded in his jherri curled multi parted gumby hair cut for a sleek bald crown and wore an all silk red suit with gold chains like Slick Rick. Fire didn't look a day over 16, his hair was cut low to a Caesar with a half moon part. The scar on the back of his head was his only mark of age. He wore a Calvin Klein Jean suit and a forest green champion hooded sweater to match his purple and green Nike Huarache's. He hardly had as much jewelry as Magnum only wearing a long Cuban link with a diamond studded gold Lion's Head and his old C.M.K. pinky wring from back in the days.

They reached their destination and got out of the yellow cab exuding an energy that commanded the attention of the street corner's hand to hand hustlers. You could tell these guys were important. Just the determined look on their faces cleared a path through the bustling street corner. Foot soldiers and salesmen alike got out the way of the two "rude bwoys from the yard *(yard-Jamaican slang for the ghetto)*." They entered "the dungeon" proceeding to walk towards the back as Star had instructed them. Magnum recognized his old friend instantly. He was sitting at a table with three men, Cutty, Dex and Cry Baby, all a little older than Fire. Fire followed Magnum bumping through the crowd squinting through clouds of lamb spread marijuana. As soon as they were within arm's reach of Star's table Cutty (*Star's henchmen*) quickly stood up gripping the gun on his belt, he pushed Magnum back with one hand and said "A bwoy why you com so close fer ya wan dead?!" in a demanding tone. Fire stealthily steps forward and puts his blade against Cutty's larynx simultaneously grabbing Cutty's gun off his belt and pressing the barrel against Cutty's gut. Fire "Pussy clod bwoy move from mi uncle de fi mi chop R blood clot head off, ya don know de general" he pushes the blade forward just enough to draw a little blood. Star slowly waddles to his feet and says "Easy nah Cutty dem bwoy de Deadly Lion dem a work wit we, so just tress back understand." Cutty tries to back away but Fire moves forward with him applying pressure with the gun and knife preparing to take Cutty's life. Star "De bwoy pure fire fe real him jus like Bulla Ayo Fire let de bwoy Cutty go him don know yas a Lion." Fire's slanted eyes were looking at Cutty blankly as though he had already envisioned him dead, Fire then shot a look at Magnum and let go of Cutty but he tucked the gun in his jeans. The men sat down, Cutty embarrassed and insulted walked away gunless. Cutty was definitely a killer but was small time compared to Fire and Magnum. The men sat down and greeted the other two men sitting (*Dex and Cry Baby*) a six foot tall chocolate goddess named Sasha came to the table to serve them 5 Guinness stout beers. Star speaks with a joint of weed hanging off his lips "Fire me hear nuff good ting bout you mi an ya fader are like brotha an brotha. Me know him from long time an mi know say him neva want him son fe grow up like we, but me happy ya grow up still rude bwoy. Me Magnum an ya fader don brush off nuff people so me know say ya com from a good breed. Understand me." Star extends his arm and touches fist to fist with Fire and brings that same fist to his heart in a salute like manner. "But dis nah bout re-union dis bout war na de lickle Spanish bwoys from de hill and dem general a ole mon name Sopa him keep nuff gun mon round him too. Understand me? Mi feel say me an dem bwoy can't live in a de same place. Two big fish can't exist in a de same pond. An right now dem bwoy murder nuff a we solja." Fire "Mi ready fe murder Star." Star leans back in his chair seeming more relaxed and less animated stroking his knotty beard that resembles a Lion's mane. Star "Me hear you lickle Bulla, tree bwoy ya mus kill, if ya won get ta Sopa –name Freedom, Stud and a next bwoy name Pistola. Dem bwoy de Sopa main gun mon an all a dem disrespect we an de firs one me won dead is de bwoy Freedom. Him fuck up nuff business fe we understand me? Murder dem family an every other blood clot ting round dem we afe make a statement. We mus make dem Know! Deadly Lion. 50 tousand blood clot dollar for every one a dem general or lieutenant or boss ya kill ya understand me!" Fire, Dex, Cry Baby and magnum all give Star a reassuring nod as he continues. "Now for de next couple a days ya gwon relax drive roun get used to de city mi hav a niece lickle place fe you relax an catch a vibes." Star then had Sasha the waitress escort the two men to an all black tinted Lincoln town car that they would be using for their stay. She took them a couple of blocks away to an apartment complex where they would stay temporarily and Sasha conveniently lived across the hall. The four hit men adjusted to the Big City real quick and had already decided how they would pair off for the Hits. Magnum and Dex were supposed to go after Freedom, and Stud while Fire, Cutty and Cry Baby were designated to go after Sopa and Pistola.

Fire was in a zone, a lot of New York memories resurfaced, he wanted to visit his family in Brooklyn, but no one made an effort to reach out to him so he figured they must not care. He missed his mother because she was the only person that could calm his flammable heart. He knew that one day he would come of age and return to New York. Bulla also missed his son but would never over extend himself in an emotional manner. So instead father and son ignored each other and that's just how it was. Fire never felt a feeling of love or affection from his father and all he learned from him was how to conquer and for that he was grateful but from the day they sent him to Jamaica he vowed to never set foot in his parents' home again. His mother would cry many a nights praying herself to sleep, Fire was just like his father and now she fears for both of their lives.

Fire felt that Star was old and weak, he heard the fear in his speech. Fire internally plotted on taking over the New York chapter of D.L.P. after he crushes La Compania. Fire's mind flew to the earlier days of his childhood, he wondered about his old friends, he wondered if he'll ever see them again and if he does will things be the same after so much changing for him since he last saw them.

BYE BYE COMSTOCK

-THE year is 1998 and Supreme has finally been granted Parole, and Freedom continues to keep a tight hold on Upper west Harlem. Anticipating Supreme's release Freedom has built up his C.M.K. organization, taking most matters into his own hands and asserting himself as a feared boss. He was silently preparing to over throw his parent organization La Compania but Supreme was the last missing piece. Mean while Star has rallied his forces to end C.M.K. and La Compania.

- (I love) Niggas with heat, (I love) niggas that's deep/Niggas that regulate the streets (sho' nuff)/Mic blessin, Smith and Wessun caressin/ (First Family) With the Desert Storm impression/The lesson: I advise if your not ready to ride on the homicide side, nigga slide! I Luv Lyrics

Artist: M.O.P. - Billy Danze

Album: First Family For Life

Freedom sat in his brand new Navy Jaguar S-type Saloon reciting every word of the song, it was a classic music to him, like the score for the cinema that is his life. Freedom took long inhales from his cigarette patiently waiting for Supreme to exit Penn Station's bus terminal. Reg is in the passenger seat talking shit as usual but there was tension in the air thicker than mud. Reg still couldn't figure out why he never saw a sign that Freedom knew of his trickery. Reg speaks between gulps of Moet he was always wearing Versace and Coogi since Biggie Smalls was rapping about it. Reg "Yeah nigga can't wait to see my nigga Basil, I mean Supreme! Nah mean son we going to need dat nigga in the street." Freedom ignores Reg's senseless gibber and continues vibing to the music. Reg "Well what we going to do with this nigga? What he going to do for us son?" Freedom can't figure out what is more aggravating, Reg or the wait. Freedom "Supreme is the god ya hear me?! He gonna be in position to do what ever the fuck he wanna do. Stop questioning me B, you getting on my nerves." Reg shrugs his shoulders and takes another gulp of Moet. Reg "Aight son damn, why all ya God body niggas always so serious?" Suddenly Freedom spots Supreme walking out the terminal looking lost so he roles down the car window. Freedom "Ayo Preme! Preme!" Supreme recognizes him and starts jogging toward the car. Freedom turns to Reg- "Yo, you could get in the back seat God." Reg "Come on son serious?" Freedom "Fuck you mean serious? Nigga get in the back seat." Reg moves quickly and bumps into Supreme who stops to admire Freedom's jaguar. Supreme "Damn God you doing it like that, when can I start?" Freedom "Relax God in due time, first we going to celebrate then get down to business, get in!" Reg "Damn Supreme how you got so big son?" Supreme "What fuck you mean nigga you sound like a bitch! I was locked bitch, that's how I got so big!" Reg sat silent in the back seat, boiling on the inside, he felt disrespected and wanted to grab Supreme's locks and punch him in the throat. Supreme had preconceived animosity towards Reg so he turned around and challenged him. "What Nigga! What's the problem hugh, you got a problem then jump nigga!" There was a brief silence while the two men stare each other down then Supreme extends his hand and flashes that super star smile. Supreme "Yo I was just fucking wit you yellow nigga, you know you my man from back in the day god." Reg returns the handshake faking as though he didn't want to shake Supreme's hand but secretly he was grateful because Supreme gave him a way out of a situation that would ended up costing his life. Supreme turned to Freedom "Yo, God I'm with you now, it's on now God." Freedom "Yeah well first we got to go shopping." Supreme "Nah God I need food I'm starving." Freedom "Aight let's go get breakfast at "No Pork on my Fork" on 125th street B." Supreme "Yeah, no doubt God I appreciate all that shit. Even when I was locked up you was on point god, we brothers. We still C.M.K. god, you got my loyalty for real, all these Judas ass niggas gonna fall God." As though he were sending Reg a subliminal message, it was apparent that the 210 pound long haired dread was definitely Freedom's trusted enforcer. The rest of the ride is spent talking about old times and blunt smoking and they all agreed to meet up later to celebrate Supreme's home coming.

Chyna Doll

FREEDOM dropped Supreme off at his parents' house in east Flatbush. Supreme's family were no way near ecstatic to see him and for him the feeling was mutual. He just needed a place to shower and change clothes any way, he definitely didn't plan on trying to move back in. Supreme left most of his new clothes in Freedom's trunk he just kept enough for the day. It felt good to be home and the first thing on his agenda was to find Chyna his childhood sweetheart, the woman who stuck bye his side during his seven years behind bars. Chyna didn't know he was getting out and he wanted to surprise her. He showered and threw on his brand new Black Pelle Pelle and black Tranzetta gortex boots to match and a yellow and black Pittsburgh Pirates jersey with the fitted Pirates hat. He stuffed the two thousand dollars spending money that Freedom gave him into his pocket. He took his Comstock issued green overalls and white Reebok classics and threw them into a garbage bag so he could throw them away and started towards the door. Supreme's mother sat on the living room couch while his father just stood there silent. Supreme felt no remorse as he walked out the door, he knew he would never return there and his parents seemed to know it too. He still did not give a fuck, the only people that took care of him was Chyna and Freedom so they were the only people he considered family. He hopped in a Haitian gypsy cab and took it to Bedford ave and Clarendon road Freedom's old block where Chyna still lived. His stomach bubbled like a dozen piranhas were in his gut, he was nervous, the last time he saw her was a month ago. He hadn't had a chance to kiss her and hold her without some sleazy correctional officer eyeballing them in years. Supreme thought back to all the warnings Freedom had given him; he told him to inform Chyna before just popping up out of no where because he could never really know what to expect. Supreme's arrogant ego would not allow him to accept the possibility that Chyna may have started seeing someone else after all those years. Despite the fact that he heard little rumors here and there about Chyna having a relationship with some older dude. The closer the cab got to his destination the more his stomach bubbled and his thoughts flashed quicker.

Chyna was a tall slender girl with slanted eyes, her features were slight yet chiseled, she wore plenty of gold and spoke with a Trinidadian accent. She kept her hair in short blond finger waves and her smile could light up any rainy day. Chyna and Supreme broke their virginity together; he never doubted that she would be the woman that he would eventually marry.

He got out the gypsy cab and surveyed the block it felt like a totally different world every thing looked different and the buildings that once seemed huge appeared a lot smaller now, I guess it was because the last time he was here he was a couple inches shorter. A chill came over him for a second when he thought about how he was just blocks away from Pat's place of death. It was not a feeling of guilt or regret it was the feeling of wisdom and coming of age. When he looks back at it, he doesn't feel bad about Pat's death at all. He walked down Bedford with his long locks that hung a little past his shoulders bouncing with his stride. Stomping through the ghetto like the modern day urban Paul Bunion.

Maybe it was coincidence, fate, or even karmic law but he bumped into Chyna walking hand in hand with this dude in front of her building. Chyna's mouth dropped to the floor in pure shock because she couldn't believe her eyes, as though she saw a ghost in the flesh. The guy who she was with was named Cash, some older Jamaican hustler from the block who won Chyna's affections by spending money on her. The piranhas inside Supreme's stomach died all at once, his narrow eyes drew together and angled in towards his nose while he walked towards them. Cash must have been fore warned because he had a defensive posture, Chyna was melting inside wishing she had a shell to crawl in and hide. Her relationship with Cash was never anything serious it was supposed to be temporary but she still developed strong feelings for him. Her feelings for Cash were minute in comparison to her deep adoration and love for Supreme. Supreme was engulfed with rage and hurt and he let Chyna know it and spoke to her as though Cash was not even present. Supreme "This is what you were doing the whole time I was locked up bitch?!" He pointed at Cash like an object rather than a person. Supreme gives Chyna a back hand slap that sends her careening to the ground. Cash makes a move to defend her but is met with a Rikers Island style gem star razor ripping across his fore head down his cheek ending around his lip. If you would have seen the act it was as though Supreme was painting a letter C on his face with a paint brush. Cash's face was slit wide open and what's worse is he didn't even notice it until the blood started pouring over his eyes.

Supreme "You don't want to fight right now bitch, fix ya face!" It was a though he controlled Cash's cut with mental telepathy because the blood shed seemed to grow more intense. Cash could do nothing, though he was consumed with anger he knew that if he tried to fight Supreme in this state he would ruin his face, his best bet was to leave and retaliate another day. Cash extends his hand out towards Chyna "Come on!" Chyna responded with tears flooding her eyes "No, I can't." Cash takes one last look at Supreme to get a photographic memory of him and turns away and jogs off before the razor swinging battle cat strikes him again. Supreme grabs Chyna by her inner bicep like an angry parent subduing a rowdy toddler and pulls her to the curb where he stops a cab and shoves her into the back seat. Supreme "Yo driver take me to Manhattan 190th street and Wadsworth terrace!" he pulls out a hundred dollar bill "Here that's for you just take me where I need to go." The cab driver steps on the gas, grateful for his generous tip. Supreme lights a cigarette to calm his nerves while Chyna just stares out the window crying. Chyna speaks with a trembling whimper. Chyna "I'm sorry, Basil I …… just felt lonely." Chyna's eyes turned into little tear flooded slits in her face as she peered deep into Supreme's spirit. Supreme "You could have told me the truth. Why you make me come home to this bullshit? You were my queen, now I look at you as a bitch!" Chyna "Don't say that Basil I love you, but what was I supposed to do for 7 fucking years. Didn't I always visit you on the regular? Didn't I bring you money and send you shit all the time? Did I ever abandon you?" Supreme "Yeah you helped me out a lot but you betrayed me when you ran and fucked that nigga! After all the lessons I sent you, you'd think that you would have more respect for yourself than that or at least have respect for me!" Chyna "Fuck you Basil I don't love him I love you." Supreme "You know niggas warned me but I ain't listen, I should have listened. I can't believe you played me like that." Chyna "I was going to break up with him before you came home." Supreme "That's why I surprised your ass! You dirty bitch." Chyna yells back at him "Well then fuck it, let me out the fucking cab, I'll just go home!" Supreme raises his hand to slap her; she resiliently looks him dead in the eyes challenging him to do it. Supreme turns away as if to resist his violent impulse but it was really to hide his tears. Chyna reads his actions and grabs him with her slender arms nestling her face on his chest as she talks softly while playing with the peach fuzz on his chin. Chyna "Basil I'm so sorry, please understand that you are the only one I want to be with." Supreme's pride wouldn't allow him to speak but he understood, he gently took her hand from his chin and firmly held it. Their relationship was not altogether mended but the worst part was done…………

SMARTEN UP STREETZ IZ WATCHING

BACK at Freedom's apartment he was preoccupied playing with his four year old daughter Rain. Samaya was in the Living room cleaning up preparing for their company, this is the first time anybody visited since they got the apartment. Samaya was anxious to meet the Supreme she had heard so much about, she knew that Freedom trusted no one so just the fact that he has such great trust for Supreme is a testament to his character. Samaya was putting together a genuine soul food dinner; fried chicken, collard greens and baked macaroni and cheese, when the door bell wrung. Freedom buzzed them in knowing it can only be two people.

Supreme and Chyna came to the door, you could tell something was wrong with Supreme, he had fire his eyes and he was smoking a cigarette like it was the only thing calming him down. Chyna's face was red and her right cheek was bruised. Freedom always had a knack for reading people and he had a good idea of what happened without Supreme telling him. He just invited them inside and hoped that he and his wife's hospitality would bring them some type of peace. Samaya was just as aware as her husband and noticed Chyna's bruise and Samaya also could fathom what took place but was glad that at least the couple seems to be trying to work things out.

Samaya was some what familiar with Chyna because she

would go with Freedom to drop money off to her for Supreme's commissary, but they never had a chance to really talk to each other. Chyna sat quietly on the couch wallowing in guilt, but seeing Rain added cheer to her demeanor. Chyna "Oh my god who is this pretty little girl?" She got down on her knees to talk with Rain. Of course Rain being the performer that she is runs down her name, birthday, address and the alphabet. Chyna says to Supreme "Isn't she so sweet." Supreme confirms her statement "Yeah God the little earth is a star, you and your wisdom done good." Samaya extends her hand to shake Supreme's and says "Peace God" Supreme "Peace Earth" Supreme turns to Freedom "Yo God I didn't know, you didn't tell me that your wisdom(girlfriend or wife) had knowledge of self." Freedom "Yeah she does but she but she don't study the Earth lessons. (5% lessons for women)" Samaya "I was born Muslim but I embrace anything that helps keep my babe thinking strait and out of trouble." Supreme "True indeed, maybe you can teach Chyna something." Chyna just sucks her teeth and continues to play with Rain. Supreme says to Freedom "Yo, I know you got some of that equality you was telling me about." Freedom "Shit I got pounds of that shit, but of course I don't keep all that shit here, but I got a little something, come in the bedroom with me." As the two men get up to walk into the master bedroom Samaya hollers "Ya'll niggas better open the windows and close the door, I don't want my child catching contact!" Chyna and Samaya giggle at her statement. In the bedroom Freedom reaches under the bed and pulls out a Ziploc bag full of some light green hydroponic weed with bright orange fibers the scent filled the room immediately. He doesn't waste anytime rolling up a blunt. They sat on the bed and conversed between inhales of weed. Freedom "Damn nigga you alright, you look like you higher than a mother fucker, don't black out on me nigga, Chyna will murder me." Supreme "Yeah I'm alright God, what's on the agenda for the rest of the night?" Freedom "I told you god we going to celebrate your home coming." Supreme "That's peace, but when do I meet all them German mother fuckers you was telling me about?" Freedom "Yeah that's what I wanted to tell you B I don't want you to meet any of them yet, I don't want them to know you just yet either understand? It's the power of deception, the art of war nigga, I got a lot of enemies but they can't hit what they can't see and you're my wild card got me." Supreme just grins and says "Damn god you a diabolical motherfucker, even when we was kids you always was plotting up shit, but on some real shit, I need me a piece of all this shit. Tonight, I'm going to give you a present nigga and show you how real it is. You know that nigga Reg need to get served justice right? I know the nigga a snake God he betrayed you and I can see right through him, bitch ass nigga just used you to get close to that Sopa guy, I'm telling you and you still letting the nigga spy on you. Come on god from all that shit you told me in jail then seeing the nigga eye to eye, he gotta go." Freedom "Aright nigga chill." Supreme "The sun don't chill god." Freedom "Alright, well let's just maintain for right now and have a good time because I don't want you jumping head first into this shit take your time cause once it's starts this shit don't stop. Any way trust me nigga you going to have a fun night I got some females for you to, let's smoke this weed and get ready to pick up faggot ass Reg." Freedom passes him a ziploc bag full of weed and grabs his nine millimeter Smith and Wesson from under his bed and puts it on his hip. Supreme "Where is mine?" Freedom "Aint you on parole nigga? Just maintain for a while I got you." Supreme "I know you looking out for me but I'm supposed to be naked with no protection?" Freedom reaches into his top draw and takes out a stainless steel butterfly knife and some Trojan condoms out of his pocket and gives the items to Supreme. Freedom "Here take this that's all you'll need tonight and in case any thing gets hectic I got another nine millimeter under the passenger seat in my ride but don't fuck with it unless we really need it. Let's get ready to motivate (move or leave) god?" Supreme "Yeah I'm ready but you talk a lot of shit, just remember I'm your enlightener and I'm bigger than you nigga." They engage in laughter as they walk out the bed room, Freedom says to Samaya "Yo Ma, me and Preme bouncing give me my kiss." He puckers up his lips and playfully grabs her. Samaya "ill you smell like weed, all high and shit." As she kisses Freedom "Don't put them weed lips on my daughter either." Freedom "Yeah aight" and kisses his sleeping child on the cheek a dozen times. Supreme "Peace Earth" to Samaya then tells Chyna "You want to chill out here for a while what's it going to be?" Samaya intervenes sensing the tension and hoping to mediate for Chyna and Supreme's sake. Samaya "She going to wait for you here, she can chill." Freedom felt his wife's vibe. "Yeah god, Chyna going to chill wit Samaya cause if you my brother that makes Chyna my sister in law, we all family." Chyna "Babe I'm'a stay here and wait for you." They exchange brief hugs and the guys leave, after he closes and locks the apartment door he turns to Supreme in the hallway. "Yo what's up with you and Chyna?" Supreme "It's a long story man I'll tell you in the car." Sometimes you don't need a lot of words to describe a feeling; Freedom knew that Supreme must have caught her with another dude.

They were having a somber moment as they jogged down the steps until the sound of "Don't move, Police" made their hearts stop. There were just two regular beat cops standing in the lobby of his building. Freedom was nervous inside as his first thought was to pull out and blast at them, but these cops didn't make moves to search him. Apparently they had gotten reports that there were two burglars in the area so Freedom was required to show I.D. and tell them his apartment number which was on his driver's license. They let Supreme slide even though he did not have I.D. and the officers left the building Supreme and Freedom walked out behind them. Freedom was suspicious of the whole thing it was common for police to walk the stair cases of some buildings in the neighborhoods down the hill, and they would give out misdemeanor summons for trespassing, loitering, smoking weed etc.. But Freedom's building and immediate surroundings weren't populated with a lot blacks, or Ricans it was considered a good neighborhood. Cops usually don't make rounds in the apartment building hallways of "good neighborhoods" so why this sudden interest in Freedom's. Something was wrong and Freedom could feel it. He and Supreme threw matters of love and women to the wind and discussed the matters at hand. They both agreed that something was wrong with that whole picture and that Freedom has to pack up and move his family this week because there was an impending danger. To bad Freedom and Supreme drove off in his Jaguar and didn't notice that the danger wasn't impending, it was very present.

At the same time about two blocks away from Freedom's building is an all black fully tinted Chevy Impala 95 model. Sitting in the driver's seat was the sneaky little bastard Det. O'Neil with his brawny partner Det. Schultz next to him doing his usual chain smoking Marlboro cigarettes while drinking coffee. O'Neil uses binoculars to watch Freedom and Supreme get in the car and pull off. O'Neil while squinting threw the binoculars says "Look at this fucking nigga he's got a fucking Jag (*pulls out a pen and jots down Freedom's license plate number*) and he can't be more than 21 or 22 . While I'm 38 years old with a fucking Camry, I can't believe this shit, did ya see how the little fucks looked all over the place before he got in the car, he's a cautious little bastard isn't he." Schultz's two way radio goes off and he looks at O'Neil with a devilish grin, an unknown officer on the other end of the two way radio said-"I got its apartment it's 5k!" Schultz thanks his unknown assailant and can't help but smile. They had been following Freedom since he picked up Supreme and they knew his building but didn't know what his apartment was. So Schultz had his little cousin whose a rookie cop at the 34th precinct do him a favor and get freedom's apartment. Now the detective had the leverage they were looking for, they knew he had something to do with Jacob's apartment burning up, Hashish's death and over a dozen more. It hurt their pride that Freedom beat the charges and after his short 11 month stint in jail he's come out and gotten stronger. The Det. had a personal hatred for Freedom. Schultz "Listen I got a plan……the leader of D.L.P. offered me a pretty penny if I could get Jamaal's address, once these niggers kill each other we'll swoop in and put an end to the nigger war and make a take a couple mill in ." O'Neil "I get what your saying but with all these homicides that are about to take place how do you know the Feds won't come poking they nose up our ass." Schultz speaks with his cigarette in hand "You know what I don't know how you have the fucking most homicide cases solved in our whole precinct and you don't know your dick from your ass. The Feds are already watching Sopa, they just haven't moved on him yet, I'd say he's got a couple more months. O'Neil "So we are just going to capitalize on the whole situation." Schultz "Now you got it, these cock suckers going to self destruct real soon and there is going to be a lot of loose money lying around now let's go talk to that monkey Star." -----

Mean while else where Freedom and Supreme make their way to pick up Reg, Supreme is smoking a blunt big enough to make Red-Man have a heart attack when Reg entered the car. Reg was all dressed up, he loved to wear those colorful Coogi sweaters. Reg "Yo what up, anybody ever tell ya that ya look like brothers? Any way what's up for tonight? We need ta go ta Sticky Mike's." Freedom "What's the fuck is Sticky Mike's B? I aint going to no fucking strip club." Reg "Nah son Sticky Mike's is a dance hall club nigga?" Freedom "A Jamaican club yo you working for them D.L.P. niggas or something you trying to get us shot the fuck up?" Reg "Nigga the club ain't uptown it's down town Manhattan damn near Brooklyn I go there all the time I don't never see no D.L.P. niggas, it mostly be Brooklyn niggas and them Jamaican bitches be showing a niggas love." Reg taps Supreme on the shoulder trying to coax him into making Freedom agree. Supreme "I don't give a fuck as long as we fuck with some bitches and get some pussy." Freedom "Aright fuck it let's go to Sticky Mike's then but I'm telling ya niggas now if I don't feel right and a nigga front I'm bodying (kill) something." Supreme "Like I said nigga, I don't give a fuck I just want to fuck with some bitches." Freedom "Oh trust me we going fuck with some dime bitches later. OOOhh shit you know what I almost forgot? Everybody in the whip got shines except the God (*Supreme*)." Supreme "That aint nothing god I'm a get that, fuck around I catch a jukes tonight." Freedom "Yo, check the glove compartment for me B." Supreme reaches into in and pulls out a 34 inch 14 karat gold hand made Cuban link with a solid gold number 7 pendant flooded with princess cut diamonds identical to Freedom's chain. Supreme quickly threw it on and gave a look of gratitude. Supreme "Damn God this shit is ill god, thanks." Freedom "That's ta show you that you my brother and the chain is an exact duplicate of mine because you my equal. So all the shit I got a Jaguar all this bullshit, you gonna have it to."

Reg was left out the conversation for the rest of the ride, and Supreme's passenger seat pimping antics made the ride go quickly; yelling vulgar compliments at female pedestrians was Supreme's fun, but you can't blame him he hadn't been able to see a woman (*aside from Chyna and the female corrections officers*) in 7 years. They found a parking spot but before they got out and walked to the club Supreme said something that would stick in Freedom's head for the remainder of the night. "Yo god I'm going to fix one of your problems tonight." Freedom looked perplexed by his statement and the rest of the conversation was non verbal Supreme shot his eyes side ways as though pointing to Reg (*unnoticed by Reg*) and Freedom quickly nods his head in disagreement. Supreme then let it be known out loud "That's going to happen whether you wit me or not, we going to start cleaning up nigga! Fuck that."

See Supreme was very hot tempered and never had much tolerance for snakes and would not tolerate a traitor in the mist of his family. All Freedom could do was silently disagree, because he knew that once Supreme makes up his mind it is pointless to try and stop him. Reg "Yo ya niggas starting to scare me son, fuck is ya talking bout?" Freedom "Nah that was some other shit, ain't nothing." Reg "Let me find out ya niggas is fucking or some shit." Everyone starts laughing except

Supreme who just stares at Reg through the rear view mirror giving him a sinister grin that even gave Freedom a chill.

The three of them made their way into the club skipping the line. Freedom quickly gives the bouncer 3 hundred dollar bills and the bouncer ignores the gun on Freedom's waist.

The exterior of Sticky Mike's will fool you with its raggedy appearance while the interior was a totally different story. The first floor level had a full bar on the left hand side, lounge chairs and table. On the right in the middle was a set of stairs that led down to the dance floor in the basement. A thick aroma accompanied by foggy mist of marijuana filled the air. Reg started to roll up a blunt, while Freedom squints hard scanning the bar for enemy faces. Freedom purchased a bottle of Hennessey and two bottles of Moet. He gave the bottle of Hennessey to Reg and kept a bottle of Moet giving the other to Supreme. He wasn't sure what was going to happen later but he knew he needed for Reg's senses to be dulled and for Supreme's to be sharp and enough Hennessey will dull your senses.

> *"Woman nuh waan nuh bait// Dem nuh guh feel violate if yuh accelarate pon a date//Dem wha yuh infiltrate //Woman dem wha yuh tear down them wall and dem gate //Yuh nuh hear whey mi state [repeat] [Verse 1:] Woman nuh wha nuh coot, from a knock boots// Whey yuh want yuh fi tell her to tear off di suit//Dem nuh want nuh dude, whey never dey inna di mood// And dem nuh wha nuh little boy wit nuh girl attitude"---song—Infiltrate—by Sean Paul.-*

The whole place vibrated to the exaggerated bass of the D.J.'s sound system. All the women wore the sexiest clothing leather or latex boy shorts, high heel stilettos boots, and or cut up dresses that show everything. Women of all shades of brown adorned themselves with perfumes; scented glitter lotion and every different hair weave conceivable. Freedom and Supreme fit in well with the crowd, the Rasta men who walked by gave Supreme the fist and said "Yes king". The "rude bwoys" who walked by gave those matching diamond studded number sevens the eye, were met by the beams from Freedom's cold black gaze that simply meant "I will kill you." The ladies were definitely taking a liking to them like they were celebrities. Reg was the first one to pick a girl to grind on despite being one of the shortest dudes in the club. He picks the tallest chick to dance with but that was Reg he was a clown by nature. The three eventually made their way down the steps to the dance floor. As soon as they hit the floor two women aggressively seized them like prey. They were both clad in patented leather cat suits and high heels one was dark skinned in all red and the other brown skinned in all black. They manipulated their rhythmic movements of as though each butt cheek had a mind of its own, they moved there vagina around to the point of almost having sex on the dance floor. Their seductive dance movements make music, sex, and the body one. "Bwoy ya know ya mus a come home early Koof! Awah ya try do disrespect Shelly Koof!" The ladies sung Shelly Thunder's classic word for word.

Even though Freedom was somewhat engulfed with this juicy butt worshipping his man hood he still kept his beady eyes surveying the darkly lit dance floor. He was always aware that the enemy can be anywhere and anyone the only thing he feared was being caught off guard. Off in the far opposite corner by the DJ equipment was three young dudes who seemed to take notice of Freedom. He took notice of them as well. It was Cutty, Cry Baby and Fire who Freedom did not recognize, what he did recognize was Cutty tapping the other two on the shoulder and pointing him out. Cutty says to Fire and Cry Baby

"See dat bwoy de a Freedom dat one a di most important bwoy we mus kill ya understand?" Fire subtly reached in his pocket to get his twenty two caliber handgun filled with hollow slugs. At the same time Freedom sort of walked through the woman he was dancing with delicately pushing her to the side, Supreme followed him instinctively. Freedom covertly pulled out his glock and rested it against the back of his left thigh so that it remained unobvious to part the other party goers. Fire moved forward while Cry Baby followed him with gun in hand and Cutty in the back round.

The club basement was so dark and murky that no one noticed this wild western stand off. Fire bumped his way through the crowd like the little bully he was while Freedom humbly excused himself through the jam packed crowd as not to alert any one of his gun in tow, he likes to do things as quiet as possible. When the two warriors met face to face there was a silent moment of recognition. Both men were clenching their weapons anticipating the homicide. They recognized each other before either of them could draw their gun and execute as they have done so many times in the past. Fire quickly dropped his 22 caliber in his pocket and Freedom tucked his nine in the small of his back. Then Fire opens gives his long lost comrade and hand shake that leads in to a manly half hug. Fire "I can't believe dis!" Freedom "Fuck you doing out here nigga?" Cry Baby is confused by his cohort's actions until Fire leans back and tells him "Mi brethren dis from long time, tell Cutty we afe finish de business later ,right now mi ago chat wit mi brethren dem n try a lickle negotiation understand soldier!" Cry Baby and Cutty didn't necessarily agree with Fire's decision but he out ranked them and it was pointless to kill him because his family ties would extend every resource possible to destroy you. So they accepted Fire's command.

Fire looked over Freedom's shoulder at the tall menacing dread locked shadow-"Dat de bwoy Basil? Blood clots look at de big man!" Supreme also recognizes him and it becomes a big C.M.K. re-union. Freedom suggests that they go out side and have a talk. Through everything that took place Reg was still dancing some female oblivious to the situation. Until Freedom tapped him on the shoulder Reg looked like he saw a ghost when he looked at Fire but he quickly snapped to his senses and followed them out side. As they walked to the car they stopped at a 24 hour store to buy some Dutch Master cigars to roll up some blunts and snacks but strangely enough Supreme bought Hefty garbage bags. Every one but Freedom disregards this action as him just picking up something for his place but Freedom knew there had to be more to it than that. They brought each other up to speed on what's been going on while they walked to Freedom's jaguar and got in a discussion commenced over weed smoke. Fire "So Basil yo Rasta Mon now eh you know bought Selassie I, Jah n dem ting der?" Supreme "Nah I aint no Rasta but I'm still righteous God body" Fire "Still youz a righteous mon wit dread some a consider you a dread still king." Freedom "Wow God you still a little dude you aint grow at all." Fire "Yeah lickle mon big gun and if a bwoy try tes mi ago rinse mi gun inna him blood clot face understand see mi." Freedom "Damn nigga you aint changed a bit just got worse." Fire "All a we afe get worse fi make life better ya understand?" Supreme "So what brought you back to America after all this time?" Fire "Just a business trip ya know America have de bes money dread." Freedom was curious as to what type of business. Fire "Mi feel say ya ask me a foolish question my business your business de same and by de look a de jaguar and de chains mi feel say every one doing good business chaw!" Freedom "I know you aint talking bout me you fly ass little nigga." Fire was decked out wit navy blue Polo shirt wit a pair of royal blue suede wallabee Clarks and an solid 42 inch 14 karat gold Gucci link with a big Lion face pendant adorned his neck. Fire "But truthfully Basil and Jamaal mi have sumting fe tell you." Reg "Damn I heard nobody call ya that in a while, I'm bugging right now looking at ya niggas all grown up. Like I remember when ya was some bad ass little niggas but I ain't know ya was going to grow up to be like this. Ya niggas changed a lot yo." Freedom lights another blunt "We grown men that's all, Yo Fire so you bouncing wit us?" Fire "Mi really wan chill an everyting but mi have mi brethren inna de club still." Supreme to turns to Fire "Yo you know today my first day home from jail for that Fat Pat shit." Fire "For real so dis ya first day home eh?" Fire digs into his pocket and passes Supreme a wad of cash. "Here go a lickle sumtin fe help you get settled." Supreme "Thanks God peace." Supreme stuffs the money in his pocket without counting simply being grateful for the gesture. Fire inhales the weed smoke through his mouth and exhales from his nose and says to Freedom. Fire "Mi really have fe tell you something. Jamaal." Freedom makes eye contact to sensing the urgency in Fire's voice but he had a gut feeling that fire worked for or with D.L.P. Freedom "Aright so put me on." Fire "De bwoy you see inna de club, dem bwoy paid fe kill you, Mi a Deadly Lion understand so you and my organization have war. Mi luv you like a broder still so mi afe tell you right now de bwoy Star put nuff money on ya head and any bwoy dat run wit you."

An intense quiet fell over the passengers and for a moment

Fire thought he might have sealed his own death certificate. Freedom just grinned as though it did not even surprise him. Freedom "Fuck them niggas I don't give a fuck about none of them God! You think I don't know them niggas want me dead? They been trying to kill me for years and they can't so all that other shit aint even relevant. I just want to know who you wit us or them? I need to know that right now or we walk away from each other tonight as enemies." Fire "De D.L.P. is mi family but you and Basil are mi brethren, so mi can't just turn my back plus mi really no like de bwoy Star an mi feel say I can do a better job. So mi wan give it some time an mi ago take over Star's operation. An we tree can run the whole a blood clot uptown but firs mi gwon chat to dem bwoy say sumtin bout sum truce business an den we set-up Star real nice eh." Freedom nods his head to agree while he continues smoking. Supreme remains silent this moment is a sensory over load, the last time he saw Fire was the day he killed Pat. To hear something that makes him feel like he must kill Fire puts a sour taste in his mouth. Supreme always knew since childhood that Fire could not be trusted and only thinks of himself. Could Fire's characteristics have changed in his young adulthood deciphering this was purely a matter of trial and error but in this stage of the game an error might cost a life or lives. Supreme knew this was a touchy subject. He thought of Pat's death as favor for C.M.K but it was for him and Freedom because as kids he and Fire never liked each other at all. The stakes are higher now because they are both grown men who have the power to take a man's life away. Their only bond was Freedom he always played the diplomat between them, they shared a mutual respect and love for him.

Supreme's head was tilted down his long dreads seem to

cloak his features and his eyes disappeared under the shadow of his Pittsburg Pirates hat. Supreme "Yo, Fire I hope you ain't planning no snake type shit god." Fire "Listen because mi nah wan tell you a nex time mi loyal ta C.M.K. understand mi! Mi nah deal wit no botty bwoy informer business. Mi nah betray you king." Freedom "Remember I knew Fire before I knew ya'll niggas so I know if he say he wit us then he wit us!" Fire and Freedom exchange beeper numbers while Freedom drives him back to the club every one exchange's pounds (*handshake*) before Fire exits. Freedom instructs Reg to roll another blunt and jump into the front passenger seat while Reg continues get drunk off the Hennessey. Even though Freedom believed Fire to a certain extent he thought it would be foolish to go back in the club and be in the midst of those other two D.L.P gunmen. Their was no way they would all be comfortable in the same place knowing there is some one who has definitely murdered one of your allies and probably wants to murder you, some feelings are beyond reconciliation.

It's a Pity

FREEDOM takes the Brooklyn Bridge to Brooklyn; it's been a long day of revelations for Freedom and Supreme. They understood each other's thought waves holding eye contact through the rear view mirror. It was morbid humor to wonder if Reg had any inclination of his impending doom. Today was Reg's day of redemption, as he sat slumped in the passenger seat with a blunt hanging from his lower lip he was nodding like a heroin addict in a state of mid consciousness between being awake and asleep. Freedom gave him the Hennessey and kept him smoking blunt after blunt for the single purpose of making Reg as incoherent as possible. The Jaguar rode slowly down Jay Street into the D.U.M.B.O. Development Under Manhattan Bridge Overpass area. They kept their eyes scanning the windows for police as they road passed the York street F train station. This area was filled with trendy lofts, warehouses, storage and power plants and factories there was an ever present scent of car exhaust from the near by overpass. The buildings were blanketed wit grey soot that matched the cobble stone streets adding to the areas overall gothic look. The streets were empty except and occasional drunken partygoer.

Supreme began to pull out a bunch of garage bags and tie them in a knot, the crackling sound of bags did not even stir Reg who was settled into a drunken slumber by then. Freedom finds a nice quiet spot by a dumpster. Supreme speaks in a monotone

"Yo you ready God? Freedom "Yeah B" Supreme "So then hold his hands" Freedom wasn't sure what method Supreme would use but he knew it definitely wasn't going to be pretty. Freedom leans over into the passenger seat and puts a tight grip on Reg's wrists pressing them against his lap. It was important to grab Reg's wrist because although he wasn't a killer he was a knock out artist. He woke up groggy but slightly startled and barely has a chance to say "What the fuck!" before a suffocating hooded mask of four bags are thrown over his face smothering him. He struggled, attempting to fight for his life. It was like they were trying to tame a wild bull at a rodeo. He wrestled one of his arms free giving Freedom a solid wallop to the eye, hard enough to hurt and stun Freedom but not enough to save Reg's life. Freedom gained slight control over his hands as Supreme applied more pressure using his body weight as leverage simultaneously pulling and twisting the bags. Reg's body slowly went limp like a wrestler in a submission hold ready to tap out except this hold isn't until submission it's until death. Freedom was grabbing his wrist so tight he could feel the tempo of Reg's pulse slowing down as if his heart beat faded out like a requiem song. Freedom had to hit Supreme's arm to break him out of his trance when Supreme let go Reg's laminated head flopped forward into the dash board. Freedom punched Reg in the face out of spite Supreme says "Hold up God I'm going to break his neck to make sure he dead." Freedom agreed but silently wondered was Supreme careful or just ruthless? This was not the movies this was real life, it's not as easy as Jet Li makes it seem. Supreme grabbed Reg's head with both hands, while Freedom braced Reg's shoulders, Supreme twisted Reg's head to the right pulling and yanking at it until the passenger seat almost broke. Then Reg's head almost spins all the way around and there was this terrible crunching sound reminiscent of a farmer twisting the neck on a live chicken (*multiplied by ten*). Supreme looked satisfied while Freedom was sweating and a little out of breath. Reg's head did not even bobble forward towards the dash board it slumped to the side leaning against the window; a broken splinter of bone was beginning to protrude from the left side of his neck. It was a gruesome ordeal that made Freedom nauseas, he was accustomed to shooting he has never stabbed a person to death, he has never felt a man die in his arms. While Supreme adapted to the feeling of his enemy dying in his arms as he strangles them to death or pushes his blade through their flesh.

Freedom "Look at this nigga God, something is wrong with you, can you help me get this bobble head nigga the fuck out my car?" Supreme "Right here god?" Freedom "Yeah nigga, police ain't coming over here, they patrolling Farrugut projects, niggas be bugging over there. We'll just dump the nigga in the dumpster right there." Supreme "I see you was really the one that had this whole shit planned out." Freedom "Yeah we gone set the nigga on fire to to destroy any DNA we might have left on the nigga, know what I'm saying?" Both men proceeded to lift Reg's body out of the Jaguar and threw it into rusty greenish brown dumpster like a 200 pound puppet. Freedom grabbed some lighter fluid out of the glove compartment and emptied the bottle into the dumpster with a lit pack of matches causing the dumpster to turn into a furnace cremating Reg. They jumped in the car and pulled off, there was a casual silence in the car as Freedom swerved through back streets to jump on the Brooklyn Bridge.

Any one can wave a gun and shoot a person but a true killer can suck the life out of you with his bare hands. Freedom has gone toe to toe and worked with some of New York's most dangerous killers and he has never met one that would rather choke a person to death than shoot him except Supreme. Supreme "See god that's how I do! Imagine what I'd do to a nigga with a gun." Freedom "Relax nigga, what's this the second time you caught a body or something?" Supreme "You a funny nigga but you don't know, a lot goes on behind prison walls, so nah this ain't my second…..It's deeper than all this murder shit ' I want you to know that I'm here to hold you down god, Reg was a traitor so he had to get it and peep how we see the god Fire for the first time today, of all days, do the knowledge to that god trust me, Fire is a snake and he chose to show his head, I peeped how he had the little biscuit (gun) on him. That nigga was supposed to have killed you tonight nigga remember that, don't sleep on that nigga god cause word is bond I'll *(kill)* send that nigga to the essence before I let something happen to you God." Freedom "I hear you but let's get one thing straight; Fire is family nigga, he may be a shiesty nigga but he ain't no traitor, Fire would rather shit on a nigga to his face then do some back stabbing shit, Fire is family nigga and he would never betray us!" Supreme "Alright, so you say but when he does I ain't got shit to say, watch! I got a feeling I'm a have to kill that nigga! Speaking of that wassup, when I'm'a meet this Sopa dude?" Freedom "Relax B you going to meet his niece tonight hear me? This is going to be the grand finally to your first day home; she got a cute little home girl with her and she going to show you some love. You know what I'm sayin god, this your first day home I ain't want you to body something (kill someone) an all that, we was just supposed to have a good time know what I'm sayin." Supreme "True that God, but I did have a good time we just did what came natural."

It is a pity; life has a way of dealing out something called "Karmic Justice." You know , it's like whatever fucked up shit you do comes back to bite you in the weirdest places. Freedom had no idea O'Neil and Schultz had his home under surveillance, and he definitely did not know that dirty cops sold his address to Star. While Freedom and Supreme were having there wild night out Samaya and Chyna were showered with bullets.

The night started out with the girls gossiping for hours probing each other for secrets. Chyna spoke well of Freedom saying "He was the only guy on our old block who didn't try to talk to me." Samaya "Not me he was up under me every time he saw me at first, I thought it was goofy then, I don't know but out of no where he just got sexy, he's a good man with morals you know." Rain was sleeping with her head rested firmly on Chyna's lap, children have this way of looking so pure in their slumber.

Star was the bloodthirsty gung-ho type and wasted no time utilizing his newly found information. Despite Magnum's advice to watch Freedom for a while first, Star insisted on showering Freedom's apartment with bullets, he didn't care whether Freedom was home or not. His motive was planned; he figured if Freedom is there then he dies, if he's not there then freedom's family dies and it will still throw Freedom off balance. He wanted to make an overall statement to Sopa because Freedom was the key to his strength. Star had a special hatred for Freedom and considered him a traitor for being a black man who kills for Dominicans; he actually lost all respect for Freedom when he learned C.M.K. was backed by La Compania.

Star sent Dex and Magnum to shoot up everything, and they were packing some heavy artillery equipped with a sawed off double barrel shot gun, Tech-9's, totes leather gloves and black stocking caps under their skully-hats. The two henchmen crept slowly up the block in a raggedy old Buick that looked like a hunk of metal trash on the outside but was a race horse on the inside. The engine's transmission and inner workings were all brand new and state of the art.

They militantly parked in front of the building. Magnum walked over to the building with his shot gun tucked away in his black Bear goose bubble down coat while Dex carried his Tech-9 tucked under his hooded sweater. Magnum began to wring different buzzers impersonating a policeman through the intercom. Samaya heard her bell go off but she ignored it assuming it was pressed mistakenly since no one ever came to her place. Some idiot actually believed Magnum and buzzed them in. Samaya asked Chyna to put Rain in her bed, so they could finish talking. As Chyna tucked Rain into her bed with her pink blankets Chyna fantasized about what it would feel like to raise a family and have Supreme's child.

Dex and Magnum ran up the steps with their guns in tow, their thoughts were blank the mission to massacre at all cost was the only focus. They had no idea that they were about to reek havoc on a child and two defenseless women.

Samaya felt comfortable around Chyna because she never really got to know any one who had so much information about her husband's childhood in Brooklyn. Chyna looked to her for advice since she was mature and well grounded. Samaya sat on the couch waiting for Chyna to be done with Rain. As Chyna exits the bedroom and walks into the living room, a loud shotgun blast ripped through the apartment door. Samaya jumped up off the couch ran straight towards her bedroom. In times like these maternal instincts kicks in, her child's safety was the priority. The shot gun blast was followed up by the rapid fire that spewed from Dex's Tech9 escorted by sparks and smoke, slugs riddled through the door shattering porcelain lamps and tearing the leather couch to shreds. Samaya practically knocked Chyna over as she ran and snatched Rain out of her bed ducking into the corner behind the dresser to cover Rain with her own body. Chyna quickly crawled into the corner with Samaya seeking some sort of shelter from the shower of bullets that has already overcome them. They cried silently as shards of plaster and wood from the walls caused a dust like powder to blanket the room. Samaya knew there was a gun in the house and Freedom taught her how to use it but it was all the way across the room. With shots ricochcting every where it would have been suicide to try and retrieve that gun. Samaya thought she heard a brief cease fire. Wondering what could the mysterious gunman be doing?

Dex and Magnum reloaded their weapons as they stepped through the tattered cavity that used to be a door. Before Samaya thought to move she heard the sounds of foot steps crunching through debris. Samaya's eye's screamed out in fear as she lay atop of Rain who was silent but shaken with terror. They hid on the blind side of the dresser like Jewish refuges cowering in hiding during the holocaust. Strange enough little Rain did not make a sound, tears dripped from her face as she nibbled her pacifier. Her bright brown eyes were wide open sparkling like the moon on a clear night she seemed at awe with the intensity of the situation. The two searched the different rooms in the apartment for victims or hidden survivors, all the while shooting up television and stereos, just being destructive for the hell of it.

Dez poked his head in Samaya's bedroom for a brief moment and spotted the girls in the corner curled up in fear.

Samaya stared boldly into his face as if to embrace death and Dex was over come with the spirit of mercy because something in his heart said "these girls don't deserve this." He quickly turned away from them like a hungry vampire suppressing his blood lust going back into the living room to meet up with Magnum. Samaya listened carefully as the men spoke Dex said "Na mon dat room empty." Samaya let out a low sigh of relief as she heard the men leave; like thieves in night.

Samaya was a true soldier even though she had never been through such an ordeal she quickly rose to her feet and gathered her senses because Freedom always talked to her to prepare her for days like this. She knew that all of Freedom's guns and money had to be transported somewhere fast before the police get there. She grabbed a kilo of cocaine wrapped in plastic she quickly rips the seal open and flushes all of it down the bathroom toilet spilling a little on the floor in her haste. She gets Freedom's money stash out of their safe and grabs a suitcase ordering Chyna to get Rain dressed. Samaya crammed all the money, guns, and and Rain's clothes into the suitcase. Samaya snatched Rain from Chyna and hastily made her way out the door. As they jogged down the steps Chyna noticed that there was blood all over Samaya's shoulder she couldn't tell if it was Rain's or Samaya's.

Samaya stops to check Rain's little body for holes or scratches then suddenly she feels a burning sensation in her chest and shoulder. In the mist of all the excitement she didn't notice getting hit with some of the shot gun barrel pellets and 4 rested in her left shoulder blade area. She continued on stopping in front of the building passing Rain to Chyna. Samaya "Okay carry Rain I got a plan." Chyna and Rain alike had tears streaming from their eyes. Chyna "But you bleeding you got to go to the hospital." Samaya "I know that calm down and listen to me bitch damn! Can you drive? Aright here's the keys (Samaya leads her to the old Audi) I don't even care get in the back seat. (She pops open the trunk a places the suit case in the trunk and gets into the passenger seat) Alright Chyna drop me off at the hospital then drive to Jamaica Queens, 168th street and 89th avenue building 8815 apartment 8B. Tell my aunt every thing that just happened, leave the suitcase in the car and leave Rain with them and make sure you page Freedom 911. Tell the black bastard what he put me and his daughter through, here is my aunt's phone number." Chyna replies with a head nod soaking up every detail of Samaya's instructions driving down Wadsworth terrace making a left on 181st street and takes Broadway to 168th street Columbia Presbyterian Hospital. Samaya "Okay let me get out right here, I'll be okay." She looked a little pale and her garments appeared soaked in red dye. Chyna "Let me help you inside okay." Samaya "No! if you come in there they going to ask you questions, I'll be able to make it through the door (turning towards Rain who has never felt so terrified) aunty Chyna gonna take you to Queens okay baby, I got to go to the hospital okay, I love you." She gives her daughter a kiss and gets out the car. Chyna watches as Samaya nonchalantly strolls into the emergency room. Chyna prays in her head as she drove off, admiring Samaya's strength in the mist of all that turmoil. Every one in the emergency stared at this unusual woman who looked like a war torn Middle Easterner in full Islamic garb minus the veil. Samaya is exhausted she could barely muster up the strength to speak to the security guard "help me, I've been shot."

It's truly a Pity that while Samaya was in surgery to save her life Freedom was some where else committing adultery with

Mercedes. She was an enchantress who had learned to infiltrate almost every aspect of Freedom's life. Mercedes has been his mistress for 4 years. He seems to have genuine feelings for her but if you asked him he'll tell you "That's just my little ride or die bitch." But the truth was he had developed strong feelings for her that rivaled his loved for Samaya. He coped with his guilt by tricking himself into believing that he was simply using her for convenience and information.

Mercedes knew her role and played it well, they had it all mapped out, both women were hardly dressed with their hair in pony tails prepared for a night of alcohol, weed and sex. Jocelyn was Mercedes best friend and she was a petite flower with huge sensual breasts, small eyes, a perky little round butt and long brown hair that fell to her waste. Jocelyn was the type of girl who at the age of 22 could still pass for a 15 year old high school girl. Supreme clicked with her instantly but it was already set up that way, The girls had been waiting for them for hours. Jocelyn used to mess with Stud but he was physically abusive so she had to get away from him. Freedom and Mercedes wanted to give Supreme and Jocelyn time to get better acquainted so they crept into Mercedes bedroom and left their company in the living room. Mercedes had a lot of critical info for Freedom, and she advised him to have a discussion with Sopa because he was beginning to loose trust for Freedom and the growth of his C.M.K. organization was becoming a threat. He was getting too big for his britches and his father / son relationship with Sopa began to fade. It seemed like Freedom no longer consulted Sopa about important business decisions. This was all apart of Freedom's plan to assert his independence but Mercedes words bothered him because he did not predict that Sopa would catch on to his hidden agenda. He spent years preparing for this conflict and apparently the battle was at hand. He paid close attention to her every word with no visual reaction as none of it really surprised him until she told him that Sopa was planning to have him killed as soon as the D.L.P. war is over. She whimpered every word mixed with tears and saliva as though it pained her to speak. Ultimately Sopa would have killed Freedom a long time ago sighting him as a growing nemesis but needed him to be victorious against D.L.P. Freedom engulfed with rage grabbed Mercedes by her arms and demanded to know how she came to learn Sopa's plot. She admitted that the Sopa ordered her to spy on Freedom and that she would be the one contracted to kill Freedom. She claimed that in the process of her spying she fell in love with him. She begged him not to expose what she had told him. That night he did not even get the urge to have sex with her and had it not been for his buddy having sex in the other room he probably would have left to contemplate a way to utilize this new info to his advantage. As a matter of fact he was thinking about killing her not knowing whether she was telling him the truth or setting him up. She gently placed her head on his lap and unzipped his jeans. She looked up at him with her bright hazel eyes and spoke in her gentle seductive Dominican accent. "I give you my life Papa I would never betray you, I would do anything for you even kill and you can trust me but you better watch Reg. I see you ignoring me I know you got a lot on your mind." She stroked his erect penis and started gently kissing the tip with her fluffy pink lips, she teased it for a while before plunging his head into her mouth and deep throating his manhood. She sucked and caressed his penis until he ejaculated in her mouth. Where most women would have stopped, she continued slurping sucking and swallowing every bit of semen that Freedom had to give until he fell limp.

There was a brief moment of quiet until Freedom's Motorola pager went off at 4:00 am in the morning, only Samaya or Sopa would page him that early in the morning. He picked up his beeper and saw Samaya's aunt's home phone number followed by 911. He quickly grabbed Mercedes house phone and frantically started dialing the number, Mercedes looked on in concern seeing the worried look on Freedom's face.

Samaya's aunt Sharada answered the phone "Hello who's speaking?" Freedom "Freedom" Sharada "Oh it's Jamaal I hope your happy." Freedom "Why what happened?" Sharada "They shot up your apartment." Freedom interrupts "Where is Rain? Where is ……" Sharada "Samaya is at the fucking hospital but Chyna and your daughter are right here." Freedom "What hospital?" Sharada "Columbia Presbyterian" Freedom hung up the phone and pulled his pants up giving Mercedes a three word explanation "Samaya's been shot". Mercedes was obsolete to him, he had to get to his family. Freedom quickly threw on his jacket and screamed out to Supreme "AYO! Preme we out!" Mercedes was right there while he spoke on the phone; it was obvious that something bad happened to Samaya. The way he was rushing to her aid in her time of need made Mercedes jealous inside because it reminded her that she could never take his wife's place in Freedom's life. Supreme was up and ready, he came to the door with a pleasant smile on his face that swiftly disintegrated when he read Freedom's face. Supreme threw on his jacket and to the satisfaction of both females the guys stopped to give them a kiss goodbye as they exited.

About five minutes after Freedom's departure Mercedes' phone wrung again it was Chyna she must have pressed *69 on

Sharada's phone to recover the last phone number that called in. Mercedes picks up the phone "Hola" Chyna "Yeah can I speak to Freedom or Supreme?" Mercedes "They aint here whose dis?" Chyna "This Supreme's wife and Freedom's wife's sister now who the fuck is you?" Mercedes "None of your business bitch." Chyna "Aright bitch don't think you can't get seen bitch stay away from married men bitch!" Mercedes "Well if they so happily married then why them niggas was here eating pussy all night?" Chyna "Aright bitch where you at?!" Mercedes "I don't got time for this shit." and she hangs up the phone.

Columbia Presbyterian hospital across the street from where the ruins of the Audubon theatre is exactly where Malcolm X died. The building number 5 on 167th street and Broadway on the 8th floor room 508A at 6:00am. Freedom's eyes bounce up and down following the green lights on the heart monitor. Two pellets tore through Samaya's left lung and a third traveled downward almost reaching her heart while the forth pellet had to be removed from her shoulder blade. Dr.Weiner, the surgeon on hand explained the details of Samaya's operation and punctuated the fact that if she arrived any later she would have been dead. Either she would have bled to death, her lungs could have collapsed under the flood of blood through her capillaries or she could have simply choked on her own blood. Why hadn't he been there to protect her, instead he was with another woman. Guilt and anger are two emotions that have power to consume you, make you wallow in it until there is nothing left of your insides, like your heart has dropped down to your abdomen and you can still feel it beating. There is a pulse of heat from your hair line to your upper eye brows forcing you to squint and grimace in misery. Trust me, whenever you get these feelings they will either destroy you or make you sinisterly focused.

There was at least three I.V.'s in both of her arms, Freedom recalled what he almost forgot about Samaya, and that was her elegant beauty which was unexplainable with words. Her light reddish brown skin seemed pail and her cheeks looked slightly sunk in. He felt her hands and for the first time they felt rough. He did not want to wake her but he wanted answers, he needed clarity, he had a feeling that the police were involved. Still it had to be more to it than just a bunch of dirty cops, it had to be Star or Sopa who had his place shot up. Anger filled his heart as he had day mares (day dreams + nightmares) of the horrors Samaya must have experienced. Samaya appeared so peaceful and angelic in her state of temporary sleep. She reminded him of his mother as he remembered her from his youth. That's when he could not hold back his tears as they showered his face and his guilt grew. He recalled the things his mother went through because he didn't have the power to save her, and once again he had failed another woman he loved. Emotions are brutal; they speak a pure truth that reminds you of just how wrong you are. Freedom had a dilemma besides needing answers, he still wasn't sure he could leave Samaya alone in the hospital out of the fear that some one might want to finish the job. He trusted Supreme to stand guard but he might need his presence on the street with him. After spending hours by her bedside Freedom took a moment to step out side of Samaya's room.

To Freedom's surprise there was an entourage waiting for him. Sopa stood wearing his usual beige suit and Stud towered to his left while the young Carhartt wearing gunman Pistola was to the right. Supreme came from behind the guys and stood by Freedom. Supreme is very cunning and receptive he was just sitting in the car waiting for Freedom to check on Samaya. When he saw these three men walk into the same hospital building as Freedom did, he got a funny feeling and followed them. His feelings were correct because they ended up going straight to Samaya's floor.

There was a brief stand off, Freedom could not figure out whether to pull out his black nine millimeter and fire or just say "what's up". He peered into Sopa's eyes wondering if he tried to have him and his family killed last night. Freedom wiped the tears from his face and broke the intense silence with a comment to Supreme. Freedom "Yo Supreme if this was chess it would be us two kings versus the king (*Sopa*) the rook (*Stud*) and a knight (*Pistola*). Every one just grinned except Sopa and Supreme because they both truly understood the nature of his statement. Freedom gave Supreme a full lay out of Sopa's structure. Sopa "And how are you Jamaal?"(*Gives Freedom a hug, and looks up into his face*) "How is Samaya doing?" Freedom "She's alright she gon' be okay, she just been through a lot and needs a lot of rest. How did you find out so fast anyway?" Sopa puts on a grin reminiscent of a television evangelist. Sopa "Come on Jamaal you forgot that nothing can happen in Harlem without me finding out, I just wish I could have prevented it." Sopa's all knowingness and ability to throw money around made him a scary opponent. This was Sopa's way of keeping people of balance. Sopa "You know we have a lot to talk about and this is not the place. I brought Pistola with me so he could guard your wife while we go talk." Freedom had a weird gut feeling but he wasn't sure if this was a set-up or not but he was comfortable with Pistola guarding Samaya, Freedom gained much respect for him since the shoot out at Club2000. Freedom "So Pistola's going to stay out side the room until she's able to leave?" Sopa "Yes and don't worry about police I've thrown enough money around." Stud and Sopa start to walk towards the elevator Freedom turns to Pistola and shakes his hand and pulls him into a half hug and he says something low enough for only Pistola to hear Freedom "You're the only one I really trust." Pistola looked puzzled, but Freedom said that for a reason. They shared something in common; they both had reason to kill Sopa. The rumor on the streets was that Pistola was Sopa's illegitimate son.

Apparently Sopa was having an affair with Pistola's mother, when she threatened to tell his wife he made her disappear. Pistola can still remember the night he over heard Sopa arguing with his mother before they left him alone in the house for a while. The next morning she never came home and from that day on Sopa took Pistola under his wing like a son. No one would dare speak about it in front of either of them for fear of being killed but behind closed doors the rumors wrung out with a slight hint of truth. Sopa insists that Pistola's mother was a hooker who could not care for her fatherless child and one night she overdosed on drugs so out of sympathy he adopted her son. That's Sopa's truth but the real truth was that she was his mistress, not a hooker but a school teacher. When she demanded that Sopa acknowledge Pistola as his child or she would make it known, her fate had been sealed.

Pistola "Yo ya'll could at least get me a pretty nurse to keep me company, damn B." Freedom smirked as he walked toward the elevator with Supreme and the rest of them. Supreme is suspiciously calm to not know what was hell is going on.

They took the elevator to the lobby, Sopa and Stud got into their black BMW and Freedom and Supreme followed.

Freedom hasn't even had a chance to see Rain yet, but he had to speak with Sopa. As he drives he can feel the tension emanating from Supreme.

Supreme "How ya Earth (wife) ,she alright god?" Freedom "Yeah she going to pull through, at least that's what the surgeon said." Supreme "You know who did that shit right?" Freedom "Who? Supreme "Them fucking Jamaican niggas and Fire. I'm telling you do the knowledge, we just seen the nigga for the first time and all the sudden niggas shoot up your crib (home). You believe in coincidences? I don't, they set you up, them niggas at the club wanted to merc us God (kill us) but they got shook, matter of fact they probably been watching you." Freedom agrees with him "Yeah and why they do some hurb (punk) shit and try and body my family you know?" Supreme "So you know what we got to do right God?" Freedom "Yeah we got to get rid of them niggas once and for all." Supreme "We got to hit that nigga Fire first." Freedom "But God we still ain't sure he had something to do with it." Supreme gets frustrated and raises his voice "You ain't sure but I am, and on some real shit God ain't no way that nigga ain't know about it and if he was really going to ride with us then why he didn't leave the club with us. Man that nigga loyal to them Jamaican niggas and if you don't realize it now then you will when your 6 feet under! I mean the niggas peoples shot your wife nigga! They tried to kill your seed nigga! Only thing left for the nigga to do is shoot you himself! Only mother fuckers you can trust is sitting in this car right now and that's me! We got to kill that nigga fuck all that family shit!!" Supreme's mannerisms and comments made Freedom feel like he was back in prison. There was no need to reply, Supreme was brash and abrasive but that was his way of showing tough love. That's why you need a strong team, so you have someone to lean on in times of need. Freedom paid close attention to the twists and turns of the high way and he could tell they were following Sopa to the White Stone area of New York. Supreme, forever inquisitive "Where the fuck we following these Germans to (derogatory name for Latinos) God?" Freedom "We going to White Stone nigga, it's a good area, mad nice houses and shit. I'm going to tell you when we going to hit these niggas we aint going to do that right now though, we going to have a little meeting and see what this nigga talking bout." Supreme "He going to let me in his house?" Freedom "Yeah he doesn't usually let niggas in his house unless he got something real important to tell them or if he knows they won't live much longer." Supreme "So which one is it for us?" Freedom "I don't know but I hope he has something important to tell me but let's just be read for any thing. See the old dude looks at me like a son but I know he think I'm getting to big to control, I know him though, he probably wants to warn me face to face before he tries to have me killed." Supreme "I don't give a fuck, I just don't want to walk into a set-up." Freedom reaches under the passenger seat and pulls out a nine millimeter identical to his own and passes it to Supreme. Freedom "You know how to use it right, I know you like stabbing niggas and brutal shit. (*Freedom laughs*) Supreme "Come on God who you talking to." Supreme takes the gun off safety and cocks back the gat putting a bullet in the chamber then tucked the gun in front of his johnson pulls his jersey over the handle and turns to look at Freedom. Supreme "My pops taught me how to fuck with "God U Nows" (*guns*) when I was little. I'll take this whole shit apart and put it back together." Freedom grins "Yo you never cease to amaze me god, just keep that on you in case shit get out of hand and if you pull it use it and use it right cause the niggas we fucking with right now got plenty gun skills, hear me." Supreme takes great heed to his partners words "I hear you son."

Sopa had a magnificent home, it was a mini mansion with all black 12 foot steel gates surrounding 3 acres of land filled with manicured bushes, grass, flowers and trees. When you drive up to the gate entrance there are two huge white guys in all black suits who look like off duty police officers which should be of no shock to you. They practically run to the car to greet Sopa while Sopa activates the automatic lock on the gate entrance. Allowing his and Freedom's car to enter the circular drive way that ends atop a hill where Sopa's house sat, the place was a huge neo-brownstone, it had that authentic brick structure but the design was very modern. It had at least three levels with 6ft tall glass windows. The indoor/out door pool was beautifully shaped like an S *(for Sopa)* custom made by Aqua-Tech. There were armed La Compania soldiers roaming all over.

Every one parked along the circular drive way and walked up the steps to Sopa's main entrance with doors that were made of thick glass and it had a automatic lock that rested in Sopa's hand. The four men walked through the doors and followed Sopa. The main lobby had pure marble tiled floors, to the left was a state of the art kitchen, in the middle was an oak wood spiraled staircase that led to the second floor. Straight down the hall was Sopa's library where he held his most important meetings. As Freedom and Supreme followed Sopa into the library Freedom stared off into the corner at a plain metal door that was imbedded in the outside of the stairwell. This door was cold and ugly, Freedom felt it was blemish on the beauty of the house. He caught a strange feeling of dejavue as he heard the faint rustling sound of chains and growling muzzled dogs behind the door. All of the sudden his memory went back to the day Hashish was killed, Freedom was blind folded but this is exactly where he was. Freedom felt insulted and angry, his mood changed but he tried his best to hide it. The library had books from wall to wall. Mostly military biographies of infamous tyrants like Genghis Khan, Hitler, Hannibal, etc... A large red wood desk stood in the middle of the maroon carpet and redwood chairs to match. This room had no windows Stud came in the room with cups and a bottle "Mamajuana", a roots liquor found in the Dominican Republic. The bottle looks weird as hell, it was a clear bottle the same size as a 5th of Absolute vodka filled to the top with what appears to be wood chips, herbs, and spices. To state it plainly it looks like a black green brownish potpourri but stinks like hashish and liquor. Freedom can remember how his mother Margie had a similar bottle. The four men sat down Sopa looked at Freedom and poured four cups of Mamajuana. Sopa takes the first shot, Supreme lights up a cigarette keeping his peripheral vision focused on Stud. Freedom took a shot of the roots liquor and kept his left hand slightly on his gun. There was eerie silence, unitl Sopa spoke "Jamaal you know I have a great deal of love for you, but your beginning to act like your not a part of La Compania, all I hear about is this gang C.M.K. what is this about Jamaal. I hear every one calls you Freedom, did you ever stop and think that you owe me your freedom? If it wasn't for me Alshaun would have buried you under the prison. Do you think I don't notice that you are starting to branch off?" Freedom takes a long cold look at Sopa. Freedom "What if I want to branch off and do other things Sopa? You can't possibly think that you can still control me I've spilled blood all over the streets of Harlem for you the past several years, all I've ever given you was my undying loyalty and you're going to start questioning me at a time like this?" Supreme and Stud remain calm but are clearly ready to anticipate and follow up on their partner's next move, the tension was building. Sopa removes his genuine Panama straw hat and folds his hands like a distraught father who is about to lecture his son. Sopa "Where's Reg at Freedom, I haven't heard from him since yesterday morning, that's not like him." Freedom "You know what happened to him, don't you?" enraged Sopa "No one kills one of our own without permission Jamaal!" Freedom "He was not one of our own he was one of yours, he was a spy and a coward, Sopa do you really think I haven't figured this shit out yet? Hashish never betrayed me, it was Reg who betrayed me, you just wanted to be able to manipulate me to help you gain control of Harlem." Sopa grins like Satan himself and claps his hands together as though he were applauding at a live performance. Sopa "So finally the little morenito thinks he's a man, you know I made you who you are, I gave you power and it seems like you are going to force me to take that from you." Supreme "What mother fucker!?" Instinctively every man in the room draws his weapon each millisecond turned into infinity. Would there be death was not the question, who will die was!!! A shoot out at point blank range seems more like genocide than homicide doesn't it?! There's a difference between a warrior and a warlord and it is times like this that we bare witness it.

Instinct-*(noun or adjective -ref. The Merriam Webster Dictionary)*-A largely inheritable and unalterable tendency of an organism to make a complex and specific response to environmental stimuli without involving reason.-

It is important to think, but sometimes just taking the time out to think can cost you your life. There are no thoughts in this library now, only instinct, split second reactions and reflexes. Every man in that room had to use their gifts to the fullest, Sopa was one of the greatest hit men in the Dominican Republic and the natives considered him immortal, a living legend that could not die. The people of San Cristobal said that Sopa was a favorite of the Saint Aria (*Voodoo*) warrior god Chango. Maybe that's why Sopa never wore a chain, instead he wore rosary beads that he switched from time to time but never removed were his red and white beads and he definitely did not allow them to be touched. They must have been sacred to him, in times of war it was said that Sopa moves like a man possessed and bullets seem to simply miss him.

Sopa threw his red wood antiques chair at Freedom with his left hand while aiming his gun with his right. Freedom ducked under the table pulling Supreme to the ground with him while Stud and Sopa opened fire. Freedom jumped up and shot Stud directly in the chest but he did not fall. Supreme got up firing at Stud, as both men turned towards Sopa he had already reloaded and let off a shot that hit Freedom in his shoulder causing him to fly backwards and fall to the floor, Sopa jumped behind Stud's body and used it as like a human bullet proof vest. Supreme retaliated emptying his clip into Stud's huge frame which caused Sopa to collapse to the floor blanketed under the weight of his human bullet proof vest. Freedom was still lying on the floor trying to reload his weapon. Supreme lifted him to his feet and said "God we gotta bounce we're fucking out numbered!" When they rushed out the library door, two La Compania soldiers came charging at them, Freedom raised his right hand and picked them off like it was a video game. Supreme stopped only briefly to take a gun from one of the dying La Compania soldiers and they continued to speedily walk to Freedom's car. They expected to be greeted by a dozen guards but to they're surprise all the guards were at the front gate where you can hear the thundering rapid fire sound of an automatic assault rifle. Freedom jumped into the driver's seat of his Jaguar throwing his nine millimeter hand gun on his lap. He sped down the circular hilled driveway and he came to find scattered carnage of La Compania men even the off duty police guards were murdered in combat.

Pistola stood at the bottom of the drive way with a smoking AK-47 automatic rifle and he was targeting Freedom's car until he noticed that it was Freedom and ran to the side of the car. He was out of breathe-Pistola "I came to help you out B, I knew Sopa was going to try an kill you! I was supposed to wait for his orders to kill your girl!" Freedom "What about Samaya?" Pistola "Her family came right after ya'll left, it was her mom, brother and some girl named Chyna." Freedom "Get in!"

As Freedom sped he felt momentary relief as they struggled to catch their breath. Every one was in a zone, a trance of some sort with Freedom being wounded yet very calm during this time of adversity. The jaguar skid on to the high way at 80 miles per hour as Freedom continued to increase speed. Freedom can feel the blood seeping out of his left shoulder and he had to keep twiddling his fingers to stop his left shoulder from falling completely asleep.

If you ever get stabbed or shot you can't panic or you'll die quicker, be calm, and if you can move then move with purpose and precision. Freedom knew that he must do whatever was necessary and he had two individuals riding shotgun who were truly loyal to him. It was vital to show true leadership he had to be calculated and cold enough to kill without regret or remorse without hesitation or emotion.

To slowly watch a man die and look into his eyes as he leaves this plane of existence is the primordial nature of man. When man is reduced to his simplest form, he respects force. Every thing in nature respects the power to kill. The ability to destroy is more respected than the ability to build. Although man will follow and love the greatest builder they will ultimately fear and worship the destroyer because that is the vision of power. People love and adore birth and genuinely plan or let it happen but in the case of death this is something no one plans to do and most would take any measure to directly (not overtly like by not participating in drug addiction, promiscuity, etc.) avoid it at all cost. So a true master, a true leader does not love birth or fear death, instead these emotions do not affect his course of action in the least. He does not think in terms of rewards and penalties, but of plans and goals. Murder has no more significance than a mere pen to him as they are both tools to him. A leader doesn't think as an individual does because his thoughts are for the entire group which he leads and he would easily allow one to die if it ensured the survival of a hundred. True leaders will implement any possible tactic needed no matter how horrible as long as it will ensure victory. They must be prepared to take the same terror they give. In fact to be truly effective they must appear to be immune to pain or death. To convince others of his power he must first convince himself by embracing death and pain as though it were his lover, he must find comfort in conflict and pleasure in pain. A leader must prove his immortality.

Freedom's introspective thoughts anchored his soul down to his body and although he felt himself drifting in unconsciousness, cold chills engulfed his body. He still managed to hide his agony from Pistola and Supreme. Supreme turned to

Freedom "Yo you alright God, we need to get you to a hospital." Freedom seemed relaxed and melancholy steering his Jaguar "Nah B we gotta do something real quick. Yo Pistola you got another clip for that AK?" Pistola is a gun fanatic who is always down for whatever "No doubt what's up B?" Freedom "We going merc them Lion posse niggas." Supreme grows deeply concerned "Son is you crazy you just been shot god we going to the hospital!" Freedom "Them niggas tried to kill my wife and seed (child) god! I'm going to this bar on 145th where all them niggas be at and I'm mercing Fire, Star and all them niggas usually I plan shit but fuck that shit right now, them niggas gotta get got! Now if anybody in this mother fucking car ain't down tell me now so you could get the fuck out!" Supreme "Aright God if this is what you want to do I'm with you god no matter what." Pistola puts his hand on Freedom's shoulder –"I got you primo." Just the feeling of Pistola touching his shoulder gave him a sharp pain, Freedom could feel his shoulder getting cold and his mind was barely balancing on the edge of consciousness. It was only a matter of time before he would pass out from the painful flesh wound. Technically he should be in to much pain to go anywhere but Sometimes your inner strength over powers the bodies physical limitations. Freedom "Good now can one ya twist up a L (*roll a blunt*)."

Freedom drove up to Famous Fish on St. Nicholas avenue and 145th street right next to "The Dungeon"—bar/drug spot. It was about 1:00 pm on a Saturday, Freedom and Supreme haven't gotten a ounce of sleep, the corner was flooded with cocaine and weed salesmen and women. Of all the blocks the D.L.P. controlled this was definitely their strong hold. No one would come and shoot up the bar just like no one would come to Sopa's billards and shoot it up. I'm not talking about punching or stabbing some one, that took place all the time but a hit squad like attack in broad daylight was rare. The two nemesis drug organizations had a sort of respect for each other's base of operations. A person would have to be completely out of his mind to rush "The Dungeon" with all the artillery that's in there. It would definitely be a big shock to Star and that's exactly what Freedom wanted to do, use the element of surprise. Freedom can still remember when he moved to Harlem and was buying quarter pounds of weed from D.L.P. He raises his shaking bloody hand to his lips and sucks in the cannabis sativa smoke while eying the bar.

Freedom "There's like 7 or 8 workers outside on the corner (*points at the workers*) watch that nigga (*pointing to Cutty who is leaning against the wall*) he got the biscuit on him B. Pistola you rush the front hard and push into the bar, Supreme stay close behind him and watch his back. Shoot that nigga leaning all the wall first and them worker niggas will run. Ya'll go in there Pistola you know what Star look like and Supreme you know what Fire look like ya'll get to them niggas quick don't give them no time to get to they guns I'll be right here by the back exit. I'll catch whoever comes out the back, and then we ghost B." Supreme "Yo god, you sure about this? Are you sure this will work?" Pistola throws the extra clip in his AK-47 assault rifle before he interrupts "Stop doubting him B, shit I'm going in first and I ain't saying shit." Supreme seemed to be getting a little angry at Pistola. Supreme I aint talking about us, I'm talking about him. "Yo gods are sure you can do this?" After taking a long pull from his blunt. Freedom "I can do this God-alright."

All three men get out the car Freedom's blood has stained the seat he zips up his jacket in an attempt to conceal his blood soaked black Guess shirt. By standers scattered in fear at the sight of Pistola marching toward "the dungeon" entrance with AK47 in his arms as though it was legal. In a matter of seconds the corner was cleared out except Cutty who seemed to be leaning in the cut waiting for the opportune moment to draw his gun but Supreme took him out with one shot. Freedom stayed outside by the back exit while Pistola and Supreme rushed into the bar. Pistola was a brutal young man with a hair pin trigger on his automatic Kalashnikova AK-47 capable of releasing 600 rounds per minute he had a drum magazine allowing him to hold at least 75 rounds of rare Chinese (7.62x39) ammo.

"Limb by Limb mi ago cut dem down sen fi de hacksaw take out dem tongue. See di see di seed di hit mon a come" song Limb by Limb – by Cutty-Ranks. The song seemed to be a fitting score for the massacre that was taking place. The dungeon was filled with members of D.L.P. Pistola kicked the door in with Supreme right behind him the music was so loud that everyone barely noticed the commotion at the door. Until the music was abruptly cut short by the tumbling bullets that ripped through the sound system, and Pistola's aim did not discriminate man and women alike were being gunned down as he showed no mercy. Star, Fire, Dex and were sitting at the V.I.P. table in the back near the exit. Pistola looked like a Dominican Rambo spraying bullets rotating in a semi circle raining bullets on bar patrons and D.L.P. members alike. Supreme was being very specific with his shots, though his bullets were limited he still managed to clean up behind Pistola covering his blind side. Pistola was charging towards the V.I.P. table. There was a brief shoot out, Star and the rest of the men at the table moved for cover trying to get a clear shot but they were caught off guard and out gunned. Wooden tables were turned into mere splinters and saw dust and liquor bottles shattered into rigid air born glass shards from the deadly Chinese bullets. There was no innocence in this bar but there was a few customers coming for product, thirsty chicks looking for high rolling drug dealers, drinkers, and the rest was all D.L.P. still no one was spared. Even the bartender felt the buzz saw like sensation of having his head torn off. Absolutely no one escaped this whirl wind of bullets with their life except Fire and Star who is wounded. Fire wants to attempt to go behind the bar and get some heavy artillery but there is no way he'll make it and if he tries to take a shot at Supreme or Pistola he'll definitely be over whelmed by their fire power. Fire was a trooper in every sense of the word, he went for the kill and fired until his gun was empty, Star laid a couple of paces away wounded. Fire looks at Star for a brief second and grins and winks his eye at him because although Fire was ready to retreat out the back door he could have helped Star get out but why, when he'd rather see him dead. Fire made his way to the door crouching down while everyone else was dropping like dominoes. Fire had to step over Dex's body and caught eye contact with Supreme who began shooting directly at him but couldn't hit him. Star wasn't so lucky slugs tore threw his skull making his locks resemble blood soaked sponges mixed with corned beef hash. Between the exit door and the street there is a dark hallway. As Fire closed the door behind him the bullets followed ripping through the door creating little passages of light that slightly illuminated the passage way. Fire was distraught and confused, he knew him and Supreme didn't like each other but he never suspected that this would happen, he was just with him last night. He ran and kicked the exit door to the street to meet his final fate. Freedom smacked him with his gun as soon as he burst through the door. The sheer impact split his forehead and hurled him backwards. Fire was dazed seeing darkness and sparkling lights. He regained his vision only to see his childhood friend standing over him pointing a gun at his bleeding fore head. Fire screams out with blood all over his face "A you like mi broda why ya wan kill mi eh? Pussy hole! Traitor bwoy!" Fire spat globs of blood with every angry word. Freedom grabbed Fire by his collar with all the strength he could muster in his wounded arm and put the nozzle of his nine millimeter on Fire's lips. Freedom did not yell he just looked Fire straight in the eyes and said. "So now you don't know why I'm doing this right. You fucking snake you'll even lie before your death fucking coward ass nigga." Fire screams out grabbing Freedom's wrist "I should have murdered you last night!" Before Fire could finish his words there was two nine millimeter bullets entering his mouth and exploding out the back of his cranium, the gray matter splattered against the concrete pavement. Fire's hand went limp as it released Freedom's wrist. It was a weird feeling as he looked at Fire's distorted head all deformed and swollen. For the first time Freedom felt some remorse for his victim—"What have I become" he thought to himself as he gently lowered Fire's head to the ground. He placed his hand over Fire's eyes to close them. Freedom's eyes got a little watery but he fought back the tears. Fire had been extinguished, this is what had to be done, can't cry now cause what's done is done. Supreme was already sitting in the blood soaked driver's seat of Freedom's Jaguar with the engine running. Supreme yells out the window "Come on God let's be out!!!" Freedom's eyes dart from Fire's quivering corps to Supreme and Pistola as he jogged back to the car.

Supreme speeds making sharp turns and running red lights doing his best to get Freedom to the doctor. Freedom sat in the passenger seat zoned out, he barely had enough strength to raise his cigarette to his lips. Freedom calmly turns to Supreme and speaks as though it were his last dying words "Now take me to that hospital on 168th street. Just drop me off I got to see my wife before anything. I'll be out of commission for a while I need you and Pistola to hold it down for me Ya'll all I got." They say real thugs don't cry but Supreme let the tears flow. Supreme "No doubt god, I got you." Pistola "Don't worry I'll get rid of the guns and we switch cars after we drop you off aright B." Extraordinary circumstances or tragic events tend to draw peoples closer especially when they've had to face adversity united. Freedom, Supreme and Pistola solidified their bond stained with innocent blood and baptized in fire as Fire himself was sacrificed so that C.M.K. might be reborn and replenished.

THERE'S NO PLACE LIKE HOME

SOPA'S sole purpose for bringing Freedom to his house was to kill him. He knows how Freedom's mind works and it was at a point of no return, Freedom was growing out of his control. In most instances Sopa usually issues a warning to his co-workers that seem to be leaning towards insubordination but in the case of Freedom he had to kill him without warning. He knew that the worse thing you could do with Freedom is give him time to plan. He assumed Freedom would be in a vulnerable state after what happened to Samaya but Sopa's merciless tactics were unsuccessful. A regular hit would have been easier but Sopa revels in the personal kill and truly derived pleasure from killing.

Sopa laid under Stud's dead body still fearful, wondering if Freedom knew he survived and would finish him off but then again he had too much security, Freedom couldn't have gotten away. They must have been murdered on the way out Sopa thought as he pushed Stud's huge body off his own. There was blood all over his eggnog colored suit he took off his blazer and burst through the library door rushing up stairs to his bedroom. It was a superb master bedroom to say the least; he went to his safe located in the upper right hand corner of his walk in closet behind what appeared to look like a fuse box. He opened the safe to retrieve a briefcase full of money, key's to a safety deposit box and a dozen fake passports and visas. He changed his clothes then took a quick break and thought it peculiar none of his security came to check on him. When he took a look at his surveillance monitor he saw a gruesome display of his personal security guards mutilated bodies sprawled all over the entrance and he couldn't believe his eyes. Freedom and Supreme actually made it off his property alive. In light of the current circumstances there was no need for him to stay around and think things over plus his uppity neighbors have probably called the police already. Sopa had to disappear and regroup, gather what soldiers he had left and strategize. He grabbed his brief case and ran down the steps straight to the kitchen, he turns the knob on his gas stove oven all the way up. Then he went to the bathroom and grabbed a bottle of rubbing alcohol, he went back into his library and poured the alcohol allover the red wood desk and carpet. He lit the desk on fire before jogging to his garage to retrieve his personal vehicle. For times like this it was a plain gray Toyota Camry 95 model, something that would not attract any attention. Sopa was a master of illusion and knew how to cloak his presence very well. He jumped into his car, sped down the circular drive way leaving his luxury home to go up in flames.

Sopa laughed talking to himself out loud "I guess I taught him to good." Sopa has taken losses before but never like this. He made the terrible mistake of underestimating the monster he created and because of this one mistake every thing fell apart. Sopa had already felt the federal government and the local police were crossing the line going from excepting payoffs to attempting extort him. It was definitely time to become a ghost, wise old men live long and make cautious moves. Sopa decided he was going to charter a plane under the name of one of his business associates and go hibernate in the Dominican Republic until the smoke cleared but he would have to re-claim his status in the trenches of San Cristobal "el campo". He had powerful friends back home, they don't intend to bump heads but things happen. Sopa belongs to an elite conglomerate of ruthless Dominican drug lords and killers who call themselves "Sangre de Jesus". They are known for using unorthodox yet brutal tactics from witch craft to poisons to eliminate problems. Sopa was the second eldest, a man named "Caldo" was the eldest of the blood brotherhood and secret alliance. They still seemed divided into two subdivisions, one following Caldo the other following Sopa. Sopa wasn't sure that his grip hasn't weakened in his absence, but the way things were going he had to get out of New York and manage what remains of La Compania from afar.

NUCLEAR-FAM*ILY-FISSION

PLACE: the 30th street precinct on 151st between Amsterdam and Broadway it's been a normal morning for Detectives Schultz and O'Neil. They seemed at ease sitting at their desks drinking coffees, silently gloating over their handy work pleased with the generous payment they received from Star. Until the police lines were wringing off the hook. Every call was someone who witnessed a shoot out that took place at the bar called "The Dungeon" on 145th street and St. Nicholas, and it had to be direct result of their own work. Schultz scarfed down donuts like cookies and speaks with his mouthful. "Let me ask you a question O'Neil? How long you think it's going to take us get that Jamaal kid?" Schultz washes down his hardly chewed donut with a gulp of coffee. "Cause he fucking gets away wit murder and is controlling every drug house in our district." O'Neil "We need a good witness!" Schultz "Just so he could kill another witness, I'd rather do it the easy way." Schultz stared down at his desk looking at a photo of his deceased father in honorary uniform that died in the line of duty. Schultz felt a sense of purpose as he gazed at his life long idle. He wondered if his father ever resorted to being a dirty cop to make ends meat. Schultz thought of the times before the invasion of the crack epidemic and the law enforcement profession was actually respected.

O'Neil looks at Schultz and says "I got an idea, let's go

grab that Reg kid and get him to talk, that kid is soft, he'll rat." Schultz "You know what let's go into the field and see what we can dig up." The detectives began to gather their things to go out. Schultz never leaves the precinct without putting his bulletproof vest on over his T-shirt and having at least two guns holstered. While O'Neil never wears a vest and usually keeps one firearm on his person and a shotgun in the trunk of his car, he throws on his navy blue blazer and they make their way towards the door.

Before the detectives could leave, the door swung open and Captain Vural and federal officer Paul Shaw barge in. The captain was an over weight "Danny Devito" look alike. There was always some type of stain on his tie from his glutinous ways and to add to it, he was a Napoleonic asshole. Now the man next to him, federal officer Paul Shaw was a dressed in a navy blue Ralph Lauren suit with a navy blue tie to match. He stood 5'11 with an athletic build, white, in his mid 30's with bright grey eyes and a military hair cut. You could clearly gather that Mr. Shaw was definitely a military man by his demeanor and posture.

Cpt. Vural spoke directly to Schultz and O'Neil "Listen guys we got the feds on us, they want that "purp" yous been after. So I tell Mr. Shaw here, yous guys would be the best people ta help him apprehend this guy. So he's going to hang out with you guys today alright, apparently they got a hard on for a couple of these lowlifes in our district." Shaw speaks with a slightly southern twang yet articulates himself well, he shakes the detectives' hands and introduces himself.

Shaw "Well I've been debriefed on this and Jamaal a.k.a. Freedom character, but he is not at the base of this investigation, he's just a high ranked soldier in La Compania. Our main focus is the leader Sopa but we can't seem to be able to nail him on anything but tax evasion. Right now we got enough evidence on this Jamaal kid to put him away for at least 10 years, but I know he's got the kind of information I would need to take down Sopa." O'Neil interrupts "So you're hoping that Jamaal will give you the nail for Sopa's coffin." Shaw "Exactly I have to take him into custody and I hear you two are the best people to find him. I got a lead that his girl friend is in the hospital. He's got to stop there or we could question her on his where a bouts." Schultz and O'Neil don't appreciate the feds coming in and infringing on their territory but they have no choice but to smile and cooperate. They were personally concerned with the extent of Mr. Shaw's investigation and does it encompass police corruption as well as criminal activity. This whole investigation can turn into shambles if this federal officer happens to turn over the wrong stone, but they knew the feds would move in sooner or later. The best thing they could do was stay close to Shaw and make sure he didn't find anything that'll put them in the mix. O'Neil "Well I guess we should all get going hugh?" Shaw "Let's got to the hospital where this guy's girlfriend is and sniff around, see if we can find his where a bouts." The two detectives follow federal officer Shaw out the precinct.

"Stumbling holding my neck to the god's rest// Open flesh burgundy blood covered my guess// Emergency trauma black teen headed for surgery// Could it be a out of state nigga tried to murder me?"--- song –So Simple Then—album—36 Chambers—song-by Ghost face killah and Raekwon the Chef. The song blared out of Freedom's sound system and the entire Jaguar rattled with the heavy bass driven rhythm. The song seemed to fit the mood of the moment. Supreme was driving reckless trying his best to get his wounded comrade to the hospital. Freedom was fading slowly into

unconsciousness the long drags from his cigarette seemed to help him cope with the excruciating pain in his left shoulder. He was freezing cold inside to the point where he was shivering. Even through all the blood loss he still felt a unique mental numbness as though he was pleased with himself. Their was an eerie calmness in Freedom's eyes, he was prepared to relax and embrace death yet his love for Samaya and his child must have fueled his soul, inspiring him to stay alive. Fatigue was overcoming him and his lungs hurt with every breath. Freedom never felt helpless like a child before, ironically his state of serenity derived from the bliss and absolute tranquility gathered from anticipating a chance to confront The Creator. Your reality is dictated by your actions which seemed to haunt every man's soul. Even if a man never utters a word to any one of the sins he has committed there will always be two entities that will always know your every sin, those two are God and you. There is no hiding from the burden of your own guilt and Freedom's life style was weighing heavy on his shoulders, the streets were closing in on him. The 5 %(*not a religion–it's a way of life*) nation considers the black man god (*which can vary by interpretation*) the maker, the owner, the cream of the planet earth father of civilization god of the universe. Muslims call him Allah/ Catholics and Christians call him God etc. The highest power has many names but no matter who it is or what it is, in times of need most people call on it, except Freedom. In his times of need he always called on himself to be the ultimate judge and jury for his own personal convictions. Inside Freedom figured he had done to much wrong to ever redeem himself spiritually, so to call on any one but himself in a moment of adversity would have been hypocritical. In Freedom's eyes he was already a condemned man, yet there are still times when the highest power's presence is undeniable and as mere men we are mentally inadequate to completely decipher his ultimate plan.

The Jaguar came to a screeching halt in front of Columbia Presbyterian hospital's emergency room. Supreme turned to look at Freedom, and Pistola sat quietly in the back seat and despite his expertise in murder he still isn't a mature enough to deal with emotions and was at a loss for words. Supreme "Want me to help you get in there God?" Freedom unlocks the car door and speaks in a low wounded whisper "Yo stop being stubborn, let me do this, you and Pistola got a lot of shit to do just come check me later in the hospital alright nigga, peace." Freedom gets out the car and closes the door Supreme gives his brother one final look as he walks away like the last wounded warrior on a war torn battle field. Freedom turned and walked towards the hospital entrance he figured he would at least go and see Samaya before he went to the emergency room. Clearly he was delirious walking into the building a security guard attempts to help him noticing his blood soaked jacket. Freedom only shoots the hospital security officer a cold look as though he could kill him with a death ray from his eyes while he pressed the button for the elevator. Freedom caused quite a scene in the hospital lobby as patients and staff a like were unable to get him to the emergency room. What they did not understand was that Freedom had a burning desire to be near Samaya, this desire was so great that he totally disregarded his own life just to have a moment with her. The security guard did not necessarily know how to deal with the nature of the situation and assuming that Freedom was some bleeding insane man he felt the best course of action would be to radio for back up. Freedom got on the elevator while the bewildered security guard and hospital staff looked on.

Det Schultz O'Neil and federal officer Shaw pulled up to the hospital entrance. Shaw had already done his homework so he had Samaya's room number. The three men crudely parked in the ambulance entrance as only police can do and get away with it. When they entered the hospital flashing their badges they were engaged by the hospital security who were waiting for the elevator to go and restrain a crazed bleeding mad man who can't find his way to the emergency room. The three officers automatically had a gut feeling they knew who this wounded mad man was so they graciously offered to detain him for the hospital security.

The elevator doors opened and Freedom slowly walked out the doors pealing off his sticky blood soaked leather jacket and drops it on the ground. He looks down the hall towards Samaya's room and tries to walk as fast as possible but he can't, things are beginning to really shut down his vision is fading to black with little sparkles of light appearing in the air like ferries. Freedom spoke to the higher power as he walked down the hallway ignoring the weird looks people gave him. He just kept murmuring Samaya's name begging his higher power to save her from death and in those same thoughts he rebuked the creator questioning why was he cursed him with this wretched life.

Federal officer Shaw and the two detectives stepped off the elevator. Schultz sees Freedom and automatically draws his weapon and cocks it, the numerous hospital staff members gasp at the sight. Schultz screams "Freeze bitch turn around!" Freedom ignores Schultz and doesn't even turn around he just smirks to himself and continues his slow turtle like walk. Schultz

"I'm not fucking around Jamaal!" Shaw and O'Neil draw their weapons as well; a gracious nurse who had been walking behind Freedom with the idea of helping this bleeding man quickly ducked out the way for fear of being shot. Nurse "Officers he's hurt and in a state of delirium. Please don't shoot! Let us help him! Please!" Schultz was disappointed when Shaw directed him to put his gun away when he noticed the trail of blood that followed Freedom and the blood soaked leather jacket on the floor. Schultz and O'Neil could tell Freedom was wounded but they were looking for a reason to kill him and if so many people weren't around including the federal officer they definitely would have. All the commotion in the hallway made Chyna come out of Samaya's room when she opened the door tears flooded her face as she asked Freedom what happened to him then she saw the officers behind him and yelled "What the fuck is going on?" Freedom was oblivious to every one the officers pursuing him, the staff members trying to come to his aid, even Chyna and Samaya's family seemed like a group of deaf mute shadows from Freedom's point of view. He had tunnel vision with the angelic sight of Samaya as the beaconing light at the end. He stumbled past Samaya's mother who was looking on in fear and confusion. Freedom laid his eyes on his princess, his sleeping beauty and leaned over to gently kiss her cheek while she slept. His eyes closed the moment he kisses her and his hand seemed to release it's grip on the bed railing and his blood smeared all over her white bed sheets as he collapsed to the bed and then slid down to the floor.

God gave Freedom exactly what he wanted "Peace".

Freedom lost consciousness, his vision turned jet black and through the fog of unconsciousness he could hear the sound of Chyna's weeping, and Samaya's mother arguing with the officers, as they turn his collapsed body over and cuffed him before the medics could even begin to help. All these terrible sounds melded into a tragic symphony of "ghetto life". The terribly chaotic yet harmonious melody's volume seemed to gradually get lower and lower. Freedom's inner ear seemed to loose track of the tune until its faint sound faded into nothing and Freedom could not see, feel, or hear. A slight grin fell over his face as though his spirit sent one last message thanking the outside world for finally giving his physical vessel a chance to rest.

THE END FOR NOW--